THE TAKERS

SHIRLEY O'NEIL

This is a work of fiction. Names, characters, places, and incidents are products of the author's imagination or are used fictitiously and are not to be construed as real. Any resemblance to actual events, locations, organizations, or persons, living or dead, is entirely coincidental.

World Castle Publishing, LLC
Pensacola, Florida

Hardback ISBN: 9798247343677
Paperback ISBN: 9798891265189
eBook ISBN: 9798891265196
First Edition World Castle Publishing, LLC, March 3, 2026
http://www.worldcastlepublishing.com

Cover: Cover Designs by Karen
Editor: Karen Fuller

Chapter 1

Ponderosa pines, native to Washington state, cast shadows across the asphalt road leading to an elementary school as a driverless electric transport pod carried Abby Muse to her requested destination. A sense of foreboding filled her as she gazed out of the pod's clear body at the forest flanking both sides of the road. The smell of pines filtering in through the pod's louvered windows filled her lungs. Abby breathed out slowly, trying to let her anxiety go. She glanced at an empty seat where her five-year-old son, Dillon, would sit on the way home after his first day at school.

The pod parked in the school's vacant lot. Then she realized what seemed odd. *It's noon,* Abby thought. *Did school let out early? The schoolyard is empty.* When the pod door opened, Abby climbed out and followed the sidewalk to the path leading to the main entrance. To the right, a sandbox filled with monkey bars, swings, and slides appeared unused except for a plastic toy dump truck buried halfway in the sand. A breeze startled her, ruffling her hair, and the swings swayed as if the ghosts of children played. Tree leaves rustled in the forest beyond the field. A dark storm cloud in the distance glowed as it released its lightning. She quickened her steps.

Abby opened the double doors, wondering why the halls were empty and the lights were off. All of the offices were vacant. Her footsteps echoed down the hallway as she proceeded to Dillon's classroom and pulled open the door to find the room dark and unoccupied. Terrified that the worst had happened, she looked for clues. The only light in the room came from a wall of windows that looked out over the parking lot. When a flash of lightning lit the sky, she noticed a small handprint on a pane of glass, and she tried to make sense of it. *Were they trying to escape?*

Her heart nearly stopped when she heard movement behind her. She turned to find a man standing silently.

"I'm Doctor Will Henderson," he told her. "I'll take you to your son. Give an order to the pod. Enter the word *clear* so it will delete your retrieval information. Then enter the words *wrong address* to conceal your arrival. Tell it to wait for new instructions. Hurry. We don't have much time."

Abby reached into the back pocket of her jeans and grabbed her cell phone. Without hesitation, she entered the commands.

"Come with me," Doctor Henderson told her.

"Where's my son?" she asked, putting the phone back into her pocket.

He raised his finger to his lips and turned toward the door.

She followed him down the hallway to an empty showcase standing against the wall. Doctor Henderson retrieved a key from his shirt pocket, placed it into the cabinet's keyhole, and turned it to the left. The mahogany case swung forward, revealing a hidden door.

He opened it and went inside. "Hurry. They're coming." Doctor Henderson waited for her to enter, then reset the showcase to its former position and closed the interior door.

Abby gazed around the empty room, searching for Dillon. "Where's my son?"

"This way." He crossed the room with Abby shadowing him and stopped at a storage closet. Reaching up, he tugged on a dangling string that turned on a light. Again, Doctor Henderson unveiled a hidden door, opened it, and stood aside, allowing her to enter first. "There are stairs. Watch your step."

The soft light lit nearly all of the staircase. She held on to the rail and descended into darkness. At the bottom of the stairs, she waited for him to join her. When he reached the final step, she asked, "Why have you brought me here, Doctor Henderson?

Where's my son?"

"You can call me Will."

She turned at the sound of a door opening and saw Dillon standing with a young woman, the room behind them filled with bright light. Tears welled in her eyes as he rushed toward her and threw his arms around her.

A second later, he took her hand. "Hurry, Mommy. We have to hide." He led her to the woman who held the door.

Will trailed.

Abby heard whispers and laughter before she saw sixty children sitting on the floor, watching cartoons on an old-fashioned flat screen TV.

"This is one of our teachers, Miss Carson," Will said. "She'll watch Dillon for you while I show you around and answer your questions."

"You're Dillon's teacher," Abby said. "I met you a couple of days ago when I enrolled Dillon in your class."

"Yes. I'm keeping the children entertained while we wait."

"Wait for what?"

"I'll show you," Will said. "This way." He led her to a surveillance station. An array of monitors lined the wall. "Have a seat." He pulled out a chair for her next to his, and she sat.

The monitors showed a multitude of views of the school grounds, entryways, and windows. The interior images displayed a live feed of every hallway and door.

"This is extensive," Abby said. "Who are you expecting?"

"The government's kidnappers."

A chill engulfed her. "The Takers," she whispered. "I placed Dillon in this school to keep him away from them." She knew that children ready to enter kindergarten were removed from their parents' custody by the Takers and placed into a government-run school. *A place no one can find,* she thought.

Will nodded. "Did you see a dark thunder cloud heading

this way?"

"Yes."

"They're on hovercrafts in front of the cloud."

"So, you're saying they control the cloud?"

"Somehow, yes. The cloud is used as a weapon. Over years of surveillance, our team found that the Takers can control the exact location of lightning strikes, destroying buildings, and killing anyone who defies them."

"Heaven help us," she said.

"I remembered," Will said, "when it began years ago after the Board of Education started changing the curriculum. The parents protesting the teaching of controversial material were met with the government's promise that they'd replace the Board of Education with the Federal Bureau of Education. Now Congress is in charge of hiring all teachers and controls the content of the school's curriculum for all ages, elementary through high school."

"Something had to be done. Most of our children couldn't even read."

"For now," Will said, "the government has eliminated just the local elementary schools across the country, replacing them with their own institutions, teaching kindergarten through sixth grade. All children older than twelve remain in their local junior high and high schools."

"That doesn't sound so bad except it's a wolf in sheep's clothing," Abby said. "They forcefully take our children at age five, kidnapping them is more like it. That's a lot of children across our country who've been taken. There must be more than one school. Have any others been found?"

"Not one."

Scanning the monitors, Abby saw no one on the school grounds and not a soul in the hallways.

"This is one of the many closed elementary schools they

patrol," Will told her. "We're aware of the signs the Takers unknowingly give before they arrive. Did you notice anything unusual on your drive through the forest? Maybe an odd feeling like something was wrong?"

She thought back. "It was strange that I didn't hear the children playing outside."

"No. I meant an eerie silence in the surrounding woods. It's subtle, easily missed. I don't believe the Takers realize it happens. By the time they reach their destination, the wind picks up, and they never seem to detect that all creatures in the forest hush as if trying to become unnoticed. I know it sounds like a scene out of a science fiction novel. Look." He pointed to a monitor. Three hovercrafts softly landed on the field behind the school. Moments later, men dressed in gray, their slim-fitting suits resembling body armor, walked toward the school, each carrying what looked to be a weapon in their hands.

"They stole my oldest son, Ethan, when he was five years old and murdered my husband, who tried to protect him," Abby told Will. "Ethan's eleven now. I miss him so much."

"I'm sorry." He cleared his throat. "You've moved here now, and we protect our own."

"Thank you," she said. "But how can anyone compete with their technology?"

"You should come to one of our meetings."

"Give me a time and place and I will."

The monitor showing the parking lot gave them a view of one of the Takers examining the pod. He stepped away from it, seemingly satisfied it held no interest. He joined the other two, and they entered the school through the main doors.

"We're safe," Will told her. "This room is totally soundproof and undetectable by their life force sensors. As you know, we teach the children in secret. And the Takers don't know we're here."

"Why do they want our children?" Abby asked. "Who gave them the right to take them from us?"

"We're searching for those answers, too," Will said. "Questioning everything is a good habit to have. Don't believe anything anyone tells you. Be aware of your gut feelings, weigh the evidence, and make up your own mind. You're invited to join our meeting, but we're not going to tell you what to think."

"Gut feeling?" Abby asked. "Like sensing the silence?"

"After a while, it will become as easy as breathing," Will said. "You just need to read the signs. We'll help you with that."

The live feed showed the Takers walking slowly through the hallways, opening doors as they searched.

"Do they do this every time?" Abby asked.

"Yes, since the government closed all the public elementary schools ten years ago. They're not worried we'd be teaching classes. They're looking for the children."

Chills went up and down her back. She watched the Takers complete their search and leave. "Now what?" Abby asked.

"We wait until the cloud is miles away."

She glanced at the monitor showing the parking lot. "Why was I the only one who drove to school?"

"We contact each parent when we know the Takers are coming."

"Why wasn't I called?"

"An oversight. The person who gave you the information packet at enrollment was supposed to record your phone number. I'll make sure it doesn't happen again. You did get the packet, didn't you?"

"Yes. I have questions about the code words and phrases. Do you really think the government is monitoring our phone conversations?"

"We know they are."

"In California, after my son was taken and my husband

was murdered, I thought they were eavesdropping. I even made sure Dillon wasn't anywhere close by when I was on the phone, so they couldn't hear him in the background. I didn't know if I was paranoid or having a mental breakdown. It was getting close to his fifth birthday, the same age as my eldest when he was taken. I felt we had to run. So, we moved here."

"That doesn't sound like paranoia. It sounds like you followed your instincts," Will told her.

"I've been running on adrenaline, jumping at shadows."

"I can guarantee you won't be alone any longer," Will said. "Remember, the information the office gave you is extremely important. You're going to have to memorize the code words and phrases. Until you do, when I call you about the meeting, it will sound like I'm asking you out on a date. Just play along."

"Who can I trust to watch Dillon when I go? I don't know anyone in town."

"Who told you about our school?"

"Chad, the guy who delivers my groceries. The day I moved here, he said the types of food I ordered led him to believe I had a child. I tried to deny it. He assured me he wouldn't tell anyone. Then he told me about the school."

"I'll send word to his wife to get in touch with you."

"Thank you." She glanced at the security screens. "Is it safe to go now?"

"Yes. I'll lead you and your son out." He grabbed a pencil and paper. "Give me your number, and I'll call you about the meeting." He passed her the pad and pencil.

She wrote the information down and handed it back to him.

"If you decide to go, I'll pick you up. The location's secret. I'll have to blindfold you."

"Seriously?"

He smiled. "Just joking. But you can't tell anyone. For

some insane reason, there are still some out there who are faithful to the government. And as you've witnessed, the government's Takers have ways to kill which appear to be death by natural causes or an accident."

"When Dillon was born, I kept it a secret by having a midwife deliver him instead of going to the hospital, where they keep records. If the government had knowledge of his birth, they would've taken him by now. I know how to keep secrets, and I'll keep yours if you keep mine."

"That's a given." He turned and gazed at the children watching cartoons. "You're not the only one who's hiding their children."

Abby and Will stood. Dillon joined them, and they walked to the parking lot.

She reprogrammed the pod with her address. Then, she and Dillon drove home.

Abby smiled at her son sitting next to her inside the pod. "How was your day?" She hoped he hadn't been frightened.

He giggled and told her about his new friends and what they learned today. Then he recounted how Will led them to the basement. "We played a game called hide from the monsters."

A tear streamed down her cheek. *He doesn't know.*

"It's okay, Mommy. It was just a game."

When the pod brought them to their front door, Abby cleared the transporter memory and sent it back to its home base. She watched it drive toward the thick woods that hid their house from passersby on the main street. Then she took Dillon's hand, and they went inside the house.

While washing dishes a couple of hours before dinner, Abby looked out the window and saw the deliveryman drive up and park in front of the house. He grabbed two bags of food from the bed of his truck.

Abby went to the door. "Thanks, Chad." She took one of the bags.

"My pleasure, Mrs. Muse," he replied, following her inside, carrying the rest of her groceries. "Did you enroll your son in the school I told you about?"

"Yes. I can't thank you enough for your help."

"Our community is small, and we watch each other's backs. Mrs. Yeller, not far from here, got a call from her son, Vance. He was taken seven years ago, and he told her he'd be coming home."

"That's good news," Abby said. "It gives me hope that I'll see my eldest son again."

"Vance isn't the only one to return. A girl, whose family lives on the edge of town, came home a few weeks ago and found she had a little brother she'd never met. Two hours after her return, the Takers came and took him away." He set the grocery bag on the kitchen counter. "We were lucky. Her brother was about to be enrolled in our school. If he had been, she would've told the Takers. Then there would've been war."

Panic filled her. *If Ethan comes home, will I have to choose between him and Dillon?* "That's a living nightmare."

"Don't let the children's innocent faces fool you. Be very careful who you trust." He reached into his shirt pocket, pulled out a folded piece of paper, and handed it to her. "If you need someone to talk to, you can trust my wife. She wanted me to give you her number. Maybe our sons can have a play day as long as they keep out of sight. I need to get back to work before they start asking questions. Take care. If they send anyone else to deliver your groceries, I'll give you a heads up. It will take time before you know who's who in town."

"Thanks so much, Chad. What's your wife's name?"

"Holly."

"Tell her I'll give her a call."

He turned and walked back to his truck.

When he drove away, she closed the front door. While she put things away, mixed emotions brewed images in her mind. Abby thought about how fortunate she had been to find friends and what terrors could happen in the blink of an eye. She caught herself putting the dish soap into the refrigerator as her thoughts focused on what could transpire if she received a call from Ethan.

The phone rang. She jumped. *I'm not ready for this,* she thought, imagining she'd hear Ethan's voice on the other end of the call. She picked up her phone and stared at the caller's number with trepidation until she realized he wouldn't be calling from a local phone. "Hello."

"It's Will."

Abby released a deep breath.

"I'm calling to see if you'd like to go out with me tomorrow night. Dinner and dancing."

"I'd like that. Nowhere fancy, I hope."

"No. Just a casual night out. Jeans and a T-shirt will be fine. I'll pick you up about 6:30."

"Do you want my address?" she asked.

"I know exactly where you live."

"Why doesn't that surprise me?" Abby said.

"I'll see you then."

"Yes. Bye." She ended the call and dialed Holly's number. "Hello. This is Abby Muse."

Abby kissed Dillon goodnight, turned the lights off, and left his room, leaving the door ajar. She wanted to tell him that Holly's son, Jack, would be coming over tomorrow, but she knew that it's always the innocent little things that have a way of creating problems. *Why does life have to be so difficult? I always have to rethink every move before we make it. It would be so much easier if I could just tell Dillon about the Takers so he could understand.*

She went to the kitchen, opened a can of soda, retrieved the school packet from the kitchen table, and headed to the living room. She set her drink on the end table and plopped into the chair in front of the fireplace. The glow of the lamp next to her illuminated the pages of information the school office had given her. As she flipped through them, Abby pulled the code list from the stack and set the rest of the packet on the floor. Sipping her drink, she studied the code words and phrases, drilling them into her memory.

Rubbing your left shoulder means the cause is great. She continued to read the list.

Chapter 2

The next day at Abby's house, while their children played in Dillon's bedroom, Abby sat with Holly in the living room, drinking sweet iced tea and trying to make sense of the world.

"So, the children are taken when they're elementary school age and returned when they're twelve years old." Abby set her glass on the end table next to her chair. "Why aren't they taking the junior high and high school students, too?"

"Nothing makes sense," Holly said. "Why does the Takers School exist at all? Why didn't they leave things the way they were and have the teachers they hire work at the local schools? And why are they hiding their elementary school?"

"Their parents should be able to get answers," Abby said.

"The ones we've talked to said they tried to contact the Federal Bureau of Education, but each time they were denied any information."

"It sounds like they're covering up something."

"Exactly," Holly said. "What are they hiding?"

"Why do you think it's just the elementary-aged children that are taken from their parents?" Abby asked.

"In my opinion, it's because the young are innocent and still trust adults. They're easy to manipulate."

Abby pictured Ethan in her mind, wishing she could see what he was doing right this moment. "The hardest part for me is not knowing where they've taken my son, and not knowing if he's being well cared for."

"The children who've returned home are healthy. But when questioned, they can't recall any details of the school, which sounds strange to me, since they have total recall of their curriculum and the teachers they had. And when asked to go into detail about what they've learned, everything they say is so generic and vague. I could be overly suspicious because I was trained to question everything for so many years, but something doesn't feel right."

"I agree there's more to it," Abby said. "The Takers on hovercrafts who control thunderclouds worry me. Why would they use lightning as a weapon? Why are they killing to get our children?"

"The Underground is searching for the answers," Holly said. "Meanwhile, we keep our children out of sight." She drank the last of her iced tea and set the glass on the table next to her. "We need to get going. We'll come back after dinner tonight so you can go on your date with Will."

"You know it's not really a date," Abby said.

"Yes. But make sure you convince the government's loyal followers that it is. Eventually, you'll learn who can be trusted and who's a threat. Until then, don't let down your guard." She stood.

Abby went to Dillon's room. "Jack will be back later to play, Dillon. He and his mom will stay with you while I go out for a short time. Come on, Jack. Your mom's waiting."

From the kitchen window, Abby saw Will pull up in a blue truck with a signage wrap reading Kelly's Dairy on the side. She went to the front door and opened it when he knocked.

"Come in," Abby said. "I'm waiting for Holly. She's on the way." She led him into the living room.

He sat in a chair across from her.

"I'm surprised to see you driving a dairy truck," she said.

He chuckled. "The police won't stop farm gas-run vehicles. They're protected under the Petroleum Equipment Act. It allows farmers to drive gas-run vehicles without fines or restrictions. I never worry about getting pulled over."

"Smart," Abby said. "Pretty soon, the government will ban cow manure."

Will laughed.

"That must be Holly." She excused herself and answered a knock at the door. "Thanks for this," she said as Holly entered.

"Not a problem," she replied.

Abby led her into the living room. "You know Will, of course."

She nodded.

"Holly." Will turned to Abby. "We'd better get going. We'll try not to stay out too late."

"There's no school tomorrow," Holly said. "It won't hurt Jack to stay up past his bedtime."

"You're much appreciated," Will told her. "Tell Chad hello for me."

"There are snacks in the refrigerator," Abby told her. "If the boys run out of energy, Dillon can show you how to work the video streamer. His favorite movie is *Star Wars*. It never gets old. And, in case of a fire, I have an accordion folder with important papers in it by the back door."

"Have fun, you two," Holly told them as they left.

Will opened the passenger door for Abby, and she climbed inside. He went around the truck, got in, started the engine, and it roared to life. He followed the road through the woods until he came to the main street.

"I like the way your house is shielded from the public," Will said. "Does Dillon play outside at all?"

"There are woods surrounding the backyard, too," she told him. "I let him play there. It's not good for him to be kept in the house all the time. We lived in an apartment in California, and he stayed inside for years. He has much more freedom here."

"You're lucky to have the privacy."

A lake surrounded by tall white pines flowed under the

bridge they drove over. A bald eagle soared in the cloudless blue sky. "I've been troubled about something Chad told me," Abby said. "He said that children who return home aren't to be trusted. I've been worried about what would happen if Ethan, my eldest, comes home and finds he has a brother."

"I wouldn't worry about that until he calls," Will said. "If he does come home, we have ways to know if he's dangerous."

Dangerous, she thought. Abby felt her eyes water and took a deep, calming breath. "I'm not ready. How could I ever be ready?"

"Try not to think about it," Will said. "Allow yourself to have a good time tonight, and remember you're not alone."

Thank God for that, she thought. "I haven't had a close friend in five years," she told him. "Today was Dillon's first playday."

"Things are looking up," Will said. "I'm taking you to Suzie's Diner. She has the best fried chicken in town. Fresh off her brother's farm. She and her husband are one of us. The place gets lots of business. The information she gathers from the government's kiss-asses is as good as gold. She'll catch us up on the latest so we can share it with the others at the meeting."

Abby glanced at Will. "Holly told me that we should act like this is a real date to convince the moles. I thought I'd let you know before I grab your hand while we walk. I'm not that forward."

"Glad she mentioned it. I didn't want you to be alarmed if I put my arm around you. Just for appearances, of course."

"Of course."

"We can use physical contact as a signal too," Will said. "Squeezing your hand can mean danger. An arm over the shoulder can mean watch what you say."

"What if we're not standing next to one another?"

"I'll raise my hand, rub the back of my neck, or lick my lips, and so on. We can work out the details."

"If nothing else, we'll convince everyone that we can't get enough of each other," Abby said.

He smiled. "Nothing wrong with that. Another thing. How well can you shoot a gun?"

The hairs on her neck stood on end. *Will I have to shoot someone?* "I've never held a gun in my life."

"That has to change. Even though they haven't taken our right to own guns away, as much as they've tried to, they've made it mandatory that anyone who buys a gun must take shooting lessons within ten days after purchase."

"That seems like a logical law," Abby said.

"You would think so. But as soon as you make an appointment for target practice, you'll be put on a terrorist list and monitored. The Underground is keeping one step ahead of the government and has mobile shooting ranges in remote locations. While Dillon's in school, we'll go to one, and I'll teach you how to shoot."

"It may be fun," she said.

"It may save your life," he replied.

She stared out the window.

Will cleared his throat. "It's all-you-can-eat fried chicken night. Suzie's will be crowded. It will give me a chance to show you who's a threat and who you can trust. We'll take a booth, even if it means waiting. I'll sit next to the window, and you can sit next to me so I can squeeze your hand whenever a government loyalist walks by. The faster you know who to trust, the easier your life will be."

"I hope I can remember their faces," Abby said.

"Not a problem. Suzie covers the walls with customer photos. The locals love it. It's one of the ways she gets to know everyone. That and her gift of gab. She sends copies of the photos to us so we can put faces with names."

Once past the tall pines, in a clearing off the main road,

Abby spotted the diner. "It looks busy."

"Best place to eat in town," Will said.

As the sun set, casting its golden hues across the sky, the red neon Suzie's Diner sign above the door illuminated the parking lot. Electric pods filled ninety percent of the parking spaces. Only two other petroleum-run cars were parked in front of the diner.

Will pulled in on the side of the building. They got out of the truck and walked around to the entrance. He opened the door for Abby and led her to the register.

A hostess took them to an empty booth near the door and gave them each a menu. "Your waitress will be right with you," she told them before dashing away.

"This is perfect," Will said. "Let's get our orders in so we can concentrate on our surroundings."

Abby nodded and studied the dinner choices.

A woman in her late thirties, carrying an instant photo camera, came to their table.

"This is Suzie," Will said. "Suzie, this is Abby."

"Nice to meet you," Suzie said, snapping her photo. She put the undeveloped snapshot in one of the big pockets in her pink, flowered apron. "I hear you're from California."

"Yes," Abby said. "And I don't miss it a bit."

"Since Abby's a stranger in town," Will told her, "I'm showing her the nightlife to get her acquainted with the locals."

"Lucky lady," Suzie said. After the photo developed, she removed it from her pocket and placed it on the table in front of them. "This town is attracting lots of strangers lately. For the life of me, I don't know why. The only thing to do here is watch the cows graze."

Will picked up the photo and tucked it into his shirt pocket.

"I bet you're in a hurry," Suzie said. "I'll get your waitress. I'll be around again to make sure you have everything you need."

When she walked away, Will whispered to Abby, "She slipped me a couple of other photos. We can check them out when we leave. Too many eyes in this place."

"Is it unusual to have strangers in town?" Abby asked.

"You caught that, too. She wouldn't have mentioned it if there wasn't something odd about them. We'll probably learn more when she comes around again."

Abby glanced at the menu. "What do you recommend?"

"The pot roast will melt in your mouth. The prime rib is the best in Washington state. And like I said, the fried chicken is to die for."

"I can't remember the last time I had prime rib," Abby said.

When the waitress came over, they placed their order.

Will scanned the room. "Try not to stare. The booth on the right side of the restroom door. That's Harvey Smelt, his wife, and their eldest son."

When she saw him reach under the table, she felt him take her hand and squeeze it hard. She leaned, looking toward the restroom at the far end of the aisle. "If you'll excuse me," she told Will, "I'll be right back." She placed her napkin on the table, stood, and walked to the ladies' room. Abby glanced at the booth on her right, getting a good look at Harvey and his family, then entered the ladies' room. To complete her ruse of needing to use the restroom, she waited before leaving, washed her hands, and listened to the conversation of two women in the stalls.

"I'll pick you up at eight in the morning, Marylin. The protest starts at nine. Make sure you wear your hiking boots."

"I'll be ready," the other woman replied.

Abby dashed into one of the stalls and closed the door before either of the women walked out of theirs. When they had left the ladies' room, Abby returned to Will and plopped into the green-tufted leather seat next to him.

"What's wrong?" he asked.

She took his hand and squeezed it.

"Where?" he asked.

"The bathroom," she whispered.

"Marylin Dowser and Betty Hill," he said. "Care to explain?"

"Those two were talking about protesting in the morning. In California, protesters broke store windows and set buildings on fire. I'm sure it's nothing."

"I wouldn't say nothing," Will said. "You've got good instincts. They're Harvey Smelt's neighbors. Watch out for all of them, even the son."

Harvey and his family stood and walked toward the register. He stopped at their table. Tilting his head at Abby, he said to Will, "She's a nosy woman."

"I'll have a word with her," Will told him.

"Best you do," Harvey said.

Out of the corner of her eye, Abby watched them walk to the register. When they left, she repeated, "I'll have a word with her?"

"Sorry, but I have to keep in character. I get along with Harvey by agreeing with him. By doing that, I find out what's going on in the county. Everybody knows him. That doesn't mean I like him." He rubbed his left shoulder. "The cause is great."

Abby thought about Dillon and the other children at his school. "Yes. The cause is great. I guess I'll be required to take acting lessons, too."

"I'd call it survival classes," Will said.

The people in the booth next to theirs stood and left. Will didn't squeeze her hand.

"Why do you think Harvey said that?" Abby asked Will. "I didn't look at him and his family more than anyone else. I made sure I was careful. What did I do wrong?"

"You're right. That wasn't it. Marylin and Betty stopped by his table before they left the restaurant. Think back. What exactly did you do while they were in the ladies' room?"

"I wasn't planning on using the restroom. I just wanted to get a closer look at Harvey, his wife, and son. When I went in, I wasted time by washing my hands so he wouldn't think it was odd that I went in and out so quickly. I didn't know Marylin and Betty were in there until they started talking. I hurried to an empty stall and closed the door so they wouldn't know I heard them."

"It didn't work," Will told her. "Most people wash their hands after they leave the stall."

"Was that it? Really?"

"Or it could've been the way you darted into a stall."

"I wouldn't say darted."

"Okay. It was the way you ducked into the stall. Anything unusual triggers a reaction."

The waitress set their meals on the table, asked if they needed anything else, and stepped away.

Will gave Abby a nod whenever a government loyalist walked by their booth.

Fifteen minutes later, the waitress brought more fried chicken to Will. Most of the customers left before he had his fill. Only half the people who walked by their table got the nod.

"Am I right to assume the town is divided?" Abby asked him.

"Yes. But not all of them are dangerous."

Suzie returned to their table. "There were three men dressed in suits who came to breakfast this morning. I asked if they were just passing through. They said they had business in town. That's all I could get out of them."

"Thanks, Suzie," Will said. "I'll pass their photo around at the meeting. Someone must've seen where they were going or where they came from."

"If I learn more, I'll let you know," she told him.

When Suzie stepped away, the waitress returned with their check. Will paid, then Abby and he left.

Chapter 3

The headlights on Will's truck lit the darkness, casting light on the towering trees along each side of the pavement and the road leading to the county line. Three miles down the road from the diner, Boot Kickers Country Bar stood like a glimmering island in a sea of night. As they drove closer, Abby watched electric transport pods and gas-run vehicles coming from the north and turning into the well-lit asphalt parking lot.

Will pulled in and parked next to a pickup truck. He went around and opened Abby's passenger door. She got out and gazed at an eight-foot palomino statue rearing up on its hind legs on the roof above the Boot Kickers sign. Floor to ceiling windows along the front and side of the building allowed her to peer inside at a multitude of tables and chairs surrounding a large dancefloor. Will pulled open the entrance door for her and took her hand, leading her to a table in a corner near a window. An array of framed antique tavern ads covered the wood-plank walls next to their table. At the far end of the dancefloor, a stage with two microphones, a few speakers, and a set of drums waited for the band.

"When the music starts, follow me," Will told Abby.

The tables surrounding them soon became occupied. The waitress, wearing tight jeans and a plaid short-sleeved shirt, worked her way around to their table.

"What can I get you?" she asked.

"I'll have what you're having," Abby told Will.

He ordered two beers, and the waitress walked away as a tall man wearing a black cowboy hat joined them. He sat next to Will.

"Abby, this is Nat. Nat, Abby."

He tipped his hat. "Pleased to meet you. I heard you're from California."

"Yes. It seems word gets around. Everyone I've met so far knows who I am."

Nat smiled. "You know what they say about small towns."

Will reached into his pocket and pulled out the photos of the men in suits. "Have you seen these three? They came into town this morning and ate breakfast at Suzie's."

"As a matter of fact," Nat said, "they're sitting at the bar as we speak. I came over to tell ya that our plans have been postponed until they leave."

"Good to know." Will glanced around and whispered, "Does anyone know what they're up to?"

"Someone saw them coming out of the county orphanage this afternoon. It'll be a topic for discussion."

The orphanage, Abby thought. *The children.*

Will slipped the photos back into his pocket as the waitress approached with their drinks. "Good to see you again," Will told Nat when the waitress set the drinks down. "It's been too long."

Nat stood. "Hope we run into each other again. I'll leave ya be so you can enjoy your date." He gave Will a wink and walked away.

Will paid the waitress, and she moved on to the next table.

"Is it really that bad in this town?" Abby asked Will. "I feel like I moved from a dangerous situation to a horrific one."

"I think you're opening your eyes for the first time," Will told her. "It's happening everywhere. If you didn't know the lengths the government will go to make the people bend to their will, then you've hidden yourself away from the world, along with Dillon. I'm sorry. That was harsh."

"Harsh, but true."

Four members of the band took the stage. A woman wearing a blue dress and boots carried a fiddle, a man sat at the drums, and two men wearing cowboy hats and holding guitars stood in front of the microphones. The lights dimmed, and a spotlight washed over the stage.

Will and Abby remained seated, sipping their drinks as the music started. Customers from the surrounding tables rose and headed to the dancefloor.

"Would you care to dance?" Will asked Abby.

"I haven't danced in over five years."

"The two-step never goes out of style," he said.

"What about the meeting?"

"They'll find us." Will stood and offered his hand.

He led her into the middle of the floor. She placed her left hand on his shoulder and offered him her right. They flowed to the beat of the music and circled the floor.

Just before the song ended, Nat, dancing with a dark-haired woman, leaned toward Will. "The suits are gone. See you in a few." He led his partner off the dancefloor.

Will took Abby's hand, and they walked back to their table. "We'll give it about five or ten minutes to make sure they don't come back in."

As they finished their beers, Will kept an eye on the parking lot, while Abby watched the door.

"Two got into their car, but they're just sitting there," Will said. "Where's the third one?"

Abby looked toward the door, then scanned the room. "The other's in here. He's got something in his hand that he's studying."

"The life force detector. He'll see the people in the basement who are here for the meeting." He stood and searched the crowd. "Where's Nat?"

There were too many on the dancefloor for Abby to find Nat. She glanced at the entrance door again and saw that the third man had disappeared. "Did the suit leave?" she asked Will.

"He's outside talking to the other two."

Nat came out of the crowd and walked to their table. "I don't like the looks of this," he said.

"What are they doing?" Abby asked. "Are they spying on us?"

"She has no idea what's going on," Will told Nat. "This is all new to her."

"This is America," Nat said, "and we don't plan to give up our freedom. They're hunting our children, and they know we intend to fight. They'd look under the carpet if they thought they would find the backbone of America and try to break it. Even if it is just a small meeting like ours."

"We intend to ruin their plans," Will said.

"It's their plans that we're trying to uncover," Nat said. "They're confiscating our children. We want to know why. There was an Underground meeting in Arizona a few weeks back that the Takers found out about. The warehouse where they met was struck by lightning and burned to the ground. The same thing could happen to this bar."

"Their life force detector would only tell them that there are people in the basement," Abby said. "They can't prove a thing."

"All we can do is outwit them," Nat said. "The bartender opened the door leading downstairs and placed a sign next to it reading Line Dance Classes with an arrow pointing to the basement. We have someone teaching a class right now."

"They're coming back in," Will said. "Let's hope it works."

"They wouldn't dare burn this place down with so many people in it," Abby said.

"Tragedies happen all the time," Nat told her.

"I assume the meeting's off," Will said.

"Plan B," Nat replied. "Another day, another place. We'll contact you. Oh, by the way, when they leave the parking lot, they'll be going north to the Dusk to Dawn Inn."

"Good to know," Will told him.

Nat left them and stopped to talk with others.

"Might as well enjoy the evening," Will said.

Abby watched the suits weave their way through the crowd toward the hall leading to the restroom. "Let's dance," she said. "I want to see what their reaction will be when they see the sign."

Will led her to the dancefloor. They danced over to the bar, where they found a strategic location to see the hallway and the line dancing sign next to the basement's open door.

Abby looked around. *I guess people would rather dance than drink,* she thought. All seats at the bar were vacant except a few at the far end. "Is it believable that classes could be held down there?"

He nodded. "It's not uncommon for them to have classes while the band plays on the main floor. It gives some folks a chance to catch up on the latest dance steps before joining everyone up here on the dancefloor."

She saw one of the suits go downstairs while the other two waited. It only took a minute before their friend returned, shaking his head. This time, when they left, they drove north.

Abby and Will left the dancefloor, went back to their table, and finished their beers.

"Do you think they're satisfied?" Abby asked.

"More than likely, they'll call to confirm there are classes tonight," Will replied. "All of the staff who work here are members of the Underground. They're in on the ruse. It'll be fine." He looked at Abby's empty glass. "Ready to call it a night?"

Chapter 4

Saturday morning after breakfast, Abby sat at a wrought iron table on the back porch, going over the Underground's school information packet while Dillon played. She referred to the list of code words as she read. Pet and owner's ID required, it stated. *Pet is your child. ID means DNA,* she said to herself, taking a sip of coffee. Vet administering the procedure available Monday morning. *Vet is a doctor, and procedure must mean extracting the DNA. I wonder why? I'll have to ask Will about this.*

Her cell phone, resting next to her coffee cup, rang, and she answered the call.

"It's Will. The movie's playing tonight if you still want to see it."

Movie means meeting, she thought. "Yes. I'd love to go."

"Chad and his wife will meet us at your place," he said.

"Perfect."

"I hope you had fun last night," he said. "I know I did."

"I did too." She thought she'd try a little masked conversation as well. "What happened to those three rednecks who were kicked out? Did they ever come back and burn the place down like they threatened to do?"

"No. They went back to their bug-infested hotel and never returned."

So, the Underground placed bugs in their room, she thought. "They learned a lesson."

"I know we did," he told her. "We should keep our distance from them while they're in town. They're nothing but bad news."

Bad news, she thought. *I'll ask him about it later.*

"I'll see you tonight," Will said.

Abby opened the front door for Will. "Come in." She led him into the living room. "Chad and Holly are on their way."

"We've got plenty of time." Will eased himself into a chair near the fireplace.

She sat across from him. "I was going through the information packet from the school, and I was surprised to see that Dillon and I have to provide DNA samples."

"We use DNA to find the parents of all the children who have fled the government school. If we need more information, the Underground will hack into the federal database."

"The government has a DNA database? On everyone?"

"Yes. Every citizen in the United States. And a separate one for noncitizens. We only access their data if necessary. It's too risky. We prefer to use our own files. They're kept small so they don't attract attention and are stored in hospital records in each county all over the country. It's a massive undertaking."

"Are there that many children who run away?" she asked.

"It's more than that," Will told her. "Children change as they age. A child who is taken at five years old can look completely different at age twelve. There have been cases when a child has returned home, and we've found that they aren't who they say they are. They're replacements."

Abby swore under her breath while her mind went in all directions, trying to imagine the horror. "Replacements?" She tried to visualize how Ethan would look at age eleven.

"When we first became aware, we passed the word to each Underground member to test their children's DNA once they had graduated from the government school and returned home. We discovered a common thread among the replacements. Their last samples were taken while they lived in orphanages—over a hundred different ones all across the country."

"What happened to the real sons and daughters?" Abby asked. "Are they being abused. Do you think they're dead? What other explanation is there to use replacements?"

Will shook his head. "We're still looking for answers."

She gasped and then remembered what she wanted to ask. "What's the bad news you were talking about on the phone?"

"Our town orphanage is closing for restoration," Will told her. "We suspect the older children might be relocated, but the young will be confiscated by the Takers. We're working on a plan to stop them."

A knock on the door caught her attention.

Abby went to the door and invited Chad and Holly inside. Dillon and Jack ran off to play while Abby escorted her new friends into the living room.

"Did Will fill you in on the latest news?" Chad asked Abby.

She nodded. "It's dreadful."

"I deliver food and supplies to the orphanage every day," Chad said. "I hung around while the Takers spoke to the headmistress. Her assistant, Eve, is one of us. After the Takers left, she filled me in on everything. The headmistress is about to tell the media that once repairs are made to the building, the children will be returned, and things will go back to normal. We all know that's not true."

"Chad's going with you to the meeting," Holly said. "I'll be staying with the boys."

"Eve has a plan that I want to run by the Underground," Chad told them.

"I hope it's a good one," Will said.

"She wants to burn down the orphanage," Chad replied.

Abby gasped. "She must be joking."

Will chuckled. "It's kind of ingenious. Burn the place down, save the children from the Takers, and play our own shell game."

"Exactly," Chad said.

Will stood. "Let's go. It should be an interesting meeting."

Abby and Chad followed him out to his extended cab truck. After they piled in, Will took the main road heading south.

Five miles out of town, they came to a busy mall. Will parked, and they all climbed out. Once inside the mall, they ducked into a hallway off the food court, took the stairs to a conference room, and were greeted by other members of the Underground. Abby and Will sat in the front row while Chad spoke to a group of men standing by a lectern. After a few minutes, Chad sat next to Will, and the meeting began.

Chapter 5

A Pacific breeze chased away the morning clouds on Sunday. In the afternoon, Abby set extra chairs around the patio table, made lemonade and iced tea, then waited for her friends to arrive. When she heard cars pull up, she opened the gate and led everyone to the backyard.

Dillon and Jack ran to a fort built near the tall trees leading into the woods.

"Stay where we can see you," Abby called to them.

Chad sat next to Holly, who poured him a glass of lemonade. He took a sip, cleared his throat, and said, "Eve has set up a day trip tomorrow to the Seattle Science Museum for the orphans ages four to twelve. It's perfect timing because she had the trip planned before the Takers' visit."

"What about the others?" Abby asked.

"The older children will play a soccer game against another orphanage two counties over," Chad told her. "They're not due back until later in the evening. That leaves the babies and infants. Every afternoon, the staff takes all of the babies and toddlers outside to get exercise and fresh air. Our accomplices within the staff will make a sweep to make sure anyone sick or disabled gets out safely. That's when we'll strike the match."

Will pulled out a chair for Abby. She sat, and he sat next to her.

"It sounds like all the planets are aligning," Abby said. "How big is the place?"

"It houses two hundred children," Will told her. "There will be six staff loyal to our cause going with the children to the museum. The drivers of the school buses are members of the Underground. When the fire starts, Eve will tell the drivers to take the children to the county emergency shelter. We know the place is overcrowded. We're counting on it. All of the shelters have overflowed since they opened the southern border."

"The border," Chad said. "Now that's another story. Remember when the government opened the border, and millions of people from all over the world entered our country? Do you recall the tent cities that they built in several states to house all of the unaccompanied children who came across? It made the headlines. Once they dismantled the tents, not a word hit the media about where hundreds of thousands of children disappeared to. But we know."

"The Takers confiscated the younger children," Will said. "The older ones were put into shelters all across America. Since then, all the shelters are still overcrowded. Because there'll be nowhere else to go, Eve will appear to be making a rational decision to take the children to our orphanage."

"You have an orphanage?" Abby asked.

"Yes," Chad replied. "Did Will tell you about the runaways?"

She nodded.

"We had to have a front," Chad said, "allowing the runaways to have a place to live while we search for their parents. The Underground has one in every state."

"We expect the Takers won't want to deal with the confusion once their plans go up in smoke," Will said.

"What can I do to help?" Abby asked.

"I can watch Dillon if you want to go with Will," Holly said.

"I'm going to our orphanage to collect DNA samples from the children on the buses," Will said. "I'd appreciate your help if you want to join me."

"Count me in," Abby said. "How are you going to make sure the Takers don't put your orphanage on their list?"

"Ours specializes in teens," Chad told her. "We're well known for going to extremes to track down any living relative and find the teens a permanent home. We'll never be on the Takers' radar. Our children are too old."

"We've hacked into the government systems and downloaded emails they sent to a list of orphanages across America," Will said. "We're spreading the word to let them know what the Takers are up to."

Abby shook her head. "It'll be impossible to save them all. Isn't there a way to track the children to find out where the Takers are bringing them?"

"We've tried that," Chad said. "It led us nowhere. We had a clear signal, but when we reached the location, there was nothing there except an empty field and a marsh."

"Maybe they should try again," Abby said.

"Believe me, we have," Will replied. "We sent a team out to the area, and all of them returned with headaches, rashes, swollen nasal passages, and other symptoms. We found documents stating the area was a hazardous waste dump. The marsh is probably radioactive."

"I guess all we can do is our best," Abby said.

"No," Chad said. "We need to do more than that. We need to be relentless."

"What about the runaways?" Abby asked. "Did they tell you why they ran away?"

"They all have different stories," Chad said. "But it all boils down to fear. They made close friendships over the years. Once some of their friends turned twelve, they were never the same. The runaways ran because they didn't want to become zombies."

"What was their definition of a zombie?" Abby asked.

"The twelve-year-olds' personalities changed," Will said. "It was as if their memories of the school and the people in it, especially their friends, were being erased."

"This is a nightmare," Abby said. "Every parent in America should be devastated."

Holly nodded. "The government's first graduating class will be in their mid-twenties this year. Since the founding of their school, I've noticed our children have stopped thinking logically. According to the runaways, they were taught that reasoning is another word for defiance."

"Brainwashing isn't new to our world's history," Will said. "But this time something seems different, evil in some way."

"That's why we can't give up," Chad said.

"And we won't." Will turned to Abby. "I'll be by tomorrow at noon to pick you up."

She nodded. "I'll be ready."

"It's all set then," Holly told her. "I'll come to your place and watch the boys while you're out."

"You'll see me at our orphanage," Chad said. "I'm driving one of the buses."

Abby poured their choice of another glass of lemonade or iced tea. As she sipped her drink, she looked up at the scattered clouds. "We're expecting rain tomorrow. Will that be a problem?"

Will chuckled. "I almost forgot that you're from California. You're not used to the rain. Here, it's a nuisance, but we don't let it stop us. Same with the snow. In the middle of winter, you'll see construction workers building homes. We're tough. Nothing stops us."

"What kind of work did you do before you moved here?" Holly asked Abby.

"Accounting," Abby replied. "I'm still employed by the same firm. I work online. I took a couple of weeks off to move."

"Are you happy with your job?" Will asked her. "We need someone we can trust in the school office. You'd be the school coordinator and organize the curriculum since we're not affiliated with the Federal Bureau of Education. Plus, you'd be communicating with all of our other schools across the country, and there might be a little undercover work involved."

"You're guaranteed healthcare through the Underground," Holly said.

Abby's eyes welled. "One of my fears is that I wouldn't know what to do if Dillon became ill. I've been lucky so far. But the fear never goes away."

Will nodded. "Understandable."

They all stared at her, waiting for her answer.

School coordinator shouldn't be too hard, she thought. *But, undercover work?*

"Undercover work is at your own discretion," Will said as if reading her mind. "You'll always have someone around you who can answer all your questions. Like me, for example."

"I'm assuming I'd get paid under the table."

"For tax purposes, you'll be our orphanage accountant, and you'll be receiving a paycheck just like anyone else," Chad said. "There'll be no red flags."

Healthcare and a support group. She took a deep breath. *Undercover work. Am I brave enough to go for this? I've had my job for sixteen years. Do I really want to quit? I can't pass up healthcare for Dillon.* "Okay. I'll do it."

Chad raised his glass. "To our new recruit."

Chapter 6

Looking out the window of Will's truck the next morning, Abby realized it must take a lot of water to keep all of Washington state's trees green. But the amount of rain coming down as Will drove south made it almost impossible to see the trees along the side of the road.

Halfway to their destination, Will pulled off the highway and parked in front of a diner, a pink neon sign blinking *Open* in the window. "According to the internet, this rain should subside soon," he told Abby. "Let's have a bite to eat while we wait." He reached into the backseat, grabbed two umbrellas, and gave one to her.

She opened her car door, thrust the umbrella up into the rain, and it snapped open. Looking down, she watched her step. Rain cascaded off the umbrella, making it hard to see in front of her. She trudged through the half mud, half gravel soppiness to the wooden steps leading to a sizeable porch she couldn't wait to get under.

Before entering, Abby raked her boots over the mat, scraping off the globs of mud. Inside, other than music coming from behind the double doors leading into the kitchen, the place appeared abandoned.

Will retrieved the menus resting by the register, and they sat in a nearby booth.

A moment later, a waitress came from the back room, straightening her apron. "Sorry to keep you waiting," she said. "Can I get you anything?"

"Are you hungry?" Will asked Abby.

She shook her head. "Just a cup of coffee will be fine."

"Two coffees," Will told the woman.

She returned and filled their cups to the brim. "I'll be back in a few minutes to check if you changed your mind."

"Thank you," Will said.

As the waitress disappeared behind the double doors once more, Will's cell phone rang.

"It's Chad," Will told Abby. He put the call on speakerphone.

"I'm still at the museum," Abby heard Chad say. "The children should be back on the bus in about fifteen minutes. Where are you?"

"We're about a half hour away from the orphanage," Will said. "Is the plan still in effect?"

"Yes. Any minute now. The sky's blue here. What's it like where you are?"

Will glanced out the window. "It's still sprinkling. It should be clear soon."

"Once the rooster crows," Chad said, "I'll text you a thumbs up."

"How long will it take you to drive from the museum to the orphanage?" Abby asked.

"About an hour," Chad told her. "But remember, we'll be making another stop, so add another twenty minutes."

"We'll be waiting," Will said. "See you soon." He ended the call.

After Abby and Will finished their coffee and paid the bill, they climbed back into the truck and sped away. The rain had stopped. Beside the highway, a strong breeze whipped over a lake, creating white caps that scurried across the water. Above them, the wind propelled the clouds eastward, leaving no sign of dark clouds in the west.

Fifteen minutes later, Will received a text. "It's Chad. He sent me a thumbs-up. The match was struck."

"I feel bad for all the babies and little ones," Abby said.

"They'll be watching their home burn down."

"It will only be a minor inconvenience. We have insiders at nearby orphanages who are jumping into action. They'll send them transportation within an hour and bring them to their new sanctuary. There's no need to worry." He rubbed his left shoulder. "The cause is great."

"The cause is great," Abby repeated.

Soon, she saw the Underground's orphanage in the distance. Its old-world charm gave the residence the appearance of a sixteenth-century English Tudor. Chimneys rose from steep-pitched gable roofs. Multi-paned windows looked out over the vast acreage surrounding the orphanage and its flanking wings. To the left, a lake seemed to go on forever. To the right, tennis and basketball courts were filled with children.

"It's beautiful," Abby said.

"It was built in the early 1900s," Will told her. "You'll be meeting Morgan. He's the founder of the Underground."

When they approached the main entrance, a man with wavy, white, shoulder-length hair and a full, snowy white beard came out of a wide, arched wooden door.

"Good to see you again, Will," the man said.

"Good to see you," Will replied. "This is Abby. Abby, this is Morgan. And this is his orphanage called Safe Haven."

"Nice to meet you," Morgan said. "Please, follow me." He strode beside them up a walkway lined with black-eyed Susans and held the door as Abby and Will stepped inside an oversized foyer, leading to a long hallway.

As she followed their host, Abby noticed an open door, leading to a vast library with tall redwood shelves and a multitude of tables and chairs. Ahead, in what looked to be a large room, she saw boys and girls moving furniture aside.

"We're setting you up in the common room," Morgan told them.

Abby stepped into a huge, peaked-roofed room with dark wooden beams spanning the roof's width. Fold-up tables for the DNA testing were being placed in the center of the room.

"It'll be about an hour before the children arrive," Morgan said. "Why don't I take you to the dining room so you can grab a meal and relax."

"Sounds like a plan," Will said.

"Thank you," Abby added.

They followed Morgan to the other side of the common area and through a double door leading to a huge dining hall. Its white walls highlighted the dark wooden-ribbed ceiling and the ebony flooring. Booths lined the walls below the ceiling-high windows, and round tables filled the middle of the floor. Across the room, a stone fireplace dominated the entire north wall.

"The buffet is closed now," Morgan told them, "I'll have someone bring you guests' menus." He waved to a girl nearby, cleaning the tables. "She'll be right with you. I'll be in the common room once you finish your meal. There's no hurry. Take your time."

They thanked him, and he walked back the way he came.

A woman took their orders and left.

Abby scanned their surroundings. "This place is ten times bigger than I thought it would be. When you said it was a place for runaways, I imagined there would be less than thirty children at the most."

"As crime rises, we see an increase in orphans," Will said. "We're dedicated to all children, not just the runaways."

"The rising crime reminds me," Abby said. "I'd like to get together soon so I can learn to shoot."

A smile spread across his face. "You're going to do great. You're focused and follow your gut, the traits of an excellent marksman."

"I don't want to shatter your theory," she told him, "but I

can hardly walk without tripping over my own feet."

"You're in luck then. Walking while shooting takes advanced training."

The woman who took their order returned with their meals and coffee, served them, and left.

"Have you given your notice to the California firm yet?" Will asked before taking a bite of his hamburger.

"Yes," Abby replied, dipping a French fry into ketchup. "This morning."

"I realize how hard that was," Will told her.

"I still can't believe I did it." She reached for half of her tuna sandwich. "That job was my safety net."

"Now, you have a bigger net," Will said, before taking another bite. "You won't regret it. I promise."

She ate everything on her plate. "That was good."

Will pushed his plate aside and wiped his mouth with his napkin. "We have twenty minutes until they arrive," he said, looking at his watch. "I want to get your DNA sample before they come. Dillon's can wait until I'm back at the school tomorrow."

Abby took a sip of her coffee, then set her cup by her empty plate. "I'm ready when you are."

They exited the booth and left the dining hall through the double doors.

The common room had been transformed into a clinic and a donation center. Abby strolled around the tables, surveying the merchandise. Piles of clothes, backpacks, and toys had been placed on tables. The teens had separated the clothes into sizes, and shoes were available for those who needed them.

"How in the world did you get all this in such a short time?" Abby asked Morgan.

"We have warehouses that supply all of our orphanages," he told her. "We're prepared for anything. Even the young."

"Let's get your DNA sampling over with," Will said to

Abby.

He led her to a table stacked with DNA tests. She wrote the information required on the front of her kit, handed it to Will, and grabbed a cupful of water to rinse out her mouth.

He slipped on gloves and used all four swabs in the kit to gather DNA samples from the inside of her cheek. "There. All done. Since your name is first on the list, yours will be the first to undergo the lab test. They'll run your DNA to see if there are matches from any living relatives, and they'll pass all the information on to us. At our school, we'll make a new file for you. I'll show you how it's done. I just need to get Dillon's DNA sample, send it to the lab, and get the results back to complete his file."

Down the hallway, the sound of children coming from beyond the front door sent everyone to their stations. Abby sat with Will at a DNA gathering table.

The arched double front doors opened, and Abby saw the staff, who had accompanied the orphans to the museum, leading the busloads of children inside. "There's Chad," Abby said, waving. A few more chaperones got off the bus and followed behind him.

Morgan stopped them in the hallway before they entered the common room, gave instructions, and led the staff to tables where they would help the children write their names on the kits. Five children at a time went first, left their information, and took their kits. Behind the first group, another five went forward, moving in an orderly fashion. Once the children had given samples and gotten their photos taken, they were shown where to go to pick out clothes, shoes, and toys.

When the last child gave Will his DNA sample and joined the others to look for clothing, Will and Abby stood to stretch their legs.

"That went smoothly," Will said.

"It didn't take as long as I thought it would," Abby said.

"No need to wait around," Will told her. "They'll be shown their rooms and given a meal. We're no longer needed. Let's give Morgan our gratitude, and we'll head home."

Before Will dropped Abby off at her house, he drove by the remains of their town's former orphanage. The fragmented brick exterior stood. Through the shattered windows, Abby saw the collapsed roof and charred interior. Smoke rose as the building smoldered.

"Someone will investigate," Will told Abby. "But it will look like an accident. The Underground knows what they're doing."

"It's sad to see it come to this," Abby said, gazing at the shell of the historic building.

"The children are safe," Will said. "It's the only thing that counts."

He parked in front of her front porch, and Abby saw Dillon waving in the living room window.

"I'll see you at school tomorrow," Will told her. "And I'll set things up so we can go shooting tomorrow night."

"I'm starting to feel bad about asking Holly to sit for me all the time," she told him. "I don't want to take advantage of her."

"Holly belongs to a group of our members who help parents by watching their sons and daughters. If she can't make it for some reason, one of the other sitters will fill in for her. It's what they do. The cause is great."

"That makes me feel better. I had no idea."

"You've been living here just a short time," Will told her. "You've only seen the rise in the road, not the entire size of the mountain."

"Thanks for everything," Abby said as she opened the passenger door. "See you in the morning."

Chapter 7

In the Underground's school office the next morning, Abby finished entering her personal information into her new file on the computer.

"Great," Will said. "Headquarters should have your DNA results already. We'll send them your file."

"Where's headquarters?" Abby asked.

"In Northern California," Will told her. "Near Redding."

"I've been to Mount Shasta," she said. "It seems like ages ago."

Will's cell phone rang, and he answered it. "Yeah, this is Will." He listened. "Can you send me a photo?" He listened again. "Wow. That's intriguing. Okay. That's fine with me. And you said his name is Emory Davis? I'll have a look. I'll get back to you." He ended his call and sat in front of the computer, which Abby had used to create her personal file. In a moment, a young boy's face appeared on the screen. "This is a photo of the newest runaway."

She gasped. "He almost looks like my son. Do you think his hair is naturally white? What color are his eyes?"

"Silver."

"No one has silver eyes. Ethan's eyes are blue, and he has brown hair."

"Does your son have any outstanding traits?" Will asked.

"Nothing like white hair and silver eyes," Abby said. "But he's smart. I only had to read a story once, and he could repeat it back to me word for word. He took after his dad."

"That's interesting," Will said. "Sit down, and I'll tell you more about Emory Davis."

Abby sat in an office chair next to him. The runaway's

photo remained on the computer screen.

"Emory's the same age as your son," Will said. "And he has an exceptional memory, too. He said all children who are brought to the school at age five are given a photo of their mom. He carries her picture in his shirt pocket."

"Does she have white hair too?" she asked.

"Yes. In fact, she does. But Emory knows she's not his real mom."

"Then he's an orphan being groomed to be a replacement," Abby said.

"Not in this case," Will told her. "His real mom's face is still vivid in his memory, along with the murder of his father. That's why he ran."

She stared at the picture on the screen. "Could he be Ethan?"

"He is," Will said. "The DNA test proved it. He's your son."

She placed her hand over her mouth. Tears filled her eyes. "What did they do to him?"

"We don't know yet. He won't tell us anything until he sees you."

A mix of emotions filled her. Excitement gave way to worry that he'd been hurt. Her fear for Dillon's safety weighed the same as her longing to hold Ethan in her arms again. "Where is he? Can I go to him?"

"He's being given a complete physical at one of our belowground facilities in Northern California."

"When are we leaving?" Abby asked.

He smiled. "So, you don't mind if I tag along?"

"I trust you. I know you'll tell me what the doctors won't."

"What makes you think they won't be straight with you?"

"The Underground is based on secrecy," Abby said. "Why would they tell me anything?"

He nodded. "You're right. We leave as soon as you bring Dillon home from school and Holly gets there. Our flight is already booked. When we get to California, we'll be staying for two days. Pack accordingly."

"So, you knew I'd want you to go," she said.

He grinned. "What would you do without me?"

After landing at an airport outside of Redding and collecting their bags, Abby and Will headed for the exit.

"There'll be a black truck, with a food and grain sign on the side, to your right when you go out the door," Will told her. "We're trying not to draw attention. So set your bag next to the back of the truck and scoot into the backseat."

She did as he instructed. Once settled in, she peeked out of the window and saw Will and the driver throw the suitcases into the truck bed.

Will got into the cab and sat in the passenger seat. "Soon," he told her. "It'll be soon. We landed seven and a half miles from Redding. But we'll bypass Redding and go north. We'll be there before long."

She noticed that Will didn't introduce her to the driver and knew he had a reason. *On a need-to-know basis,* she thought. *I'll just follow Will's lead and think before I speak.* "Are we going to the hotel first?" Abby asked him.

"We're not staying at a hotel," Will told her. "There's a cabin not far from our destination. Our bags will be taken there for us. We'll go directly to our meeting."

She nodded. When they passed the Redding exit, she took a deep breath to calm her eagerness to see Ethan. *I wonder if he remembers his name,* she thought. She looked out the window at the countryside but saw nothing but Ethan's face in her mind—his white hair and silver eyes. *What happened to him?*

North of Redding, they turned down a road that wove its

way through tall pines. When they came to a clearing, the driver stopped in front of a food and grain store.

A woman stood on a covered porch while a customer drove away with a truckload of hay.

Abby and Will exited their ride, and their driver drove off, taking the luggage to the cabin.

Will didn't introduce her to the woman who led them inside, closed the door, and flipped the open sign to closed. He walked with Abby to the back of the store and down a flight of stairs to a storage area. On a wall dripping with bridles, Will sought out a rein and tugged on it. The wall glided to the side, revealing an elevator door. He entered numbers on a keypad, and the door slid open.

Abby followed Will inside, watched the door close, and stood waiting. "Why aren't we moving? Is there a button to push?"

"We're being probed—facial ID, weapons search." He looked down. "Feel that?"

"No." She focused on her surroundings. Still, nothing gave her a clue that their position had changed. She felt sure that when the elevator door opened, they'd still be standing next to a wall of bridles. Instead, when the door slid aside, they were greeted by a middle-aged man wearing a white lab coat over tan pants, standing next to a younger woman in a blue dress, holding a clipboard.

The man shook Will's hand. "Nice to see you again, Doctor Henderson."

"Good to see you." Will glanced at the woman. "And you too, Mary."

"We're excited to have you here," she replied. "This must be Mrs. Muse."

"Abby, this is Mary and Doctor Roman."

Abby smiled, remembering to listen before speaking.

"Right this way," Doctor Roman said. He led them down a brightly lit corridor. "This is by no means a jail or an interrogation complex, Mrs. Muse. We've been given permission by your son to observe his behavior while he waits for your visit. Before you meet face-to-face, we thought you might like to discreetly see the changes in his appearance that you had expressed concern about. Keep in mind that he is in excellent health. I'd like to caution you to keep silent while observing him through a two-way mirror. He can't see you. We didn't tell him you're here. We want it to be a surprise so we can witness his reaction."

"I understand," Abby said, following him around another corner.

Doctor Roman stopped, raised his finger to his lips, and opened a door leading into a room with a large window.

Through the glass, Abby stared into an ordinary boy's bedroom decorated in an all-American sports theme. But her focus stayed fixed on the young boy sitting on the bed, juggling a soccer ball in his hands.

He looked at the two-way mirror, stood, walked over, and placed his hand on the glass. "Mom, it's me, Ethan."

"I thought you said he couldn't see her," Will said.

"It's impossible," Doctor Roman replied.

Abby placed her hands against Ethan's on the glass. "I'm here, baby. It's all right."

"Come with me," Mary told Abby, leading her into the hall. A step away, Mary knocked on Ethan's door.

He opened it and rushed into Abby's arms.

"I'll leave you two alone." Mary closed the door.

Ethan took Abby's hand and sat on the edge of his bed next to her.

"I almost fell over when they told me you were here," Abby said. "There hasn't been a day that I haven't wished you were home again." She ruffled his hair. "You've grown so big. I almost didn't recognize you with your white hair." She studied his face. "And silver eyes. Do you remember when they kidnapped you? You had brown hair and blue eyes then."

"I'll never forget that day. They killed Daddy, and they gave me something that made me sleep. I don't remember arriving at the school. It took weeks before I could think right."

He looked at the floor. "When I'd dream about you, it wasn't you. It was a stranger, a woman I didn't know. And whenever I thought of you during the day, I'd see her instead of you. It was like my memories of you were being replaced." Tears welled in his eyes. He reached into his shirt pocket, took out a photo, and handed it to her. "They gave me her picture and told me she was my mom. I knew they were lying. I never forgot you."

"I had no idea where they took you. No one knows where the school is. Did they hurt you?"

"No. I guess they treated me all right."

"Were there lots of children at the school?" she asked.

"Yes. The school was big. There were forty of us in my dorm room. I don't know how many rooms there were. There must've been a lot."

"Did you make friends in your dorm?"

"Friendship wasn't allowed. If anyone hung around with someone else very much, they'd make them switch dorm rooms. But Cole and I came up with a secret code. We made sure we didn't eat together, and our beds were far apart." He chuckled. "Every once in a while, we'd pick fights with each other. Nothing that would get us into trouble, but just enough shoving and name-calling to make them believe we disliked each other."

"Where's Cole now?" Abby asked.

"He's a year older than me. When he turned twelve, he changed. They did something to him. He didn't even remember me. That was scary. If they could do that to him, they could do it to me, too. I didn't want to forget you. So, I ran away." Ethan answered a knock on the door. Will stood there.

"Hi. I'm Will, a friend of your mom's. How about something to eat? Your mom and I haven't eaten anything since this morning."

Ethan looked at Abby. "Are you hungry, Mom?"

"Yes. How about you?"

He nodded.

"I thought we could take you to The Lumber Jack," Will told him.

Ethan's eyes widened. "Are we leaving?"

"You'll have to return after we eat," Will said. "You promised to answer their questions."

"How long will you and Mom be staying?"

"We'll be leaving with you tomorrow," Will told him.

Ethan looked at Abby. "Is he telling the truth?"

She grinned. "Yes. But it's essential that you answer all the doctor's questions."

"What's so important?" Ethan asked. "I've been at school, and now I'm home. It's simple."

"We'll talk more about this while we eat," Will told him. "Let's go."

"Do we have a car?" Abby asked Will.

"Have I ever let you down?" Will asked her.

Ethan stared at her as if waiting for her answer.

She shook her head. "Never."

Mary and Doctor Roman met them in the hallway.

"There is something that I'd like to speak with you about," Doctor Roman told Will and Abby.

Mary put her hand on Ethan's shoulder. "Go ahead. We'll wait here."

Abby and Will followed Doctor Roman down the hall, far enough away to have privacy.

"I'd like to keep your son longer," Doctor Roman said. "I want to run a few tests on his eyes."

Abby crossed her arms.

"No," Will said. "That isn't the plan. He needs his mother."

"But he saw her through the two-way glass," Doctor Roman said.

"There's no proof of that," Will said. "Maybe he heard her, or it could've been a good guess."

"But it's worth looking into," Doctor Roman said.

"Don't fight me on this," Will told him. "We're sticking to the plan. We'll bring him back after we eat. Ask him all the questions you want. But tomorrow he's coming with us."

"Yes indeed," the doctor said, as he accompanied them back to Ethan and Mary. "It was only a suggestion. You can't deny his eyes are rather interesting."

Abby took Ethan's hand. *I've got you now,* she thought. *And I'm not letting you out of my sight.*

Will entered numbers into the elevator keypad, the door opened, and the three of them stepped inside.

"Thank you for sticking up for us," she told Will when the door closed.

"I've known Doctor Roman for years and years," he said. "He's just curious."

Ethan looked up at the camera. "Whenever Cole and I spotted a new surveillance camera, we'd rub the corner of our eye."

Will glanced up, then back at Ethan. "You teach me your secret codes, and I'll teach you mine."

"Deal."

The elevator door slid aside. They headed back upstairs. As they passed the store register, the woman behind the counter tossed Will a set of keys. She flipped the closed sign to open once they left the store.

Will opened the front and back passenger doors for her and Ethan. A food and grain store logo displayed advertising on the side of the SUV.

While Will went around to the other side of the vehicle, Abby told Ethan, who sat in the backseat, "So much has changed since you've been gone. We have a lot to catch up on."

Will started the engine and drove back to the main road.

"Is that the right time?" he asked Will, pointing to the clock on the dashboard.

Will looked at him. "Do you have somewhere you need to be?"

Ethan rubbed the corner of his eye.

"Where?" Will asked.

"What time is it?" Ethan replied.

Will reached into his flannel shirt pocket and pulled out a handheld device. He waved it in front of the dash, and its red light showed the location of the hidden camera.

A camera behind the clock. Who's watching us? Abby wondered.

They rode the rest of the way in silence.

The Lumber Jack had a peaked green tin roof, log siding, and a red door that Will pulled open. Inside, a bar spanned the left side of the room. Tables and chairs circled a fire pit in the center, with its hood capturing the hickory log smoke, and its vent pipe soaring up to the ceiling. They chose a booth to the right. Only three people sat at the bar, and the chairs around the firepit and at the tables were empty.

"We got here before the crowd." Will looked at Ethan, who sat across from him next to Abby. "Now we can talk. I guess my first question is—did you see your mom through the two-way mirror?"

Ethan turned to Abby.

"You can trust him," she said.

"Yes. I saw her."

Will glanced down and then looked at Abby. "That changes everything."

"What do you mean?" Abby asked him.

"I want this to remain between the three of us," Will said. "I'm not going to discuss it with the Underground. If he can see through a two-way mirror, it's hard to tell what else he can see through. If they found out, he'd be put under a microscope, and they'd possibly use him for their benefit. Remember what I told you. Don't trust anyone, and follow your gut. That's what I intend to do."

The waitress approached them, gave them menus, and told them she'd be back. When she returned with three glasses of water, they gave her their order.

"Does the school know about your vision?" Abby asked when the waitress stepped away.

"Everyone gets their eyes and their hearing tested once a year. My eyes were normal for two years after I arrived at the school. I knew what my vision was like before my eyesight changed. They tested me more than anyone else. No matter what they told me or how nice they were to me, I remembered when they killed Daddy. I'll never forgive them for that. So, I made them believe my eyesight never changed."

"What differences did you notice?" Will asked him.

"I can see really far. We played archery, and I pretended I couldn't hit the target any better than anyone else. But I could see the target as clear as if it was a few feet away. I could've hit a bullseye every time."

"I'll test how far you can see," Will said, "and what you're capable of after we get home. You said it started to change two years after you arrived at the school?"

"Yes. Every night, they gave me and everyone else vitamins before bedtime. When Cole and I became friends, we decided to stop taking them for a week to see how it would affect us. They were sleeping pills, not vitamins. And since we were able to stay awake while everyone was sound asleep, Cole and I saw children being taken from their beds and brought back just before dawn."

"Did they come for you?" Abby asked.

He nodded. "When they came, they noticed I wasn't fully asleep, so they gave me a shot that knocked me out. I never found out what they were doing. I fought to stay awake but couldn't. That's when my vision began to change."

"Did you meet anyone else who had silver eyes?" Abby asked.

"No."

"If they were secretly experimenting with genetics," Will said, "my bet is they pulled someone from each dorm to do the same experiment on. So, if there were two who had silver eyes or white hair, they would never meet and talk about their changes. That way, no one would know that they were being used as guinea pigs."

"What about your white hair?" Abby asked. "Did that happen the same time your eye color changed?"

"No," Ethan replied. "One day, they came to our dorm and told us that we all had to get our heads shaved because of a head lice breakout. Everyone's hair grew back normal except mine. It matched the color of the woman's hair in the photo." He retrieved her picture from his shirt pocket and handed it to Will.

"I'd like to find out who this woman is," Will said. "Can I keep this photo?"

Ethan nodded.

"For now," Will said, "I think you should continue keeping your secret. When Doctor Roman or Mary asks you how you knew your mom was here, I suggest you tell them you heard someone walking down the hall and heard them enter the surveillance room, or it was a good guess."

"Do you think they'll allow me to sit in while they speak to him?" Abby asked Will.

"I've often sat in on physicals and mental evaluations given to runaways," Will said. "After their physicals, I'd take them to our orphanages around the country. This is the first time I've seen signs of genetic manipulation in any of the runaways. Out of all those hundreds of children we've taken in, you'd think I'd see at least one other."

The waitress brought them their meals, and once she left them, they continued talking between each bite.

"It doesn't make sense," Ethan said. "They've taught us that separating race is important. They're going to pass a law against one race marrying another."

"So, now they want to tell us who we can and can't marry," Abby said.

"It's more than that," Ethan told her. "They taught us there were seven different species of mankind at the beginning of evolution. They said we must respect nature and let the weaker species become extinct, and the strongest and most intelligent survive. If they're manipulating genes, they're going against nature. It doesn't make sense."

"It's called brainwashing," Will said. "They're turning race against race because smaller groups of people are easier to control than a united nation. They lie to hide the truth."

The waitress came back, refilled their sodas, asked if they needed anything else, and stepped away.

"Is it unusual to have a surveillance camera in an Underground vehicle?" Abby asked. "Does your truck have one?"

"Mine doesn't. I'm guessing that the truck we're driving now has hidden features because it's connected to our major medical facility. But guessing isn't good enough. I'll tell them I found one with my bug detector."

"What about the medical facility?" Abby said. "Is that bugged too?"

"Good question. I can't leave without knowing. If the medical facility has been compromised, I'll have to contact Headquarters right away."

Ethan took the last bite of his hamburger and licked his fingers.

Before they left, Will paid the bill. He turned away from the register and showed his cash card to Abby as they went out the door. "You'll need to get one of these since you're working for the Underground now. The Takers can track your movements if you use your Fed-Coin card."

"What's the Underground?" Ethan asked as they walked to the van.

"We'll talk about that later," Will told him. "Always remember that the Underground's a secret. Never mention it in front of anyone, no matter who it is, except your mom and me. The Takers have loyal followers. If word of the Underground reached the government, our country will be destroyed."

"I understand," Ethan replied.

"We're probably being overly protective," Abby said, "but we think it's best if we don't let you out of our sight. You'd better stay with us at the cabin."

They climbed into the SUV and drove back to the food and grain store.

Inside the store, Abby and Ethan stopped to admire a set of Labrador retriever puppies for sale, giving Will some privacy while he talked to the girl behind the counter.

After his conversation with the salesgirl, they followed him to the elevator in the storage room downstairs. "She told me about the camera," Will said. "It was just as I suspected. It's extra eyes and ears in case the driver gets into a sticky situation with the federal police. We'll have to watch what we say in the SUV and in the cabin until we leave."

The elevator door slid open. They stepped inside, and the door closed. It didn't take long before they came to the belowground medical complex and were met by Doctor Roman in the hallway.

"You can both sit in if you'd like," the doctor told them as he led them to a nearby conference room where Mary waited.

"Please have a seat," Mary told them.

Will pulled out a chair for Abby. Ethan sat next to her. Once they were comfortable, Doctor Roman opened Ethan's file.

"Let's start by you telling us how you knew your mom was here," Doctor Roman said.

Abby held her breath, hoping Doctor Roman would buy Ethan's lie.

Chapter 8

Once Abby, Will, and Ethan arrived at the cabin after their meeting with Doctor Roman, they thoroughly searched for surveillance equipment.

Later, they sat on stumps around a blazing fire pit as they looked out over a calm, clear lake. The sunset painted the sky yellow, red, and orange. The tall trees along the lake's rocky bank cast their shadows over the still waters. The day's heat waned, and a lone hawk glided in the tranquil breeze.

Will poked the crackling logs with a branch. "I was watching Doctor Roman's body language while you replied to his questions," he said to Ethan. "He wasn't pleased with your answers."

"I didn't notice any negative reactions," Abby said, feeling the fire's warmth kiss her cheeks.

"The brain's limbic system processes our emotions, thoughts, and intentions," Will told her. "It creates inherent non-verbal behaviors that override deceptive reactions. I watched the doctor's facial expression as he took notes. His pursed lips told me he either disagreed with your answers or was angry about your response. And as he listened to you, his pupils became small—another inherent characteristic that revealed his true feeling of disapproval."

"Why are we still here?" Abby asked, glancing around and turning back to Will. "Do we have to stay until tomorrow?"

"If we leave tonight," Will said, "it might look suspicious and could confirm the doctor's belief that Ethan saw you through the two-way mirror."

"Do you think he could tell I was lying?" Ethan asked.

"I don't believe so," Will told him. "You replied by asking

questions. It's a good way to avoid a direct lie. I laughed to myself when you asked if he read too many superhero comics. And, when you asked how it would be possible for someone to have X-ray vision, the doctor's rapid blinking told me he gave it considerable thought."

"I didn't think you looked like you were lying," Abby said.

"You answered too quickly," Will said, "but he might've mistaken it for nerves. Aside from that, you were convincing. You did great."

"I had lots of practice," Ethan said. "I've had to keep my vision a secret for so long that lying about it became easy. I'll work on talking too fast."

"Just slow it down a bit," Will said. "Don't overdo it. Responding too slow is not good either."

"Do you think the Takers are looking for you?" Abby asked Ethan.

"I don't know why they would. I've never heard of a runaway being brought back. Why would they be? If they brought them back, they'd just rebel again. And the school doesn't like defiance."

"Are you aware that each child has been implanted with a chip?" Will asked him.

Ethan felt his neck and scanned his arms. "No. Where?"

"All the runaways have one in the same place—the temporal lobe." He pointed to an area on the side of his head. "The same square shape and the same size. But yours is different. It's round and in a slightly different location."

Ethan reached up and brushed back the hair behind his ear.

"It's embedded under the cerebral cortex in the temporal lobe, but a few inches away from where the others have theirs," Will told him.

With his eyes closed, Ethan ran his fingers through his

hair and stroked his scalp. "I don't feel anything."

"You wouldn't. It's embedded. Would you mind if I take a look?" When Ethan nodded, Will walked over to him and examined his head. "There's a discoloring in the shape of a crescent moon," Will said, stepping away.

"That's my birthmark," Ethan told him.

"You don't have a birthmark," Abby said.

"It has to be. Daddy had the exact same mark."

"Your dad wasn't born with that mark on his head," Abby said. "I noticed it about a year before his death and thought nothing about it."

"Another mystery," Will said.

"Can the chip be removed?" Ethan asked.

"No," Will told him. "The area where it's embedded is where emotions and memories are processed, regulated, and stored. If we tried to remove it, you could lose all of your memories, or worse, you could go into a coma."

"Can they track me?" Ethan asked.

"As far as I know, they haven't tracked any runaways. But you're different. We'll have to keep a visual watch for flybys and strangers in your town and near your home."

"If they find him, they'll find Dillon," Abby said.

"Who's Dillon?" Ethan asked.

"I was three weeks pregnant when they took you and murdered your dad," Abby told him. "Your brother is five years old now. He was delivered by a midwife, and there's no record of his birth. The government has no idea he exists. I intend to keep it that way."

A smile spread across Ethan's face and lit his eyes. "Wow. I have a brother."

"We moved to Washington state. So far, they don't know about him."

"I'll check on our flight," Will said, pulling out his cell

phone. He called a number. "It's Will." He listened and stood. "When?" He looked at Abby as she slowly rose.

She saw his eyes widen. Panic filled her. *No, not Dillon.* She placed her hand over her mouth, and tears filled her eyes.

Will lowered the phone and returned it to his shirt pocket. He went to Abby and took her in his arms. "It's okay. They didn't find him."

She blinked back tears and stepped aside. "Where is he? What did they tell you?"

"They don't know where he is. All they know is that no one was home at your house when the Takers got there. Someone must have told Holly to run. It was probably Chad. Whatever the case may be, there's been no communication with the Underground. You can bet your house will be watched from now on."

"Either someone told them about Dillon, or they're looking for Ethan," Abby said.

"We're setting up a safehouse for you. A private jet will be waiting for us at the airport. Once we arrive in Seattle, we'll be taking a ferry to a secure location."

"I'm almost sure they're searching for me," Ethan said.

"We'll know more sometime, tonight," Will said. "For now, let's not panic."

"How did they know where we live?" Abby asked.

"We don't know yet," Will told her. "Looks like you'll be changing your name. The Underground will help you with that, too."

"Maybe we should leave now," Abby said.

"We're safe where we are," Will said. "We need to give the Underground enough time to change your identity. How do you feel about becoming a blonde?"

"I'd rather be a redhead." She gazed at Ethan. "Brown hair for him. A shade that won't make him stand out. And he'll have to have brown contacts. What do you think, Ethan?"

"Good idea, Mom."

"What name will you choose?" Will asked. "Will you change both first and last or just the surname?"

"Just the surname should be good enough," she replied. "Freemont will do."

"Abby and Ethan Freemont," Will said. "Okay. As soon as you color your hair, I'll text a photo and your new name to headquarters."

"Cool," Ethan said.

"I'll call a friend of mine who lives nearby and ask him to pick up a few things for me," Will said. "When he arrives, I want both of you to stay out of sight. The cause is great. Take Ethan into the cabin. I'll be there soon." He retrieved his phone again.

"Come on, Ethan," Abby said. "We'll wait inside."

Abby dried her hair with a towel, then looked into the bathroom mirror. The stark change of color shocked her. *Okay. Okay. I can live with it.* She plugged in the hair dryer and let the heated air evaporate the excess water, giving her red curly hair a bounce. *Good enough,* Abby thought as she cleaned up the sink. Satisfied with her appearance, she slipped back into her black short-sleeved blouse and heard a knock on the bathroom door. When she opened it, she saw her son's jaw drop.

"Wow, Mom. Cool color."

"You're next." She grabbed the sealed box of brown hair color as he stepped in front of the sink. "This won't take long. I don't have to use the entire bottle because your hair's so short."

Twenty-five minutes later, Ethan washed and towel-dried his hair.

"Let's give you a different style," Abby said, combing his hair to the side. She stood back and studied his new look. "Okay. We're finished here. Will can help you put in your contacts."

Abby went into the living room, sat by the fireplace, and

thought, *If they were looking for Ethan, it couldn't have been Doctor Roman or Mary. They knew we were here. If Dillon told any of the children at school about his brother, they might have said something to someone. Or, maybe someone at Headquarters found out I'm Ethan's mom and told.* She saw movement out of the corner of her eye that caught her attention.

Ethan stood in front of her.

"How do the contacts feel?" she asked him.

"I can't even tell they're there. Will said I have to take them out before I have a shower and before I go to bed."

"You look super," she said. "You'll fool everyone."

"We'll need to do more than this," Will said, walking up behind him. "The facial-recognition cameras won't have any trouble recognizing you."

"I've been trying to think of who'd call the Takers on us," Abby said. "Our lives are turned upside down. Have you heard from Headquarters? Do they know where Dillon is?"

"They just called," he said. "Holly took the boys through the woods to a shack along the creek about a half mile from your house. Chad picked them up and took them to a private airport just out of town, where they boarded a helicopter. Right now, Holly, Chad, Jack, and Dillon are safely relaxing in Bremerton in a house overlooking the Puget Sound."

"Where's Bremerton, and what's the Puget Sound?"

"You seriously don't know?" Will asked her.

"No," she said.

He smiled and nodded. "You're going to love the ferry ride."

Ethan took a piece of computer paper from a printer on a table by the window and snatched a pen from a plastic cup on the desk. He brought them over to a leather stool in front of Abby, set the paper down, and began drawing. "It looks like this," Ethan told her. He drew Washington's Puget Sound with all its inlets and bays, along with the islands.

"That's exactly right," Will said, looking over Ethan's shoulder.

Ethan pointed to Seattle. "You get the ferry here, and it will take you to Bremerton over there."

"Is drawing maps something they taught you in school?" Will asked.

Ethan shook his head. "I like maps. I studied the world atlas a lot during down times. I can draw the perfect shape of any state in America, or country in the world. I have a good memory."

"His dad liked geography," Abby said. "He plastered our home office walls with maps of the world."

"I remember he read me stories before bed about kings and queens, mean rulers, and how the world will look someday."

"He was a bit of a dreamer," Abby said. "It's funny what memories stick in your head."

"Make sure you burn that in the fireplace," Will told him. "We don't want to leave a map of where we're going lying around."

Ethan threw it into the fire, and they all watched it turn to ashes.

"We have some time before we go to bed," Will said to Ethan. "Let's see what codes and secret hand gestures you and your friend came up with, and I'll show you mine."

"I'll join you," Abby said. "We should all be on the same page."

Chapter 9

In the morning, Abby, Ethan, and Will boarded a personal jet provided by the Underground.

A woman on the plane greeted them.

"This is Maggie," Will said. "We didn't have the ways and means to change your appearance sufficiently, so Headquarters sent our mistress of disguise to do the job."

"What's she going to do?" Abby asked.

"You won't be able to recognize yourself when she's through," Will told her. "And Ethan will need a little work, too."

The captain joined them from the cockpit. "Good to see you again, Doctor Henderson," he said.

"Nice to see you, too," Will told him.

The captain looked at Maggie. "I'm glad I got to see her before you work your magic. She'll look completely different when you're through. You're amazing."

"My husband, the captain," she said. "I'll need time to set up, so if you don't mind."

"I'll leave you to it," the captain said. "Have a nice flight, everyone." He turned and walked back into the cockpit.

Maggie sat across from them and secured her seatbelt.

As the plane took off, Abby's hands gripped the armrests.

When the plane leveled and the fasten seatbelt light went out, Maggie rose from her seat and joined them.

"I'm really grateful for what you're doing for us," Will told her.

"Call it payback for all you've done for us." Maggie rotated Abby's seat toward the aisle. She left for a moment and returned with a cart loaded with an array of different colored makeup and brushes.

Abby peeked at a Latex prosthetic Maggie retrieved.

"I'm just going to check the fit before I get started," she told Abby. "I'll need you to close your eyes. What you'll feel being painted on your face is adhesive."

Abby kept her eyes closed as Maggie tucked the mask into the corners of her eyes and nose. She felt her smooth the mask's edges against her skin.

"You can open your eyes now," Maggie told her. "This usually takes a lot more time than I have. But it will fool the cameras and anyone looking for you." She put on a layer of nude foundation, then began blending in other shades of skin color. "If I'm not finished with both of you by the time we land, my husband will pull the plane into the hangar, and I'll keep working until I'm satisfied."

"We're not in a rush," Will told her, watching from a seat nearby. "I couldn't pass up the chance to take them across the Puget Sound on the ferry. Once we make it past the cameras, security, and all the people onboard, we'll be okay."

After she finished, Maggie handed Abby a mirror. "When you reach your destination, and you're out of harm's way, you can easily pull off the mask."

Abby studied her new face. "There's not a bit of me left." The shape of her face had changed. The dimples in her cheeks were gone. Her nose looked fatter. *Very unattractive*, she thought. *Tough, like put a hammer in my hands, and I can build a house, tough.* "What do you think, Ethan?"

"You don't look anything like you."

"Good job," Will said.

"Thank you," Maggie replied. "Now, it's Ethan's turn."

The plane landed before Maggie could finish, but it didn't take long before she completed Ethan's disguise. She handed him a mirror and a pair of black-rimmed glasses. "They're non-prescription lenses, so you won't have trouble seeing."

He put them on and laughed. "I don't even recognize me."

"Thank you, Maggie," Will said. "I owe you one."

"I owe you a million," she replied, dropping a set of keys in his hands. "There's a black SUV waiting for you just outside the hangar door. It's registered in your name." She gave him a business card. "You now work for the Teachers Union, and you're on your way to enroll Mason in junior high. I don't think you'll be stopped, but just in case." She took their photos with her phone. "Mason and Laura Freemont. My husband will have new IDs for you in just a moment."

While they waited, Ethan stared at himself in the mirror. "I can't even see where the mask and my real skin meet. It's awesome."

Once they received their new identification and climbed into the SUV, they drove off, heading for the Seattle ferry landing.

Abby, Ethan, and Will stood on the stern of the ferry as it sailed away from the Seattle coastline, heading to Bremerton. The sun shone brightly in the semi-cloudless sky. The ferry's wake left a trail across the Puget Sound's smooth waters.

Will pointed. "To the east, the Cascade Mountains are behind a bank of clouds in Seattle's background. You can just make them out. Let's head to the bow. The view is amazing."

They walked alongside the outer railing past travelers seated on benches and others leaning over the side of the ship, gazing at seals popping their dark bodies out of the glassy water. They joined several others on the bow.

Abby pulled her hat down over her eyes. *I wonder if they can tell I'm wearing a prosthetic,* she thought.

"How's everything holding together?" Will asked.

"So far, it's okay." She studied Ethan's disguise. "We're fine." She gazed at the beauty all around them. "This is spectacular."

"That's Mount Rainier to the southeast," Will told her. "North is Mount Baker and the world's largest glacier, and in the west, the Olympic Mountains."

Ethan pointed toward Mount Rainier. "The Takers are coming."

As hard as she tried, Abby couldn't see anything unusual in the sky.

"Let's get inside." Will opened the double doors leading into the passenger lounge and followed them in.

Abby gazed around at the multitude of seats. Most were empty. At a booth along the wall of windows, a woman with a small child sat next to one another, sharing a bag of chips. An elderly couple sat a few seats away from them. At another table, teenagers played cards and laughed. Others stayed outside.

"Let's go over here." Will led them to a booth on the other side of the room.

Abby stared out the window toward snowcapped Mount Rainier. A dark speck in the sky seemed to be increasing in size. The ferry engines stopped less than midway to their destination.

"What's going on?" Abby asked. "Why are we stopping?"

A woman's voice came over the loudspeaker. "We are sorry for the delay. We are being boarded. When our visitors depart, we will continue on our way. Thank you for your patience."

Abby looked out the window again and gasped. Three hovercrafts swooped down and surrounded their ferry. One hovered a few feet above the lower parking deck. Two men emerged and jumped out. Another craft glided to the other side of the ferry, while a third hovered in front of the bow.

"They're looking for someone," Will said. "They're checking the parked cars. We'll be next."

Crowds of people came in from outside, found seats, and everyone remained quiet.

Abby's heart pounded. She took a deep breath, trying to

stay calm.

"Watch the people," Will said. "Does anyone's body language tell you anything?"

Abby glanced around the room. Some stragglers came in from outside. A few passengers stood and walked around, looking out the scenic-sized windows. She put her shaking hands under the table so no one could see them tremble. Everyone seemed tense except the teens playing cards.

Ethan whispered to Will, "There's three men inside with weapons."

"Who?" Will asked.

"The bald guy looking out the window behind us, the man wearing a John Deere baseball cap near the double doors, and the skinny redhead guy sitting with a blonde girl by the other exit."

"You can see the weapons through their clothes?" Will asked.

Ethan nodded.

Two Takers came up the stairs, while two more stepped out of the elevator. Their weapons hung on the belts of their gray armor-protected uniform. They glanced about and went down the aisles, scrutinizing everyone.

One, with his hand on his weapon, came their way. His piercing eyes studied Ethan, Will, and Abby until one of the Takers called to him. Turning away, he hurried to the other side of the lounge where the others gathered around the woman with a small child.

When the woman screamed, the skinny redhead stood and reached for his gun.

A Taker pulled his weapon. "Don't think about it," he told the redhead. "This is none of your concern." He removed the young man's gun from under his shirt. "You won't be needing this." He shoved the man's gun under his belt and rejoined his comrades.

"No," the woman screamed. "Don't take him. He's autistic. Leave him alone."

One of the Takers yanked the little boy from the booth and passed him off to his team member.

The woman's pleas persisted as a Taker led her son away.

"Bring her, too," the one in charge said.

Two Takers escorted the mother out.

As the commander walked past the teenagers, he thanked them for their help.

"We thought it was our duty to report what we saw," one of the teenagers said.

"Well done," the commander replied. Before he left the lounge, he surveyed the room, and his eyes fell on Abby, Will, and Ethan.

His hesitation turned Abby's stomach.

"Thank you for your cooperation," he told everyone. Then he pivoted, went out the double doors, hopped over the ship's railing, and entered the hovercraft.

When they flew off, Abby took a breath.

"They're gone," Will told her.

The engines started while Abby stared out the window, watching the dark specks in the sky fade into the distance.

"Let's go outside and get some fresh air," Will said.

They went out to the bow. The tranquil scenery helped calm Abby's shattered nerves. She put her arm around Ethan as the ferry sailed past Bainbridge Island, turned at Point White, and followed the Port Orchard Channel along the Kitsap Peninsula before reaching Bremerton.

Abby didn't relax until Will drove off the ferry, traveled through a well-lit tunnel, and reached the main road. Her internal compass spun in all directions. Only the mountain ranges Will had pointed out gave her a clue to where in the world they were. She remembered her disguised face. "Will Dillon know who I am?" She touched the fake skin on her cheek. "This is going to scare him."

"You're right." Will drove up a hillside driveway and pulled over. "I think both of you should take off the masks before we get there."

Abby tugged on the latex, and to her surprise, it came away with little effort, but it would take work to remove the glue left behind. She glanced at Ethan in the backseat. "There are some pieces on your forehead," she told him, and turned to Will. "How bad do I look?"

He faced the rearview mirror toward her. "This might help."

She peeled away most of the adhesive before giving up. "We'll have to wash up when we get there." Glancing at Ethan, she nodded. "It's good enough for now. Let's go."

Will readjusted the mirror before driving up the driveway. When he reached a house at the top of the hill, he parked.

They all climbed out of the SUV and went to the front door.

Will knocked three times. "It's Will."

When the door opened, Dillon ran into Abby's arms. He stepped back and scrunched his nose. "There's something on your face, Mommy." He looked at Ethan. "Hi. I'm Dillon. What's your name?"

"Ethan."

With wide eyes, Dillon looked at Abby.

"He's your brother, honey."

Ethan bent down and gave him a hug.

"Are you going to leave again?" Dillon asked.

"No," Ethan told him. "I'm here to stay."

Dillon's eyes brightened, and a smile stretched across his face. He took Ethan's hand and led him into the living room. Abby and Will followed.

Chad, Holly, and Jack stood waiting for them.

"We didn't want to interrupt your reunion," Chad said.

Abby gave each of them a hug. "Thank you for saving my son's life. I'll never forget what you've done." She felt her eyes tear, and she sniffled.

"We're glad we could help," Holly said.

Chad glanced at Dillon and Jack. "Would you two give us some time to talk? It's all right if you play in the bedroom."

They ran to a room down the hall.

"The bathroom is the first door on the left if you want to clean up," Holly told Abby.

"Thank you." She looked at Ethan. "Come on, honey."

Ethan took her outstretched hand. When they reached the hallway, they found the bathroom door open.

"Close the door, please," Abby told Ethan. "I want to ask you something."

He did as she asked and turned to her.

"Do you think we should tell Dillon about the Takers?" she asked him. "You can probably remember when you were his age. Do you think he'd understand?"

"I'll talk to him if you want me to. I promise I won't scare him."

"I've always worried about frightening him. I didn't know how I'd tell him without him seeing the fear on my face. But he needs to know. Yes. Tell him."

After they both washed up, they went back into the living room.

"I filled them in on all that's happened," Will told Abby.

"We've all been through a lot," Abby said. "I asked Ethan to tell Dillon about the Takers. I know you haven't told Jack about them yet. What do you think? Do you want him to tell Jack, too?"

"I always tried to help the little ones when they were afraid," Ethan told them. "I remember how I felt."

Chad looked at Holly. "It's time," he said.

Ethan nodded, walked down the hall to the room where the boys played, went inside, and closed the door.

"I'm flooded with questions," Will said. "Who told the Takers about Abby and Dillon?"

"Headquarters doesn't know yet," Chad told him.

"Did the Takers find out that you two were involved?" Will asked.

"There was no mention of us in any of the communications that we intercepted," Chad told him. "Headquarters has ways of knowing if the government surveillance satellites are trained on our homes. They're not. And whoever it was that turned Abby in wasn't watching her house, either. If they had been, they would've known Abby wasn't there."

"So, if they didn't know about you, Holly, and Jack, they probably think Dillon is with Abby," Will said.

"Your landlord's a member of the Underground," Chad told Abby. "He told the Takers you and your three-year-old son left and won't be back for a couple of weeks."

"He told them Dillon is three years old?" Will said. "That's cool. Nevertheless, the Takers will be watching her house from now on. You can count on it."

My important papers, our birth certificates, tax records, and documents, she thought. "Did you remember to take the folder?"

Holly walked across the room and retrieved an expandable folder. She brought it back to Abby and handed it to her. "I grabbed it on the way out."

"Thank you," Abby said. "This is all so overwhelming. Thank you for everything."

Will reached into his shirt pocket and pulled out a picture of Ethan's fake mother. "Some students were given their real mom's picture, while others were given a photo of a stranger and were brainwashed into believing the woman was their mother." He handed it to Chad. "See if Headquarters can find out who she is."

Chad took the photo. "I thought only orphans were used as replacements."

"The more we learn about the Takers School, the more confusing it gets," Will said. "They changed Ethan's name to Emory Davis. More than likely, the fake mother's surname will be Davis as well."

"I'll pass along that information," Chad said as he turned and left the room.

"What stopped Ethan from being brainwashed into believing she was his mom?" Holly asked.

"His dad was murdered when the Takers took Ethan at age five," Will said. "He can still envision his father's face and Abby's, too."

"It's scary," Abby said. "He and his friend saw children being taken from their beds in the middle of the night and brought back before dawn. Then, the night before his friend's twelfth birthday, when he was going to be sent home, they took him while he slept and did something to his memory. He didn't know Ethan after that."

"Looks like the majority of the brainwashing is completed just before the children are sent home," Will said.

"So, that means the runaways weren't totally reprogrammed yet," Abby said.

"Yes," Will told her. "Now I understand why they have faulty memories. They have trouble remembering what the school looked like and details about what they were taught. More than likely, those were the memories that were manipulated over time, during the night. They were lucky they escaped the final procedure."

"It scared Ethan so bad that he ran," Abby said.

"Fear drove almost all of the runaways to escape," Will added.

Fear, Abby thought. *I know how it feels.* "Will we have to move to another town?"

"It depends on the description they gave of you and Dillon," Will said. "Hopefully, it was vague. Headquarters is going over the intercepted communications now."

Chad returned with a few documents in his hand. "You're not going to believe who that woman is." He handed the papers to Will.

Will scanned the documents. "Oh, crap."

"Who is she?" Abby asked.

"She's the lead genome sequencing scientist at DC Labs," Will told her.

"She might have been involved with his genetic alterations," Chad said.

"If she knows her son has white hair and silver eyes," Will said, "they won't be able to slip in a substitute. Their only alternative is to recapture him and make sure his memories are sufficiently altered."

Abby heard the bedroom door open and saw Ethan walking toward them. He joined them in the living room and plopped into a chair.

"How did it go?" Abby asked him.

"Dillon asked me if the Takers are monsters, and I told him yes. He said we need to hide from them. I told him that's what we're doing."

"Is he scared?" Abby asked.

"No. He said we should fight them and something about *Star Wars*. Whatever that meant. I guess it's a movie. I told him I'd watch it with him."

"He might still be too young," Abby said, "to know what danger is. *Star Wars* is an old movie, and it's his favorite. It's filled with danger. But it's just a movie."

"We can stream it if you want to watch it in the boys'

room," Holly said.

"Let's see what the boys want to do," Abby told her.

She and Holly stood in the bedroom doorway watching them play-fight with invisible lightsabers. Dillon stopped when Abby cleared her throat.

"Are you guys hungry?" she asked. "After dinner, you can watch *Star Wars* with Ethan if you want." When they cheered and danced around the room, Abby realized they hadn't been traumatized by the news of the Takers at all. "We'll call you when dinner is ready."

Abby followed Holly into the kitchen.

"We've been ordering takeout since we got here," Holly told her. She opened the refrigerator and stared at the empty shelves.

"Why don't we order pizza?" Abby asked.

"Best idea all day," Holly said.

After everyone decided what kind of pizzas to order, Chad called it in. "Twenty minutes," he told them, putting his cell phone into his shirt pocket.

"Good." Will looked over at Ethan. "Can we ask you some questions?"

"It's okay," he said.

"They gave you the picture of your fake mother," Will said. "Do you think she has a photo of you, too?"

"We had our pictures taken every year. I don't know if they gave her mine."

"We can assume that she knows what he looks like," Will said to everyone. "Instead of using an orphan, they broke protocol for some reason by using Ethan as a replacement. My guess is they want to use him as payment for his fake mom's genome assembly skills. We need to get his school records to find out what they're doing to our children. We can't let them use them as lab rats." He turned to Ethan. "Can you lead us to the

Takers School?"

"Do you know where the man found me in the woods?" Ethan asked. "I didn't have a map or anything when I ran away. They didn't allow us to have a phone or any connection to the outside. I just ran."

"Do you remember what the school looked like?" Chad asked.

Ethan nodded. "There were rallies outside every month for our sports games. We cheered for our favorite players. It was fun. But when I got really good at math, I noticed something strange. The school looked too small to hold all of the children watching the games. I kept thinking about it. There was something wrong. When my eye color changed, I saw what the school really was—a hologram."

Everyone gasped.

"What the hell?" Will said.

"How could the Takers School not be there if you've been inside it?" Chad asked.

"It surprised me, too," Ethan replied. "To go inside, we always went up the school steps in single file and through the front door. The steps seemed real, and so did the door. And everything inside was real. But I know what I saw."

"Their hologram capabilities must have advanced considerably," Chad said.

"They're going to extremes to hide the Takers School," Will said. "What else do you remember about the place? Anything else unusual about it?"

"There was a hum all the time. It bothered me when I first got there, but then I didn't notice it much after that."

"Powering that hologram would take a massive amount of energy," Chad said.

"Maybe that's what we should be looking for," Will said, "a major power surge."

Chad stood. "I have to notify Headquarters." He headed down the hall.

"And find out if they've learned anything about the snitches," Will told him.

Chad nodded and kept walking.

"I'll check and see if the pizza has arrived yet," Holly told them. "Would you like to get some fresh air, Ethan?"

"What about the delivery boy?" Abby asked. "What if he's seen Ethan's photo?"

"Not a problem," Holly said. "It's pod delivery. I have a list of all the restaurants that give you a delivery method option."

"That's useful," Abby said, watching them walk to the front door. She turned to Will as soon as the door closed. "Do you think Chad will ask Ethan about his eyesight?"

"I thought Ethan handled it well," Will told her. "Telling them that he saw the hologram didn't sound like he has super vision. If either of them is mulling over what he told them, they'd be focused on the school cover-up and location."

"You're probably right," Abby said. "I need to stop worrying so much."

"Yes, you do," Will told her. "Have a little faith."

Chad returned to the living room and reclaimed his seat. "Well, they found out who turned in Abby. It was Marylin Dowser and Betty Hill. Headquarters is finding Abby and her family a new home."

"Did they give the Takers a photo of her?" Will asked.

"No. It was a verbal description. Vague like always."

"What do you mean by *always*?" Abby asked.

Will chuckled. "I don't think there are many people in town that they haven't turned in. I'm surprised the Takers still respond to those two nut-jobs' calls."

"So, I didn't say or do anything wrong or offend anyone?" Abby asked.

"No," Will replied. "I know it feels like this was personal, but it wasn't."

"Well, it is to me." Abby crossed her arms. "I almost lost Dillon. They're dangerous." When she heard the front door open, she went down the hallway and told the boys to come eat.

Holly and Ethan set two large pizzas and drinks, along with plates and napkins, on the coffee table in the living room.

"Maybe sometime in the future there'll be payback," Will told Abby, "but not now. You have to move. I need to teach you how to shoot a gun, and then I want to show you a few moves to protect yourself."

"How long will that take?" Chad asked him.

"As soon as she and the boys move into their new place, I'm going to take Abby to the shooting range. She's never shot a gun in her life. Everything should take about a week. Why do you ask?"

"How do you feel," Chad asked, "about taking Ethan on an expedition to see if we can find the school?"

When Will looked at Ethan, Abby knew no words were needed. Will made a promise to keep Ethan's secret. If they went, others would find out about her son's enhanced vision. "We should think about this," she said. "It's too risky."

"What do you think, Ethan?" Will asked.

Ethan hesitated before he spoke, then he looked at Chad and then Holly. "She's right. It's too risky."

"True," Will said. "Even if we knew where the school he attended is, how would we get in to confiscate his records? We should let Headquarters deal with it."

Chad nodded.

Chapter 10

The next morning, Holly asked Abby, while washing the breakfast dishes, "Did Will hear anything from Headquarters?"

"Yes. They told him that they would send someone else to guard us if he wants to go home. But he said he's here already and would rather stay until we're safely home. Since they found out who Ethan's fake mother is, they've decided to guard us day and night to make sure nothing happens to him. Once we move into a safe place, the Underground will rely on their members, who appear to be half the town, to watch out for us."

"You can count on them," Holly said. "We take care of our own. Chad thinks the Takers won't be watching your old place any longer. Your landlord said that the snitches turned in two more families for no reason at all. Now the Takers are refusing to respond to their complaints."

"Too bad that didn't happen before they turned us in," Abby said.

"It means they won't be hunting for you," Holly told her. "Dillon can continue attending his school. And I'll still be able to watch Dillon and Ethan whenever you need me."

"Thank goodness for you and everyone else," Abby told her.

Holly looked out the kitchen window. "They're here to take us to the airport."

They went into the living room. Hugs and handshakes were shared all around before Holly, Chad, and Jack left.

"I don't know how long we'll have to remain here," Will said to Abby. "While we're waiting, I want to test Ethan's eyesight." He looked at Ethan. "Are you up for it?"

"Sure. Can Dillon go?"

"We can all go," Will replied.

"Where are you taking him?" Abby asked.

"There's a certain spot in the yard," Will said, "where you can see Seattle. It's approximately fourteen miles from here to there. I'll use it as a mile marker to estimate his span of vision." He went to the back bedroom and returned with binoculars. "All set."

They followed him out the door and up a trail leading to the top of the hill behind the house. Pine trees surrounded them except where an outcrop of stones formed a clearing. Below, a ferry made its way past Point White, weaving through the waterways between Bainbridge Island and a branch of the Kitsap Peninsula. From where they stood, they saw a gray image of Seattle far in the distance. In its background, the Cascade Mountains stood cloudless in the midday sun.

"What's the farthest you can see between here and Seattle?" Will asked Ethan.

"There's a really tall building with lots of glass. It's really cool. I like it the best of all of them. It has a stripped gray pyramid roof with a small square box on top of it. The box has stars on the sides."

Abby watched Will's jaw drop. He pulled out his cell phone and a minute later had a picture of Seattle's skyline on its screen. "Is this the one?" Will zoomed in on the photo, getting a close-up of the roof.

"Yes," Ethan said. "That's it."

Will looked at Abby. "That's not possible."

"Can I have a word with you?" Abby asked, stepping away from the children. "We have to be careful about making Ethan feel like he's a freak. Okay?"

"You're right," Will told her. "What if I tell him he's amazing?"

"That's fine. But don't gush. I don't want him to get a big

head either."

"Do you know how incredible this is?" Will asked.

"Do you know what a disaster his life will be if someone finds out?" she asked.

"Are you asking me to act like this is normal?"

"I'm sure he knows it isn't. Pretend it is. Call it practice. You'll have to watch what you say and how you react around others when Ethan tells you what he sees."

Will nodded. "Composure." He grinned. "Super vision. This is so cool."

They strolled back to the boys.

"Perfect, Ethan," Will told him. "Anything else?"

"I can see farther, but I don't know how far that is."

"We don't have to be precise," Will said. "What you told me you saw is all I need to know for now." He put his hand on Ethan's shoulder. "You're amazing."

"I never told anyone," Ethan said. "Not even my best friend, Cole."

"It's a good thing you didn't," Abby said. "He would've turned you in."

"Let's head back to the house," Will said.

The boys took the lead down the hill.

Will strolled with Abby. "He loves his big brother," he said.

"Yes. I know Ethan will watch over him."

Will nodded.

"Are you sure you're not neglecting your patients, doctor?" she asked.

"I work for the Underground and go where I'm needed. Right now, I'm needed here."

"I'm glad you are."

"The children in our Underground orphanages across the nation are healthy. Especially the runaways."

"What will happen to the boy on the ferry?" Abby asked. "Will he go to the school Ethan ran away from?"

"Yes, all children ages five to twelve. Disabilities mean nothing to them."

"That doesn't make sense," Abby said. "Children with disabilities have individual needs. They all can't learn at the same level." She shook her head.

"Who knows how they're solving that problem. We won't have the answer unless we find the schools." Will opened the front door for everyone.

"Maybe the younger children attending the Takers' School have something special about their DNA," Abby said. "The experimentation has to be the only reason the Takers' schools exist. They didn't have to close the local elementary schools. They only needed to replace the teachers." She felt her face flush with anger. "They're using our children as lab monkeys. Is that what's been going on for all these years?"

Will nodded. "I think we've finally solved the mystery." He locked the door behind them once they were inside. "I'll check and see if Headquarters has information yet." He headed down the hallway.

"After you have lunch," Abby said to the boys, "you can go back outside if you want to. Just make sure you stay where I can see you." She went into the kitchen and gathered what she needed to make sandwiches. While she spread mustard on a bun, she looked up to see Will walking out of the hallway with a smile on his face.

He joined her in the kitchen. "Where are the boys?" he asked.

"They're outside." She glanced out the window. "Why? What's going on?" Abby cut the last sandwich she made in half and set it on the tray with the others.

"Headquarters sent me the location of one of their gun

ranges. I thought we could go on a group outing."

"The boys, too?"

"There's no one here who can watch them while we go. So, yes." He reached around her and grabbed a black olive. "Dillon will be fine. He can wear headgear to block the noise, the same as the rest of us."

"I guess I can't get out of this," Abby said. "I probably won't be able to hit a target."

"That's why they call it target practice. You'll have fun. I promise."

She took a step back and crossed her arms. "The only reason to learn how to shoot a gun is to hurt someone. And I don't want to do that."

"No," he said. "That's not the only reason. You may have to protect yourself and your family."

She uncrossed her arms. "I know you're right. I'll get the boys."

After they finished their sandwiches, Will followed her outside and locked the front door. They all climbed into his truck. He drove off the Kitsap Peninsula by way of the Tacoma Narrows Bridge and headed away from the city. After all the turns and curves, going east, south, and west, Abby had no idea where they were. At the end of a dirt road that led them through the woods to a meadow, Will parked.

A semi-truck remained stationary. Pictures of bales of hay, along with the caption Farmer's Best covered the side of the fifty-three-foot trailer. A few yards away, a white canopy shaded a picnic table.

"Where's the shooting range?" Abby asked.

"Inside the semi," Will told her.

After Abby exited the vehicle, she saw a man slide open the trailer cargo door, walk down wooden steps, and stroll over to them.

"Good to see you again, Keith," Will told him.

"Always a pleasure, Will."

Abby noticed they weren't introduced. *Need to know*, she thought.

Keith led them to the canopy, where he asked them to sit while he went over the fundamentals of gun safety and choosing the correct weapon for a person's stature. "I suggest the smart gun for you." He showed it to Abby. "The facial recognition technology and a vocal directive tell you the laser beam's proximity to a kill shot or a target's center point by giving you a number from one to ten."

She watched as he showed her how to load and unload the magazine.

"When you receive your nine-millimeter gun, you'll use your fingerprint or authorized voice command to lock and unlock its safety device." Then he handed the unloaded gun to Abby. "I want you to load and unload the magazine and also the gun the way I showed you. About ten or fifteen times will be sufficient. When you get your new gun, you'll need to practice loading it, too."

She began following his instructions. After the fifteenth time, she felt comfortable with the weight of the gun and confident she could load it quickly.

"I'll give the magazine to you in a safer location," he told her. "Show her how to hold it, Will, while I set things up inside the truck." He gave Will a wink and left them.

"What was the wink for?" Abby asked.

"It's a guy thing," Will told her. "Stand up for a moment." When she did, he led her away from Ethan and Dillon, who watched closely. "Aim the gun at that bear crossing sign."

"What sign?" She turned toward him. "Where?"

"Just kidding. I want you to notice where you're pointing that gun."

She looked down and saw her gun pointed at Will. "This is a really bad idea."

"It's a good thing it's not loaded. Before you turn, remember to stand down. Don't let anything distract you." He showed her how to use the safety. "Always have the safety on until you shoot. Let's use that tree as a make-believe target." Standing behind her, he wrapped his arms around her, helping her to aim and showing her how to position her hands. With his body pressed against hers, he whispered. "This is why he winked."

"I thought you told me not to let anything distract me." She gripped the gun as he showed her, held her arms straight out, and used the scope to focus on the target.

He stepped back. "Make sure you put your left foot forward to brace yourself. And keep your shoulders in front of your hips. Never lean back, or you can land on your ass when you fire. Now take aim. Never put your finger on the trigger until you're ready to shoot. Do you see the laser dot on your target?"

"Yes."

The voice accuracy indicator spoke. "Seven."

"That means your shot is off center," Will told her.

She looked down the scope and concentrated.

"Ten," the voice said.

"Now, take the safety off, put your finger on the trigger, and slowly squeeze," Will said.

She did as he told her, keeping her hand steady. When she heard a click, she took her finger off the trigger, set the safety, and turned to him. "How was that?"

"Good, but you're still pointing the gun at me."

"Oh." She aimed it at the ground. "There's a lot to remember."

"It doesn't matter if the safety is on or not. Don't point the gun at anyone unless you intend to kill them." He looked at Ethan. "You're up next."

"You're going to teach him to shoot?" Abby asked.

"Do you want me to?" Will asked.

She thought about the first time she saw Ethan at the medical center and how big he had grown since she'd seen him last. Looking at him now, she could swear he had grown a couple of inches more since this morning. "Yes. Go ahead." She sat next to Dillon as Ethan joined Will.

"Did the gun hurt you, Mommy?" Dillon asked.

"No," she told him. "It only hurts you when you don't know how to use it. Remember what Will told you. It's not a toy."

They watched Will teaching Ethan, and Abby chuckled to herself. *Bear crossing.* A rustle gave her a start. She stared into the woods about fifty yards away. Thinking about bears, she began to rise from the bench. "Will, look."

He instructed Ethan to put the safety on and lower his gun. Then he turned to see what she pointed at. "Look, Ethan," he said in a low voice.

A deer and her two fawns stepped out from between the pine trees and into the open.

"Cool," Ethan said. "I never saw a real one before."

The fawns followed their mother across the meadow.

"You've never seen deer anywhere near your school?" Abby asked Ethan.

"I've never seen an animal or any other living thing around the school. I never really thought about it."

She turned to Will. "What would cause that?"

"Good question," Will said. "Let's wait until after shooting practice before we try to figure it out." He put his hand on Ethan's shoulder. "Where were we?"

When the outside lessons ended, Will led them into the semi-trailer.

Keith met them inside. He gave all of them noise-cancelling

headphones and handed Will a loaded smart gun, then said, "The safety is set on voice command and will respond to each of your voices."

"Perfect," Will said.

Keith stepped back, and Will continued with the training.

"So, you're a doctor and a marksman, too," Abby said to Will.

"A doctor needs precision and focus to be good at his profession. It makes sense to choose a pastime that demands the same control. I'm good at golf, too."

"I bet you are," she said. Waiting for him to hand her the loaded gun, she gazed at the far end of the trailer and saw the target—the shadow image of a person's head and shoulders against a white background.

Will looked at Ethan. "Would you mind watching where each of her shots hit and in what order?"

Ethan gave him a thumbs up, put on his headphones, and helped Dillon with his.

Will joined her at the firing line. She listened as he reminded her of everything he had told her outside. Then he put on his headgear and stepped back.

Abby adjusted her headphones, balanced her stance, and held her arms out straight. She swallowed her nervousness, gripped the gun, and blocked everything from her mind, focusing. She heard the vocal accuracy indicator through her headphones say *ten*. "Safety off," Abby said. She fired three times. "Safety on," she remembered to say. With her arms stretched in front of her and a smile on her face, she looked over her shoulder at Will. "How was that?"

"I knew you'd like shooting." He pushed a button on the wall, and the target slid toward them on a zip cord. "Which one did she shoot first, Ethan?"

"The first is in the right eye, you blew his nose off on

the second, and the other right between the eyes," he told him without looking at the target Will held.

"Guess you're a natural," Will told her.

Abby waited for another target to be set up, remembering there were bullets in her gun now. She kept the safety on and lowered her gun, trying not to point it at Will. *That wasn't so bad,* she thought. *But I still don't want to hurt anyone, let alone kill them.* "If I'm a natural, maybe I can just shoot somebody in the foot or leg to stop them."

"And whoever the perpetrator is can still shoot you with their gun or throw a knife at you or maybe even attack you. So, what are you going to do when the wounded intruder is still coming at you after you shoot, and he's stronger than you? Are you willing to take that chance? You'd be risking your life and your children's."

She crossed her arms and looked Will in the eyes. "I need more practice."

"We agree on that," Will replied. "But all we have time for now is a couple more rounds from you and a few for Ethan."

She studied the firearm in her hand. *I've got to be smarter than the gun if I'm going to feel comfortable.* "I want to buy one like this. Would you show me everything I need to know about it? Maintenance wise, I mean."

Will nodded. "You can count on it." He smiled at her. "It was fun. Admit it."

"Okay. It wasn't so bad." She remembered the day her husband had been killed, and Ethan had been taken, the helplessness she felt along with hatred for the Takers, and her need for revenge. Those feelings engulfed her again as she recalled that day. Turning toward the target area, she put on her headgear, took her stance, turned the safety off, and fired off a few more rounds. *Okay. I can get tough,* she thought. Her shots seemed consistent. "Safety on."

Will showed her the target. "Good shot," he said. "Your turn, Ethan."

Once the target had been reset for him, Ethan put on his headgear and took the gun Abby handed him. He stood with his left foot forward, arms stretched out, and gun pointed at the target. "Safety off," he said. After firing four times, he lowered the gun and waited for the results.

Will removed the target from the zip cord and studied it. The holes in the simulated head and shoulders were spread out. "What were you aiming at?" he asked him.

Ethan pointed to each hole. "Both eyes, his nose, and one for the grin on his face."

Will chuckled. "In that case, you were dead on. Did you picture someone's face when you pulled the trigger?"

"Yes. The dean. He always told us to follow our gut feelings. When I did, it told me he was evil and not to trust him."

"Why would someone who is trying to manipulate you tell you to follow your gut feeling?" Abby asked. "Wouldn't they be telling you to do as they say and don't think about it?"

"Getting in contact with your true feelings was a large part of the curriculum," Ethan told her. "Listening to the voices inside our head was supposed to encourage new ideas and inspire us to be creative."

"Does the chip embedded in your head have anything to do with the voices you're told to listen to?" Will asked.

"I don't think so," Ethan said. "No one's controlling my thoughts."

"Well, I have a creative idea," Abby said. "Let's head home and have a barbeque."

"Cool," Dillon said.

Keith joined them before they left. "You'll have to contact Headquarters to order your firearm," he said. "I don't keep anyone's personal information. It's too risky."

"Not a problem," Will said. "I know the procedure."

"Glad I could be of service," Keith told him. "I'll be leaving soon and going south. It was good seeing you again, Will. Have a safe drive home." He slid open the cargo door.

Once Abby stepped down from the truck and walked toward the car with the boys and Will, she noticed Keith had already taken down the tent, and he put the wooden steps by the cargo door inside the trailer.

"He never stays long enough to draw attention," Will said as he started the SUV.

"Thank you, Will," Abby said. "We had fun."

"I knew you would."

Chapter 11

After breakfast the next morning, Will went into the back bedroom and returned with a pencil and a notepad. "We've interviewed each of the runaways to get an idea of what the school looks like and what they were taught. Since your memory is better than theirs, I'd like to see what you remember, Ethan."

"Okay. What do you want to know?"

"What did your sleeping quarters look like? Were there bunkbeds or single twin-sized beds? How about windows?"

"I can draw a picture of our room if you want," Ethan told him.

Will handed him the pencil and notepad. Abby watched over Ethan's shoulder, and Will sat on a stool across from him.

He drew a rectangular room with ten sets of double-stacked beds on one wall and the same on the opposite wall. "In each sleep compartment, there's adjustable lighting above the mattress. On the inner wall, there are drawers for our clothes and school books. Each sleep compartment has a sliding door for privacy." He drew desks and chairs in the center of the room. "We could do our homework or play games on the tables. If we wanted to watch TV or a movie, each sleep compartment has a screen at the end of the bed." He kept sketching. "On this wall, there's storage for games, books, and other things to keep us from getting bored. The showers are through the doors at the other end of the room."

"Is the area well lit?" Will asked.

"Yes. Bright white light in the center of the room and soft blue in each compartment."

"What color are the walls, floor, and ceiling?" Will asked.

"White."

"Even the desk and chairs?"

"Yes," Ethan replied.

"Too sterile," Abby said.

"Where's the door going out?"

"It's in the center of the storage wall at the end of the room." He pointed at his drawing.

"There's no windows?" Will asked.

"Not in the dorm room."

"Did you wear a uniform?" Will asked.

"We had a choice of what we could wear. The pants were all the same but in different colors and with elastic waistbands. There were a lot of styles of shirts, all made with the same material as the pants and in different colors. We had shoes that we wore indoors and another pair for outside."

"What about the girls? What did they wear?"

"They wore the same clothes as we did."

"Which rooms have the windows?" Will asked.

"The dining room," Ethan told him. "There are ceiling-to-floor windows on the outer wall. And the sitting room had windows, too."

"And you've never seen an animal or any living thing outside when you look out the windows?" Abby asked.

"No. Never."

Will rose from the stool and walked over to the sliding glass doors leading out to the patio. Silently, he looked outside, then turned to Ethan. "Are you sure what you saw looking out the window was real?"

"I think so. The sun came up in the morning and set at night. The weather changed all the time, just like it did after I ran away."

Abby stood and joined Will, who had his back toward the children. "Are you thinking that what he saw through the window is a hologram?" she whispered.

"I'm thinking they control everything—what the children see, eat, and think."

"They take children from their beds while they sleep," Abby said. "They give each child a photo of a woman and brainwash them into believing she's their real mother. The school's a hologram, and possibly what they see out the window is, too. But worst of all, they've embedded chips in their head, and we don't know why."

"And the list keeps getting longer," Will said. "Well, he doesn't have to describe the exterior of the school since it's a hologram." He walked back to Ethan. "I guess we're done here."

Ethan handed him the notepad and pencil.

Will took them into the back bedroom.

"I'm going to wash the dishes," Abby said. "What are you boys planning to do today?"

"Dillon wants me to watch another Star Wars movie," Ethan told her. "I really liked the last one."

"There's a lot more after that," Abby told them as she headed into the kitchen.

While drying the last dish, she looked over her shoulder and saw Will walking out of the hallway toward her.

"Good news," he said. "Your landlord has another four-bedroom house for rent across the lake. He's not asking for a deposit, and the rent will be the same amount. There's plenty of shopping nearby. But best of all, it's nowhere near Marylin and Betty's neck of the woods."

"That is good news," Abby said. "When do we leave?"

"Now. I have to stop by our orphanage to check on a runaway who was recently found close to where the Underground found Ethan. It shouldn't take long."

"I'll round up the boys." She dried her hands on a paper towel and headed for their bedroom. When she opened the door, she noticed the movie they were about to watch hadn't started yet. "Gather all your things. We're leaving. They found us a new home."

Everyone moved quickly and met in the living room in about fifteen minutes.

Abby helped Dillon carry the pile of new clothes Holly had bought him. "We need to get a few things for Ethan," she told Will as they stepped out the front door. "He only has the clothes he wore when they found him in the forest, and the jeans and T-shirt they gave him at the medical center."

"That reminds me." Will locked the front door and opened the back of the SUV. "You'll have to sign some papers for tax purposes when we see Morgan. And since you'll be classified as an employee, he'll give you a company cash card in your name. You can't use your Fed-coin card any longer. It's traceable."

Abby glanced at her sons in the backseat. "Okay, then. We're good to go." She climbed in and sat next to Will as he started the engine. "Buckle up and lock your doors, boys. It's going to be a long drive home."

"Two hours to get to the orphanage," Will said. "And an hour to get home."

Morgan, his white hair and beard ruffling in the breeze, met them outside the orphanage by the parking lot. They followed him through a garden where students planted and tended the blooming foliage. Then they came to a side door where Morgan used a security eye-scanner, which allowed them to enter and led them down a hallway to a conference room.

Inside, Abby's attention turned to the wall-to-wall windows that revealed a panoramic view. She stood with Will and the boys, gazing out at the lake's glassy, calm waters that mirrored the tall pine trees growing along its edge. Down a long rocky beach, a man strolled with his golden retriever.

"Can we get a dog?" Ethan asked, standing next to her.

"Please, Mommy," Dillon said.

She looked at them. "Maybe after we're all settled in."

Will leaned toward her. "I have a friend who has Lab puppies."

"Of course, you do."

"A pup can keep Ethan company while Dillon's at school," Will whispered.

She lowered her voice and said, "I know, but…what happens if we have to run again? I don't know what our future looks like. Now's not a good time."

Morgan led Abby to an office. "We'll get your employment information and tax papers filled out," he told her. "The Takers are fed up with the women who reported you. They've abandoned their vigilance of all those the women falsely accused. In short, there's no longer a need to change your name."

She filled out her information, signed each document, and gave them back to him.

"As far as the government knows, you're employed at our orphanage. They'll never know you're really working at the Underground's school." He handed her a palm-sized card. "Your wages will go directly onto your company cash card."

"Thank you," Abby said.

Morgan picked up a file from his desk and led her out of the office, past an oval conference table, and stopped at a casual gathering place with a long teal couch, several chairs, and a view of the lake.

Abby sat in a gray swivel chair next to Will. The boys remained in front of the wall of windows, searching for wildlife. Once seated on the couch, Morgan leaned forward and placed the file on the coffee table in front of him.

Will handed him Ethan's sketch. "It's the sleeping chambers at the Takers School."

"Impressive," Morgan said, studying the drawing. "He's the only runaway that remembers the school's interior."

"Everything's white," Will told him. "Table and chairs, too."

"Extremely sterile, like living inside a test tube," Morgan said.

"There are no windows except in the dining room and common area," Will told him. "Ethan said he's never seen a living thing through the windows—no birds, animals, or anything that crawls."

"How strange," Morgan said. "How about the school's exterior?"

"Ethan believes it's a hologram," Will replied.

Morgan looked up from the drawing. "A hologram?"

"And since he's been at the school for six years," Will told him, "and hasn't seen even a bird through the windows, I'm guessing the view of the grounds is a hologram, too."

"Not even a squirrel?" Morgan asked.

"Only pictures in books," Will told him. "Apparently, the library's extensive. Everything they want the children to read."

"Complete control," Morgan said. He reached for the file, pulled out a photo, and handed it to Will. "Our newest runaway."

Dillon sat cross-legged on the carpet in front of the window, watching squirrels playing on a nearby tree.

Ethan joined Abby, Will, and Morgan and glanced at the photo. "He's not a runaway. He's a snitch. He told the school master everything we said or did."

"You're certain about this?" Morgan asked.

Ethan nodded.

Abby cleared her throat. "They did something to my son that turned his hair white and his eyes silver. And they gave him a photo of a woman and tried to brainwash him into believing that she's his mother."

"The woman's the lead genome sequencing scientist at DC Labs," Will said. "For some reason, he's been chosen out of all the children at the school to be sent to her when he turns twelve as a replacement for her child. What happened to her real son? We don't know if she even has one."

"It would be interesting to find out," Morgan said.

"We believe a photo of Ethan was given to her every year," Abby said. "Because of his white hair and silver eyes, they won't be able to find anyone else to take his place."

"Good chance they'll be searching for him," Morgan said.

"What if the snitch has been sent to hunt for Ethan?" Abby asked.

"Don't give the boy a physical," he told Will. "It's better if he never sees your face. He's been quarantined until he has a medical checkup, so he hasn't had an opportunity to do any damage. I'll move him to one of our other orphanages that doesn't house runaways."

"If the Takers are sending out a search party," Will said, "maybe all of the photos of the new runaways should be sent to me so Ethan can have a look."

"I don't know if I can help much," Ethan said. "No one paid much attention to anyone outside their dorm since we weren't allowed to make friends. I only noticed Alex because he's a jerk."

"He claims to be Billy Hamilton," Morgan said. "Interesting."

"Will Ethan have to hide for the rest of his life?" Abby asked.

Morgan pulled a tissue from his pocket and turned as if blowing his nose. When he faced them again, he gazed at them through silver eyes. "Possibly. I'm still looking over my shoulder."

Will's jaw dropped.

Abby and Ethan gasped.

"I believe there's more of us out there," Morgan told them.

"This is freaking mind-blowing," Will said. "Have you found others?"

"Yes. I've tracked down five. All living throughout the United States."

"And you think there are more?" Abby asked.

"Many more," Morgan told her.

"Why are you so sure?" Ethan asked.

Morgan met Ethan's eager gaze. "I can hear them."

"How?" Ethan asked.

"I escaped from the Taker's grasp when I was the same age you are, and like everyone else who has attended that school, I couldn't remember much about it. Fear of them finding me drove me to keep moving. I kept my eye color and most definitely my exceptional vision a secret. My gut told me not to tell anyone, or I'd never see my mom and dad again."

Ethan nodded.

"I made it home to find my parents were dead. They had left me a fortune—I'm talking billions. Fear of the Takers consumed my life, and I moved from city to city, from state to state." He glanced down, stroked his white beard, and chuckled. "One day, I met a man who taught me how to live in the moment. He trained me to meditate, to let go of my anxiety, to go within myself to find a path that would lead me to understanding. In the silence, a slight ringing in my ears that I thought nothing of shattered into pieces. Each piece had its own tone, unlike anything I've ever heard." He shook his head. "Tone is a trifle word. It's more like a soul's unique vibration." He smiled. "Yes, I believe that's it."

"And the frequencies you hear only come from those with

silver eyes and white hair?" Abby asked.

"Yes," Morgan replied. "When I allowed myself to expand my awareness, I was able to follow the most dominant reverberation, the one I heard above all others. It led me to the first of several who have the same white hair and silver eyes as myself."

"Where is he?" Ethan asked.

"In the mountains of West Virginia. His name is Rudy. He's twenty-six and lives in a cabin a mile away from his nearest neighbor."

"Do you keep in touch?" Abby asked.

"No. He's young and off enjoying his life. We sat and talked for days. His ears rang, too. When I told him why, it changed his life. After I left, and he heard the soul songs, he went in search of others like us. It's been years since I've talked to him."

"And meanwhile, you created the Underground," Will said.

"I couldn't stand by and let the Takers kidnap our children. There were millions of concerned Americans throughout our country who didn't trust our government. I united them and founded the Underground. We formed schools for our members' children and hid them from the Takers. And I created our orphanages as safe havens for the lost children, those who ran away from the Takers School, and those who no longer had a home to return to. Through their DNA, we've been able to find their relatives. And in some cases, we've found their parents who thought they'd never see their sons and daughters again. This orphanage grounds me. With the arrival of each child, I find hope."

"Maybe Ethan can spend more time with you after we get settled," Abby said. "I'm sure he has lots of questions."

"I would like that." Morgan turned to Ethan. "I look forward to seeing you again. And thank you for telling me about

Alex. We'll keep an eye on him."

"Good idea," Ethan replied.

"Wait just a minute," Morgan told them. He left the room, returned with a cell phone, and handed it to Ethan. "You can call me anytime if you want to talk. My number is on speed dial."

"Thank you. This is so cool." He studied it, flipped it over, and glanced at Will.

"He's never used a cell phone before," Will told Morgan. "No phones or computers were allowed at the Takers School."

"Yes," Morgan said. "I'm aware of that."

"I'll show him how to use it on our way home," Abby said. "Thank you. It's very thoughtful."

Morgan looked at Dillon. "I didn't forget about you." He reached into his pocket, pulled out a metal insignia, and pinned it on Dillon's shirt. "You are now an official member of the space patrol."

"A Star Wars badge," Dillon said.

"Yes, it does look like that," Morgan told him. "But this one's real. It was found in what was once called Area 51 and given to a commander who passed it down in his family. It was given to me as a gift. I was told it's made from materials not found on Earth."

"How do you know it's real?" Ethan asked.

"It sings to me," Morgan said. "Much like the ringing in my ears."

"Can you track it?" Ethan asked.

"Yes," Morgan told him. "I've been roughly a mile away and heard it sing. Its range has never been tested." He turned to Dillon. "Wear it all of the time. Don't let anyone take it. And may the force be with you."

Dillon stood with his shoulders back and gave Morgan a salute. "May the force be with you," he replied.

"Guess we're good to go," Will said.

Morgan walked them out to the SUV and stood waving as Abby, Will, and the boys drove away, heading to her new home.

Chapter 12

Abby stood on the front porch of her new place and looked out at the trees blocking the view of the house from anyone passing by. On the east side of the property, more trees grew along the lakeshore. The sense of privacy made her feel secure. The home had two floors and a finished basement. As Will and Chad unloaded her furniture from their trucks, she instructed them where each piece should go.

Organized disarray filled each room. And, as the men carried everything inside, the boys played in the backyard within a circumference of trees that shielded them from nosy neighbors.

"Only a few boxes left in storage," Will told her as he and Chad carried a dresser up the stairs.

"Thank you so much," Abby told them. She turned in a circle. "This place is beautiful and bigger than the other house. It's so cool."

"It's a hundred-year-old house," Will said over his shoulder as he went up the stairs. "Looks like it was well taken care of. And it has a boat dock. Time to buy a bathing suit."

She walked to the sliding glass doors that looked out over the backyard, checking on the boys. They laughed while playing soccer. She smiled, thinking, *They're going to love it here.*

"We're leaving to pick up the last load," she heard Will shout.

"Okay." Abby began going through boxes marked living room when she heard the men drive off. She started unpacking books and placing them on a bookshelf next to the fireplace. Glancing outside, she didn't see the boys. She went to the sliding-glass doors, stepped outside, and heard Ethan screaming for her. Fear engulfed her. Following the sound of his voice, she raced across the grass and through the woods to a trail leading to the boat dock. She found Ethan standing at the end of the pier, looking downstream. "Where's Dillon?" Her heart felt as if it would fly out of her chest.

He pointed at a boat crossing the lake. "They took him. Two women. One grabbed me from behind while the other caught Dillon, dragged him to the pier, and put him in a boat. I couldn't stop them. Where's Will?"

"He's not here." Abby patted her pants pockets and realized she didn't have her phone.

Ethan pulled out the one Morgan had given him and made a call. "They took Dillon," he told the person on the other end of the phone.

"Who are you talking to?" Abby asked him.

"Morgan." He listened. "No. Will's not here. We were playing soccer, and I kicked the ball too hard. It went into the woods. When Dillon went after it, he didn't come back. They were hiding behind a tree." He listened again. "In a boat. I watched where they docked, and I saw the car across the lake that they were driving. It was a red Electric L." He gave him the license plate number.

Abby lowered her head, trying to hold back the panic that started to consume her. At the edge of the dock, she glimpsed the badge Morgan had given Dillon. She picked it up, and tears filled her eyes.

"No," Ethan told Morgan. "Mom found it on the dock." He paused and nodded. "Okay," he said and put the phone back into his pocket.

"I don't know Will's number by heart," Abby said. "I need to get my phone."

"Morgan's calling him," Ethan told her. "He said they'll hack into the government spy satellite and find them."

She noticed a lump on Ethan's head. "You're hurt. What

did that witch do to you?"

He raised his hand to his forehead. "She threw me down before she ran to join the other woman. I hit my head on a rock."

Abby looked at his wound. "Are you dizzy?"

"No. I'm okay."

She took his hand and led him back to the house. She found her phone and called Will. "It went to voicemail," she told Ethan.

"He's talking to Morgan."

She paced the living room floor, not wanting to let Ethan out of her sight. Staring at the phone in her hand, she wished Will would call. *Damn witches. Just wait until I buy a gun.* "Come on, Will, call me."

Ten minutes seemed like an eternity before he walked through the door. Will had his cell phone on speaker and motioned Abby to listen in.

"We've located their electric vehicle," she heard Morgan say over the phone. "They're headed toward a small airport about five miles out of town. Our team is working on silencing their communications with the Takers."

"What's the plan?" Will asked.

"We're sending men in suits with fake credentials to intercept them. Meanwhile, we're slowing them down by interfering with their vehicle's electric relay system. Once our team has intercepted them, they'll retrieve the boy."

"What about the women?" Abby asked. "They need to pay for what they've done. Do we have to live in fear that they'll try it again?"

"Our team will inform the kidnappers that your son has a heart defect and is unable to be registered at the government's school," Morgan said. "And that their actions have put the boy's life in danger. If complications arise from their actions, they will be arrested for kidnapping and possibly manslaughter."

"Thank you," Will told him. "We'll await your call." He

placed his cell phone into his pants pocket.

"Is that all?" Tears of rage filled her eyes. "I wish I had my gun."

"Would you shoot them from a rooftop or kill them point-blank?" Will asked.

"I'd shoot them in the face."

"I know how you're feeling," he said. "I'd like to wring their necks, but we have to think smart. If we don't, you won't just have Marylin and Betty to deal with. I'm sure you know that." He put his arms around her. "You have to trust us. You can't let yourself fall apart."

She stepped back. "I'm not falling apart. I'm pissed."

"What if I promise you payback?" Will asked. "Will it ease your mind?"

She glared at him. "Don't patronize me."

"I'm not. I don't trust those two either. If they can follow us here, they can follow you to the school or to one of our meetings. But now's not the time to think about it. We have to get Dillon back, then we'll see what steps to take. Deal?"

"Deal."

"How's Ethan?"

"He has a lump on his head."

Ethan sat quietly by the fireplace, staring down at the floor.

Will went to him. "How do you feel? Physically, I mean."

"This is my fault," he told him. "I shouldn't have kicked the ball so hard."

"Do you think it's your fault that those two women have reported half of the town to the Takers?"

"No."

Will checked Ethan's forehead and examined his eyes. "You're just one of the families those two have caused trouble for."

"They must have known about Dillon somehow," Abby

said.

"Possibly not at first," Will replied. "It's their pattern. All of the reports they made accused each of the families of hiding their children. And every report was a lie. They're nuts, craving attention. I was told that the Takers don't want anything else to do with them because they've made too many false reports."

"Unless that's what they want you to believe," Ethan said. "Those two and the Takers could be working together. Maybe the Takers didn't believe the landlord when he told them the little boy who lived there was three. Didn't they check his clothes? The size would've given it away."

"Or it could be those two witches were just trying to prove to the Takers that they were telling the truth," Abby said. "Maybe they snuck into the house after the Takers left, found the size of Dillon's clothes, and discovered they were right for once."

"I'm hoping that's the case," Will told her. "If they're as annoying to the Takers as they are to everybody else who's met them, then it will take a lot of convincing to get the Takers to listen to them again."

"So," Abby said, "what you're saying is, the Takers may not respond when they tell them that they have a five-year-old boy and to send someone to get him."

"We have a couple of feasible theories," Will said. He took out his ringing cell phone and answered the call. "Yes." He listened.

Abby stared at his back as he walked away from her and Ethan. She followed him.

He put his phone into his pocket and turned to her. "I'm not waiting." Will went out the front door with Abby and Ethan trailing behind him. He went to his truck, opened the cab's back door, pulled the seat forward, and retrieved a case.

Ethan stood beside him. "Is that a nano drone?"

Will nodded. "Check it out, Ethan." He opened the case.

"We had something similar at the school. We used it to shoot darts into aerial targets spread across three acres."

"We use this one to attach a tracking device to a moving vehicle," Will said.

"Show me how it works," Ethan said.

Will explained the system, the camera, and a small arm capable of shooting pin-sized tracking darts 100 feet. "If we can get close enough and pin the tracker to the hovercraft's undercarriage where it won't be detected, it should lead us to the school."

"What about Dillon?" Abby asked. "How will that help get him back?"

"The Underground is taking care of that," Will told her. "But if the rescue fails, this would help us find him. It's always good to have a plan B."

"Failure is not an option," Abby told him. "I want my son back."

"The cause is great," Will said.

"If you'll let me," Ethan said to Will, "I'm sure I can hit the target. I ranked number one in speed and accuracy several years in a row."

"Good to hear," Will told him. "I know just the perfect launching spot overlooking the airport." He placed the drone back into its case. "Come on. We need to move fast." Will grabbed the case and put it back behind the seat. "I'll make sure the front door is locked." He headed back to the house.

Abby and Ethan piled into his truck.

Once in the driver's seat, Will pulled out of the driveway. When he reached the main road, he looked both ways and sped up as he turned, his tires squealing.

"Can't they stop the car the women are driving?" Abby asked.

"No. We can only slow them down." He placed an earbud

into his ear as his phone rang. Without speaking, he listened to the call as he rolled to a stop at a light. When the light turned green, he punched the accelerator.

"Why would they choose to take him to the airport?" Abby asked. "Do you know if they contacted the Takers yet? Do you think they'll take their call?"

"There's a good chance that the Takers chose to meet there," Will replied. "They don't like to murder someone in plain sight."

"Do you really think they'll kill them?" Abby asked.

Will nodded. "Those two women don't know who they're dealing with. When the Takers tell you to stop bothering them, they mean it. Their lives are at stake if they can't produce the child. And even if they do, there's a good chance the Takers will exterminate them just for being pests."

"I'd like to see that."

"You just may," Will said.

"Has the Underground reached the airport yet?" she asked.

"Marylin and Betty have a good head start," Will told her. "They should be going through the airport gates as we speak. The spy satellite is still fixed on their car. There's no sign of the Takers yet. We still have time."

Five miles seemed like fifty to Abby as the possibilities of failure consumed her thoughts. She tried to take her mind off of it by searching for patrol cars as Will soared down the highway.

Not far from the airport, Will turned down a side road, drove up a hill, and parked on a wooded hilltop. He reached for the case and his binoculars resting on the seat next to Ethan. "Everybody out," he said.

They followed him through the woods to the edge of a sheer cliff, where they squatted.

Abby fumed with hatred while she watched the two

women on the tarmac below park their car in front of an airplane hangar and get out. *Where's my son, witches?* She took the binoculars Will handed to her, and she lay on the dirt, ignoring a sharp rock in her side. Raising the lenses, she searched for Dillon in the backseat of the car and saw his arm, but no movement.

Will opened the case, removed the drone, armed it with a tracking device, and handed it to Ethan.

Abby glanced at Ethan as he got down on the ground beside her.

"What direction do you think the Takers will come from?" Ethan asked Will.

"From the west." Will pointed to their left.

Through the binoculars, Abby followed the nano drone as Ethan guided its descent to the edge of the tarmac, flew it to the right, and landed it behind a rock.

Ethan looked to the west. "They're coming."

"So is the Underground," Will told them. "Look beyond the hangars to the north gate."

Through the lenses, Abby saw the men driving three black SUVs. Inside, two men in each car wore black suits. She handed the binoculars back to Will.

As the black SUVs approached the first hangar, the Taker's hovercraft swooped by Abby, gradually descended, and landed.

"Underground's coming around the other side of the hangars. Good. The Takers don't see them." Will gave the binoculars back to Abby.

She watched the nano drone fly under the craft's belly.

Ethan methodically worked the controls. "Gotcha." He flew it back to the same rock where it had awaited the ambush.

"Good," Will said. "Leave it there until they're gone."

Both of the Takers climbed out of the hovercraft and walked slowly toward the women.

Abby looked at the black SUVs parked in single file, hiding

on the side of the hangar out of sight of the Takers. *They're too late.* A tear from her flooded eyes streamed down her cheek.

"I can't read the Takers' lips, but I can the women's," Ethan said.

"What are they saying?" Abby asked.

"They're pleading with them to believe them."

Abby saw three of the men in suits getting out of their SUVs. Her heart raced as her anxiety peaked.

"The Takers are going back to their hovercraft," Ethan said.

"Go," Will said into his phone's earpiece.

One of the men from the Underground rescue party snuck around the corner, keeping between the hangar door and the side of the Electric L, ducking down below the car windows out of the Takers' view. He opened the back door, slid Dillon out of the backseat, and closed the door again, keeping low.

"What's wrong with Dillon?" Abby asked. "Why isn't he moving?"

"One of the women is pointing to the car," Ethan said. "She's telling them that since they came this far, they could at least look in the backseat to see that they're telling the truth."

Abby watched the hovercraft's driver turn, walk to Marylin and Betty's car, and look inside. He returned to the women, seized Marylin's arm, and dragged her toward the craft while the other Taker grabbed Betty.

"Go," Will instructed again, touching his earphone.

With the Takers' backs toward him, the rescuer carried Dillon's limp body to the SUVs. Once the hovercraft lifted off, the black SUVs drove onto the tarmac.

Ethan chuckled. "The Takers are giving the rescuers a thumbs up. They think they're government agents." He retrieved the nano drone.

Will placed it back into its case. He touched his earphone

and listened. "Dillon's awake. He's fine."

Abby stood and shouted Dillon's name from the hilltop.

In a single file, the black SUVs reached the gate and drove onto the highway.

Will rose from his squatting position. "We'll meet them at your place."

She threw her arms around Will and hugged him. "Thank you."

He hugged her tightly and said, "We'd better get going."

Chapter 13

Will pulled into the driveway at Abby's house and parked.

Before he turned off the engine, Abby opened the car door and got out. She ran to Dillon, who stood with two of the Underground rescuers by their black SUV. Stepping back from the long hug she gave to her son, she knelt in front of him. "Are you hurt? Are you okay?"

"No one will tell me what happened, Mommy," Dillon told her.

"Let me," Ethan said to Abby.

She nodded and stood. "Your brother will tell you. He saw everything. Why don't you go inside while I order a pizza?"

"Cool." Dillon took Ethan's hand. They went to the front door, and Ethan opened it.

"I locked the door before we left," Will told Abby. He called out to Ethan and gave him a hand gesture that meant danger.

The boys hurried back to them.

Will turned to the two rescuers. "You stay with Abby, and you cover the back." Will retrieved his gun from his truck and went inside the house.

In a few minutes, Will came out, and the other man returned to the front of the house.

"It's all clear," Will said. "You boys can go in."

Ethan and Dillon went inside.

"You're welcome to stay and eat," Abby told the rescuers.

"We'd better go, Mrs. Muse," one of them said. "But thanks for the offer. The longer we stay, the more attention we'll draw from your neighbors."

Will shook their hands. "You're right about that. Outstanding job, guys."

"Thanks, Doc," the other man said. "Smart son you have there, Mrs. Muse. That call he made to Morgan is what saved Dillon's life."

"We'll all sleep better tonight," Abby said. "What do you think will happen to those two women?"

"They'll be locked up or disposed of," he replied. "My guess is the latter."

"I'll keep an eye on their house just in case," Will told them. "Hopefully, it will be put up for sale, then we'll know that they won't be coming back."

The rescuers drove away, and Abby started toward the door.

"Wait," Will said.

She turned to him. "I haven't forgotten about the pizza. You want the works on yours, right?"

"That's not it," he told her. "I locked the front door again on my way out after I searched inside."

She nodded.

"Ethan just opened it without using a key."

Abby felt the hairs on her neck stand up. "How on Earth…."

"This isn't the time," Will said, "but I think we should have a talk with him about how he escaped from the school."

Abby thought back to what Ethan had told them about running away, but couldn't remember him discussing the details.

They went inside.

Abby ordered the pizza and began clearing and moving boxes off the couch with Will's help. When Ethan and Dillon came downstairs, she saw them out of the corner of her eye. "Did Ethan tell you what happened?" she asked Dillon.

"I was rescued like Princess Leia in Star Wars," Dillon said. "What if…."

"What ifs are wishes and nightmares." Abby led him into

the living room. "You can never go back. You must always go forward."

"Ethan said it would make a good book," Dillon told her.

"Your dad used to write books." Abby plopped down on the couch.

"I remember him reading me stories at bedtime," Ethan said. "Do you still have them?"

She nodded. "They're packed away somewhere." She looked around at all the moving boxes that filled the room.

Will turned to Ethan. "Tell us exactly how you escaped from the school."

"I went through an air vent by the storage units in the hallway and followed it to where the medical doctors and nurses have their sleeping quarters. Spying was something Cole and I did for fun on the nights the children were allowed to sleep without being taken from their beds."

"So that's how you found out how to get outside?" Will asked.

"There were lots of visiting doctors who only stayed a night or two. Some of them smoked. Smoking wasn't allowed inside the school. There's an air vent in the main hallway leading to their rooms. We'd watch and timed them when they went in and out. We were just waiting for the right time to break out of the place. That was before Cole was turned into a puppet. When they did that to him, I couldn't wait anymore. About three in the morning, I dropped down from the vent into the hallway outside the doctors' and nurses' rooms. Someone left the door unlocked. I opened it and ran."

"Are you sure the door was unlocked?" Will asked him.

"I don't understand. How would I get out if the door was locked?"

"Come with me," Will said. "I want to try something."

Ethan followed him to the front door. Abby and Dillon

trailed behind them.

Will took Ethan outside, and Abby closed and locked the door. She heard his muffled voice as he spoke to Ethan.

"Your mom locked it," Will said.

Abby watched the door rattle, but it remained locked.

"Try to open it," Will said.

"How am I supposed to open a locked door?" Ethan asked.

"Just give it a try," Will told him.

Abby saw the doorknob turn and the door open.

"Did you unlock it, Mom?" Ethan asked.

She shook her head.

Ethan looked at his hands. "I didn't do anything except turn the knob."

"Looks like we have another mystery on our hands," Abby said.

"What were you thinking when you turned the knob?" Will asked him.

Ethan shrugged. "Open."

Will looked at Abby. "Who exactly was your husband?"

"What does my husband have to do with anything?"

"He and Ethan had a lot in common—their exceptional memories and their interests in maps," Will told her.

"And the scars in the same spot on our heads," Ethan added.

"Did you ever see him open a door without a key?" Will asked. "Did he have a chip, too?"

"He was cremated," Abby said. "There's no way of knowing that."

"Was his urn on your mantle at the other house?" Will asked.

"Yes."

"It's in one of the boxes," Will told her. "I remember packing it and bringing it here with our second load." He glanced around the room, his gaze resting on the boxes by the sliding glass doors leading to the patio.

"You're not suggesting that I find it and search his ashes for a chip."

"We need answers," Will replied. When the deliveryman knocked on the door, Will stood and reached into his pocket. "I've got this." He went to the door and returned with two medium-sized pizzas.

Between the four of them, it didn't take long before only one piece remained.

"Take it, Will," Abby said. "In a few days, things will be back to normal, and I can cook a real meal."

Once he swallowed the last bite, he wiped his hand on a napkin. "We were talking about your husband before we were pleasantly interrupted."

"I remember a story Daddy used to read to me about a key," Ethan said, placing the empty pizza boxes into a trash bag. "But it wasn't a real key. The key was a little boy."

Will jumped up at the same time as Abby.

"The old boxes we took from your closet are over there," he said.

Abby worked her way around her belongings from the other house to reach the corner of the room. She recognized the three boxes she had packed five years ago, the duct tape no longer adhering to the cardboard. One at a time, she lifted the top two from the pile and handed them to Will, who set them aside. Gazing at the words Bedtime Stories written with a black marker on the next in the stack, her mind flooded with memories. The loneliness she felt when she lost her husband and son on the same day resurfaced, opening the gates that held back a depth of grief that had torn a hole in her soul.

Abby blinked back tears as she reached for the box that held the memories. Pulling back the limp duct tape, she opened it and peeked inside. "This is it." She closed it. Before she leaned to pick it up, Will bent to retrieve it.

"I've got it." He made his way to the dining table, pulled out a chair, and set the box on it while he removed several lamps and other items from the tabletop, clearing a space.

From inside the box, Abby took out a book made from layers on layers of paper stapled down the center and folded in half. She smiled as she remembered the cover of her husband's first book. *Little One Note,* the title read. Below the bold letters, he had drawn a picture of a white dove. She reminisced about how he had drawn all the characters throughout the pages. "This one's about a bird who could only sing one note. There were three in this series."

"Let's spread them on the table," Will said. "We're looking for the one about a key."

"I still don't know why you think my husband would have any connection to Ethan's eyesight or how he can open a locked door. He didn't have white hair and silver eyes." She continued to unpack. "There was nothing special about him if you know what I mean. Ethan's abilities must've been caused by something they did to him at the school. That's the only answer."

Will picked up another book with doves on the cover and flipped through it. "These illustrations are outstanding. He could've been published."

"He was more into maps," Abby told him, lifting out the last of the handcrafted keepsakes and looking inside the box to make sure nothing remained. "Ah," she said. "What did I tell you? A map." She retrieved it. "He had hundreds of maps. I have them in a suitcase somewhere."

"Can I see it, Mom?" Ethan asked.

"Sure." She handed it to him.

Dillon sat next to Ethan and watched him spread it out on the coffee table.

"This is a map of the United States," Ethan said. "On the other side is a map of the world." He held up a three-foot by four-foot detailed drawing. "It's hand-drawn."

"That's cool," Will said. "Bring it here so we can check it out."

Ethan brought it to the dining table and spread it out, covering his dad's books.

"What are all these blue dots?" Will flipped it over to the world map. "There's more on this side." He turned it over again to the map of the United States.

"Every map he showed me when I was little," Ethan said, "had dots. I always thought they were supposed to be there. Here's where we are." When Ethan touched Washington state, a hologram appeared above the dining room table.

They all gasped.

"It's the entire state of Washington," Abby said.

"What the hell," Will said. "Where in the world would your husband get technology like this? What did he do for a living?"

"He was a janitor at a conservatory in northern California."

"Mind-blowing," Will said. "Do you think he got it from someone who worked there?"

"I don't know. I've never seen this map before."

They all stood staring at the aerial images.

When Ethan removed his finger from the paper, the hologram disappeared.

"What did you just do?" Will asked him.

"Nothing," Ethan told him. "I took my finger off, and it went away."

"Here, let me see," Will said.

Ethan moved aside.

Will touched the map, but nothing happened. "Try it again," he told Ethan.

Ethan put his finger on one of the blue dots his father had drawn. Instantly, a hologram of the state appeared.

The hologram blurred, then slowly became clearer as it altered its form from a state to a small town, until the 4D image of the very house where they stood hovered in front of them.

"What in the hell is this?" Will asked. "Your husband died six years ago. There's no way he would've known you'd move into this place. Is this connected to some kind of satellite?" He studied the paper on which the map had been drawn on. "I don't understand it."

Ethan lifted his finger from the map, and again the hologram vanished.

Abby tried. "It doesn't work for me, either."

Ethan touched another dot his dad had drawn. The hologram changed into the image of the Underground's orphanage.

"Those white daisies were being planted while we were there. These images are current." He looked at Abby. "How did he know about the Underground?"

"I have no idea," she replied. "Nothing makes sense." Abby shook her head. *Who was my husband?* "Fold it up. And put the books back into the box. We're taking all of this to Morgan."

"Good decision." Will repacked the box.

"Boys, get ready for bed," Abby said. "I want to leave first thing in the morning."

"We brought over your bedroom furniture and the boys' beds on our first trip," Will told her. "Everything's set up."

"Thank you, Will," Abby told him. "I'll walk you to your truck." She followed him outside.

He got into his truck and rolled down the window. "I'll call you in the morning after I let Morgan know we're coming."

"I'll sleep better after I get some more shooting practice in and have my own gun within reach. Things are getting really strange."

"We'll work on that as soon as we get back from seeing Morgan."

"Good night, Will. See you in the morning." Abby went back into the house after he drove away and double-checked to make sure she locked the front door. Then, she went upstairs to tuck the boys into bed.

Chapter 14

Abby looked out the kitchen window as she washed the breakfast dishes and saw Will pull up in front of the house. She wiped her hands on a dishtowel and went to the door. "Boys, grab your things and don't forget the map and box. Will's here."

She carried a six-pack of soda and some snacks to Will's truck for the long drive. Ethan brought the box of books plus the map and walked with Dillon, who wore the badge Morgan had given him. The boys climbed into the double cab backseat, and Abby sat up front.

"The Underground's surveillance covers a three-block radius around your home," Will told Abby as he drove away from her house.

"I'm glad to hear that," she replied.

"These things aren't just happening to you and your boys," Will said. "Murder, kidnapping, arson, and worse are happening all across the US. The majority of the trouble can be traced to the Takers."

"It feels personal," Abby said.

"The Underground trailed the hovercraft Ethan bugged and has tracked it to a mental hospital in Iowa."

"Good riddance to Marylin and Betty," Abby said.

"Oh, and by the way," Will said, "Morgan told me that the boy who Ethan said was a troublemaker ran away from our orphanage in Utah."

"I wonder why?" Abby asked.

"He's looking for me," Ethan told her.

"There's no evidence of that yet," Will said. "You just moved. How would the Takers know where you live?"

"Thank goodness for that," Abby said. "I don't want to

move again."

—

After an hour drive to the Underground's orphanage, Abby, Will, and the boys strolled with Morgan through the garden to the secured entrance.

Before reaching the door, Will asked Morgan, "Would you mind if Ethan tries to open it? He's developed an unusual trait lately."

"Let me inform security first," Morgan told him. "I don't want anyone to freak out when the alarm goes off." He made a call on his cell phone.

They stood about three yards from the door.

Morgan ended his call. "Go ahead and try it. There'll be no harm done."

Ethan walked to the entrance, turned the handle, and the door opened.

"That's not possible," Morgan said. "And the alarm didn't go off."

"We have no idea why," Abby told him.

"It's up for discussion," Will said. "Along with a couple of other things."

Morgan led them down a hallway to the same conference room they had been to before. He held the door and allowed them to enter.

Dillon went in, pointing at his brother. "He's got a map."

"I'd like to have a look," Morgan said. "Let's talk about the locked door first."

"It's unexplainable," Will told him.

"Will thinks my husband may have something to do with it," Abby said.

"How is that possible?" Morgan asked.

"There's more." Will nodded to Ethan.

Ethan spread the map across the oval conference table.

"Take a really good look at it," Will told him. "Pick it up if you want."

Morgan leaned and studied it.

"See anything unusual?" Will asked.

"Someone did a fantastic job drawing this. They probably traced it from another map and just added the dots. I'm sure of it."

"Don't be too sure," Will told him. "It was done freehand and by memory."

Morgan looked up. "I need a better look at this." He walked over to a switch on the wall and flipped it. The hanging lights illuminated the table. He picked up the map, flipped it over, felt the paper, and placed it on the table. "I don't see anything other than a damn good-looking map."

"This is strange," Ethan said to Will.

Will looked where Ethan pointed. "What happened to the dot at your mom's house?"

Ethan shrugged. "It was there before we left home."

"Touch Washington state first, like you did with us," Will said.

Ethan placed his finger on Washington, and again, the hologram of the state appeared above the conference table.

Morgan gasped. "Astonishing. And all you're doing is touching the paper?"

"Yes," Ethan said. "Now, watch this." He placed his finger on the blue dot, and Morgan's orphanage came into view in 4D above the table.

"Heaven help us," Morgan said. "Has the Underground been exposed? Where is the surveillance coming from?" He looked at the hologram from all angles.

"There used to be a blue dot showing Abby's new place," Will told him. "But for some reason, it's gone."

"Can I try?" Morgan asked Ethan. He touched the other

dot in West Virginia. The hologram changed, showing a log cabin surrounded by woods.

"Must be a silver-eyed ability," Will said. "It doesn't work for me."

"That's Rudy's place," Morgan told them. "He called me last night to tell me that he's back from his trip. He's located six more of our silver-eyed brothers and sisters in Europe who have never been taken to a school or kidnapped."

"They've never been taken?" Will looked at Abby. "That means the school wasn't responsible for the changes in Ethan."

"It couldn't be hereditary," she said. "My husband didn't dye his hair or have contact lenses."

"But they both had a moon-shaped mark on their temporal lobe," Will said.

"What else have you brought?" Morgan asked.

"Ethan's dad read him stories at bedtime," Abby said. "Ethan remembers one that tells of a key that isn't a key. It's a little boy. But we didn't find it in the box."

"I hope Ethan's the only one with that ability," Morgan said. "It's very unsettling."

"Maybe there's a clue in the stories he wrote," Will said. "The map was in the same box as his books."

Morgan flipped the map over and viewed the world detail on the other side. "There's got to be about two hundred dots on this thing. I'm going to fly Rudy out here to take a look at this. If I'm correct, this is showing us where all our brothers and sisters are. May I keep it and the books for a while?"

"Yes," Abby told him. "But I don't see how any of this makes sense."

"It's definitely a puzzle," Morgan said. He made a phone call, and a minute or two later, a woman entered the room. "Could you take this to our lab and give orders to be very careful with it. Tell them I'll be there shortly to explain what tests need to be run."

"Yes, sir." She folded it and carried it out of the room.

"I'll read each of the books," Morgan said, "and see if there's any clues hidden in their text."

"The books are numbered," Abby said. "I assume it's for a reason."

"I'll read them in order." Morgan led them to the clusters of seating in front of the wall of windows that looked out to the lake. "Now, let's see how you feel about taking a trip to DC Labs to talk with Ethan's fake mom. I thought all of us could have a talk with her."

"Just knock on her door and hope she's not dangerous?" Abby asked.

"She's right," Will said. "We need a plan."

"Before I get sidetracked," Abby said. "I want to thank you, Morgan, for saving my son's life. Will, Ethan, and I saw the members of the Underground you sent to pose as government agents. We were up on a hill overlooking the airport."

"Yes," Morgan said. "They were telling me how Will stayed on the phone with them and told them when the Takers' backs were turned."

"You're both incredible," Abby said. "I heard you're sending out another search party to find the Takers School. What are you going to do when you find it? What makes you think that they'll let you in?"

"You're right," Morgan replied. "Once we find the school, we'll need another plan."

"It's up to you, Abby," Will said. "But I think we should see what Ethan's capable of. Can he open any door? Can he unlock file cabinets? We might be able to use his abilities when we find his fake mom."

"We have the capability to tap her phone and track her," Morgan told him.

"It would be good to know if she has a routine," Abby said. "Maybe she runs or has a place she goes to chill."

"Yes," Morgan said. "I doubt the government is watching every move she makes."

"We'll have to take Dillon when we go," Abby said. "I'm not letting him out of my sight."

"We may need reinforcements," Morgan said. "I suggest Holly and Chad. I'll find us a safehouse once we know the woman's location. Between the five of us, there'll always be someone to watch the boys."

"This will be tricky," Will said. "I haven't told Chad or Holly about Ethan's abilities. Is there any way to keep that between us?"

"They don't know about me, either," Morgan replied. "It may be time to trust in others. I know Chad and Holly will keep our unusual traits a secret."

"It's up to Abby and Ethan," Will told him.

"I'm okay with telling them," Abby said. "What do you think, Ethan?"

"I think if we don't tell them, and they find out, it could ruin everything."

Morgan nodded. "You're a smart boy."

"I'll call them when we get home," Will said.

"Great," Morgan replied. "I'll do a preliminary search to locate this woman's address, find a safehouse, and gather the equipment we'll need. Two electric vehicles should suffice, so it won't look like she's being stalked. Then we'll take the second step, whatever that may be." He stood. "I'll see you to the door. Then I have to go to the lab and see about running tests on the GPS hologram map."

"I'll call you after I talk with Chad and Holly," Will said.

Ethan shook Morgan's hand before stepping into the hall.

Dillon saluted. "Thanks for saving me. May the force be

with you."

Morgan returned the salute. "The mission isn't over yet. We have places to go and things to do. I'll be seeing you soon."

Abby saw Chad, Holly, and Jack sitting in their truck as she, Will, and the boys pulled up in front of the house.

They all went inside.

"I assume you need me to watch the boys tonight," Holly said.

"Yes," Abby said. "But that's not the only reason we asked you here."

"Have a seat, you guys," Will told them.

They gathered in the cluttered living room. Ethan sat on packing boxes. Dillon took off up the stairs to his room with Jack.

Holly glanced around. "I can help you put some of these things away if you tell me where you want them." She sat on the couch next to Chad.

"No need," Abby said, clearing a chair to sit in. "But thank you very much for offering."

"Remember, we still have one more load to get from the other house," Chad said.

"We can get that in the morning," Will told him. "Right now, we need to discuss Ethan's fake mom. We're setting up surveillance to find out where she lives and her routine. Morgan, Abby, and I need your help to confront her. She may be our link to finding the school."

Holly and Chad looked at each other.

"We're in," Chad told him.

"What about the boys?" Holly asked.

"They're coming with us," Abby said. "Morgan's finding a safehouse. There'll be enough of us to make sure the boys won't be left alone."

"That works for me," Holly said.

"How soon do we leave?" Chad asked.

"As soon as we get the information needed to find her," Abby replied.

"There's more," Will said. "Something top secret."

"You know you can trust us," Chad told him.

"We found out that Ethan has unusual traits that no one can explain. When we were in Bremerton, I took him up on the ridge to find out how far he could see. He gave me details of a high-rise in downtown Seattle."

Holly's eyes widened. "Incredible."

"Wow," Chad said.

"When we were on the ferry going to Bremerton, he told us the Takers were coming way before we could even see a dot in the sky. And from the hills overlooking the airport, he saw Dillon lying in the backseat of Marylin and Betty's car."

"How is that possible?" Holly asked.

"He's not the only one," Will told her. "Morgan has white hair."

Chad nodded, not seeming to understand.

Holly jumped out of her seat. "Morgan has white hair and silver eyes?"

"Yes," Abby told her.

Chad and Holly looked at Ethan.

He waved.

"So, Morgan has the same type of vision?" Chad asked Abby.

She nodded.

"There's more," Will told them.

"How can there be more?" Chad asked.

"Ethan has the ability to open locked doors," Will said. "He opened the locked front door at this house and the one leading into the Underground orphanage."

"That's scary to know someone can do that," Holly said.

"There are others with silver eyes out there," Will said. "But so far, Ethan's the only one with the skill to open locks."

"We'll be able to enter through his fake mom's front door," Holly said.

"We have to do a few more tests to see exactly what he can unlock," Will told her. "Think locked file cabinets and safes. It may be useful during our surveillance."

"I think we should wait for his fake mom to leave for work and go inside her place to see what we can find," Abby said.

"I'll tell Morgan your idea." Will looked at Chad and Holly. "So, you're in?"

They nodded.

Will pulled out his cell phone, made a call, and put it on speaker. Everyone could hear the conversation. "I spoke with them, and they're joining us," he told Morgan.

"Great," he replied. "When will everyone be available to meet with me here?"

Chad looked at Holly. "Tomorrow," he said as she nodded.

Abby looked at Will.

He nodded.

"Tomorrow," Abby said.

"Rudy will be flying in to examine the GPS map," Morgan said. "I'm sure Chad and Holly are eager to see it."

Abby looked at Will. "We forgot to tell them about the map," she said.

"Who's Rudy?" Chad asked. "What's the GPS map?"

"I'll explain when we're off the phone," Will told him.

"It's going to blow your mind," Abby said.

After Will hung up Morgan's call, he told Chad and Holly about the map. "You'll see it tomorrow. Can we all meet here in the morning at eight?"

"Yes," Abby told him. "What time will we get home tonight?"

"Oh, that's right," Will said. "I forgot all about that."

"Holly," Abby said, "would you mind watching the boys while Will teaches me how to shoot?"

"No problem. Have you bought a gun yet?"

"No," Abby replied.

"I would suggest," Holly said, "the Glock 32. It's comfortable and has less kick."

"You spoiled my surprise," Will said. "I bought the one she used when we went a couple of days ago. It's waiting for her at the shooting range."

"All right then," Abby said. "Thanks for watching Dillon. We won't be gone long." Abby walked with Will to the front door. Before he opened it, she placed her hand on his as he turned the nob. "Thank you, Will." She stood on her tiptoes and gave him a kiss on the cheek. "Okay, let's go."

Chapter 15

Gazing out the back window of Will's truck, Abby watched for Holly, Chad, and Jack, who trailed them to the Underground orphanage. They followed Will into the parking lot and pulled in next to him.

As before, Morgan waited in front of the gardens and walked with them to the secured entrance. "Watch," he said to Chad and Holly, then made a call on his cell phone. "Go ahead, Ethan."

Ethan went to the door, opened it, and waited for them to go inside.

Chad's brows furrowed. "How did he do that?"

"We don't know," Morgan told him. "I thought while Ethan's here, we could run a test on him if his mom doesn't mind."

"What kind of test?" Abby asked.

"Nothing physical," Morgan replied. "His implant eliminates the possibility of running most tests that I'd like to perform. For now, a simple telekinesis test would be sufficient."

"What do you think, Ethan?" Abby asked.

"Sure," he replied.

They entered the conference room. The lights shone brightly upon the map spread out on the table.

A man, who looked to be in his mid-thirties, his white hair shaved on both sides of a blue mohawk, studied the map.

"This is Rudy," Morgan told them. He introduced them while they gathered around the table.

Dillon and Jack found coloring books on a coffee table by the couch and quietly kept busy.

"Rudy arrived less than an hour ago," Morgan said. "I

thought we should wait for you before we discuss the map. You're up, Ethan. Show him what you showed me."

Ethan repeated everything he had shown to Morgan, Will, and his mom, touching the blue dot, which revealed the building they stood inside.

Rudy, Chad, and Holly walked around the table and studied the four-dimensional hologram of the Underground orphanage.

Chad looked at Abby and Will. "You were right. We had to see it for ourselves. It's beyond words."

When Rudy returned to Ethan's side, Abby noticed his silver eyes.

"Is this surveillance?" Rudy asked. "Who's watching us?"

"We don't know if we're being watched," Morgan said. "It may only be a GPS showing the locations of our sisters and brothers."

Ethan moved aside. "Try it."

Rudy stepped up to the map and placed a finger on Italy. A hologram of a villa in Tuscany appeared in detail. He touched a dot in England and another in France. Rudy looked at Morgan. "What's its purpose?"

"We don't know yet," Morgan replied. "Ethan's father created it. He didn't have white hair and silver eyes, but he did have the same implant that we have. I've had the lab run tests. The drawing is molecular nanotechnology based, including the dots. I've never seen anything like it. I wanted to know if you recognized any of the locations."

Rudy nodded. He placed his finger on seven dots, calling out the names of the others he had met.

"So far," Will said. "Only the silver-eyes can reveal the holograms."

"Silver-eyes," Rudy said. "We should come up with a better name."

"Did you find any clues in the stories?" Abby asked.

"No," Morgan said. "But I believe they will reveal their purpose in time. I didn't find the one you spoke of—the key that is a little boy." He turned when someone knocked on the door. "Come in."

A woman entered, handed him a file, and left the room.

He scanned the pages within. "We have the location of Ethan's fake mom. She lives in DC, and the lab is a few miles from her home."

Ethan touched the dot in the location Morgan had described. A hologram of a penthouse on top of a high-rise appeared.

Morgan took a photo from the file and turned it around to let everyone see her home. "She's one of us."

"But can she be trusted?" Will asked.

"We have a safehouse not far from her residence," Morgan said. "Go home and pack your things. Bring what you'll need for a week. Be back here by four in the afternoon tomorrow. The place has a washer and dryer, four bedrooms, and three baths. It may be a little crowded. Hopefully, we'll get the information we need sooner rather than later."

"Why so late?" Abby asked.

"It'll be dark when we get there," Morgan said. "I don't want to be noticed if we can help it. We haven't had time to discover her routine, so we'll figure out how to approach her once we get there."

"Is there anywhere we can set up surveillance equipment?" Will asked.

"There's a tech team moving into an apartment overlooking her high-rise."

"Good plan," Will said.

"We'll be doing the footwork, following her, searching her penthouse, and such." Morgan folded the map. "I'll lock this up until we get back from DC. Why don't we grab a bite to eat in the dining room? What time is your flight home, Rudy?"

He looked at his watch. "I have enough time to eat and run."

After lunch and returning to the conference room, Morgan addressed Abby and the others. "The word telekinesis means distant movement, which is the ability to move or change the state of an object using one's mind and without using physical force on an object. To accomplish the objective, Ethan will need to access a combination of energy centers throughout his body called chakras." He placed a Newton's Cradle Pendulum in front of Ethan, who sat in a chair at the conference table. "Okay, Ethan. Try moving the pendulums."

He stared at the steel balls, but nothing happened.

"What are you thinking when you open my security door?" Morgan asked him.

"Open."

"Okay then," Morgan said. "Try thinking swing."

Ethan relaxed in his seat, focused on the string of balls, and the one on the end moved. He smiled. "Okay. I think I've got it." With what appeared to be no effort, he made one swing and then another. He moved them forward and backward, side to side, and in a circle. "Cool."

Morgan stood silently with his mouth agape and his eyes wide.

Abby and Will stared at the pendulums.

"Did I pass the test?" Ethan asked.

"That was brilliant," Morgan told him. "You have an exceptional ability to use mind over matter. This is a talent you must only share with the people you trust. Understand?"

Ethan nodded.

Turning to Abby and Will, Morgan said, "This is just a

simple test. There's no telling the extent of his abilities. No matter where you go, make sure you locate any cameras in the area. No one must know what he's capable of doing."

Will's cell phone rang, and he answered the call. "You have to be joking," he replied to the caller. "Thanks." He ended the call and looked at Morgan, Abby, and Ethan. "Remember the troublemaker who ran away from the Utah Underground orphanage? Somehow, he and Ethan's friend, Cole, have teamed up. They tried to break into Abby's house."

Abby felt her face heat as her temper rose. "What the hell?"

"The Underground surveillance caught them before they could get inside," Will said. "They said they were told to find a treasure map."

"I'll have to move again," Abby said.

"No," Will told her. "They said they weren't sure if they found the right house. Surveillance took a device from them. The boys said it was a detector. According to the timeline they gave of their quest, the detector stopped working the moment we left your house."

"So, they're calling it a treasure map," she said.

"Who else would know about the map besides your husband?" Morgan asked.

"I don't know," Abby said. "I thought I knew everything about him. Now it seems he led a double life."

"Is it possible to trace his ancestry back to see if there were others in his family tree who exhibited special talents?" Will asked.

"We can trace Ethan's and his dad's lineage back hundreds of years. But without records, deceased relatives' identities would be impossible to verify, leaving us with only folklore passed on from generation to generation. It may prove interesting, but for now, we have other things on our plate. I know you need to get home. I'll walk you out."

Before Will dropped off Abby, Ethan, and Dillon at their home in the mid-afternoon, he promised Abby they couldn't be safer. And he told her that the Underground had doubled its efforts to guard their house after the attempted break-in. Still, she jumped at every noise she heard coming from the neighbors, the lake, and even the boys' footsteps upstairs.

After doing a thorough search of the house more than once, she started to relax. *A glass of wine sounds good about now,* Abby thought. Looking out the sliding glass doors leading outside, she noticed a clock leaning against a box near her feet. *Where has the time gone? I need to unpack these boxes.*

She opened a box marked kitchen, took out a glass, went in search of a bottle of wine, and found one in a clothes basket filled with items to be placed into the pantry. Remembering where she had put the corkscrew, she rummaged through kitchen utensils in a drawer by the refrigerator and found it, uncorked the bottle, and filled her glass. *Who knows how long ago that map was drawn,* she thought. *Now, someone wants it. Why now?*

With a wine glass in hand, she went out to the living room and started to tackle the biggest boxes first. Little by little, she put things away, and the house began to feel like a home.

After taking a break and making dinner for her and the boys, Abby looked around the living room and noticed the boxes Will set aside next to her husband's locked suitcase, filled with maps. She remembered tossing a ring of keys into a box when she packed to move from California to Washington. *Maybe the suitcase keys are on the ring,* she thought. Peeling back limp duct tape, she peeked inside one of the boxes and found them. They were her husband's, and they brought back memories of the life they had together. Puddles of tears filled her eyes, and she grabbed the ring of keys.

Sinking into the chair by the fireplace, she flipped through them. Some were clearly marked with strings and tags. *Garage door, shed, toolbox….* Abby sipped her wine and looked at the locked suitcase. Setting her drink on the end table, she rose, retrieved the suitcase, and brought it back to her chair. One by one, she tried each key, but none tripped the lock. She glanced up when Ethan walked into the room.

"Dillon's asleep," he told her as he plopped onto the couch.

"I'm going to bed early myself. At least I got a lot done today. It's beginning to look like a home." She set the keys on the end table. "Don't you think it's odd that no one came looking for the map until we found it?"

He nodded. "It's weird. It's like it was in the dark, and no one noticed it until the lights came on."

"There can't be a snitch," she said. "Only a handful of us knows about the map, and I trust them all. Thinking outside the box…. What if no one knew about it until it was activated?"

"Do you think I triggered something when I touched it?"

"Seems logical," she replied. "As if any of this makes sense." She glanced at the suitcase. "Didn't you say that all the maps your dad showed you had dots?"

"Yeah."

"Do you want to see if you can open this suitcase?" She shoved it toward him.

"Sure." He placed his hand on the lock, and it snapped open.

"Don't touch anything," she told him. "Let me." She brought the suitcase to the dining table and lifted its lid. To her surprise, she found a stack of letters tied with a lace ribbon and lifted them from their resting place. *He saved all my letters I wrote him when he visited his grandfather*. Six months seemed like forever while she had waited for his return. She felt a lump in her throat and took a sip of wine.

Setting the letters aside, she took out a scroll bound with a braid of white hair. Abby's mind raced through memories, trying to recall whose hair it could be. She slipped it off the scroll and slowly began to unroll the map, setting nearby odds and ends on each corner to hold it in place.

Abby stepped back and put her hands on her hips, studying a hand-drawn map of the world. "The hologram map and this one are different," she told Ethan. "Drawn by separate people."

"You're right," Ethan said. "Maybe the hair belongs to the person who drew it."

Abby focused on the map. White dots were placed in various countries throughout the world with a sequence of numbers underlining each dot. "This doesn't make sense. What do you think the numbers mean?"

Ethan shook his head. "I don't know."

Abby crossed her arms. "Another mystery." She rolled up the map and bound it with the braided hair. Then she reached into the suitcase and pulled out another scroll. Each one that she spread on the table revealed a different country and more dots underlined with numbers. When she retrieved the last map from the suitcase, she found another puzzler. *Green dots,* she thought. *That has to mean something.* She put them into the suitcase. "The amount of work put into them tells us they're important. Until we know their purpose, we'll keep them in a safe place. Can you lock it?"

"I'll try." He placed his hand on the suitcase as he did before.

Abby heard the lock catch. *That's helpful,* she thought. "How do you feel about all this?"

"Daddy knew this would happen to me," Ethan replied. "The hologram map proves it. It shows where I live. It feels like he's watching over me."

"You're right," Abby told him. "There's more to this. Does

having these abilities bother you?"

"Not really. But I'd like to know why."

"Time will tell. I hope we get some answers when we find your fake mom." She stood. "Are you hungry? Want a snack before bed?"

He nodded.

"Let's go see what we can find."

Chapter 16

After Abby took Dillon to school the next morning, she came back home and began to pack clothes for her and the boys. In what seemed to be a very short time later, the morning surrendered to noon, and she left to pick up Dillon at school.

Once home again, the time passed faster than Abby realized. When she saw Will pull up in front of her house, she gathered their suitcases, including the one filled with maps, and hurried to let him in. "Will's here," she called to the boys. "Let's go."

"Chad and Holly left earlier," Will told her. "We'll meet them there."

They were met in the orphanage parking lot by two teenage boys who introduced themselves.

"You'll be taking two vans," one of the teens explained.

Abby reached into the truck bed and lifted out the suitcase she wanted to give to Morgan.

Will assisted her, then helped the teens take his, Abby's, and the boys' suitcases out of the back of his truck and place them into a van.

Ethan's phone rang. He pulled it from his pocket, listened, then ended the call. "Morgan knows we're here. He wants us to join him in the conference room."

They went through the side door. When they entered the conference room, Morgan met them as they walked in.

"What's this?" Morgan asked, looking at the suitcase.

"More maps," Abby told him. "We thought you might like to look at these. One is tied with a braid of hair. I have no idea whose."

Morgan waved to Chad and Holly, who sat on the couch across the room. "Come check these out."

Will set the suitcase on the conference table. "Do your thing, Ethan."

Ethan walked toward him.

"Stop," Will said. "See if you can open it from there."

"Open," Ethan said to the suitcase.

Abby heard the click.

"Good to know," Will told Ethan. He lifted the lid and stepped aside.

Abby handed Morgan the scroll bound by white hair.

He slipped off the braid and held it up. "I'll have them run a DNA test. This may be very helpful." He set it aside and began to unroll the map of the world with the white dots and spread it out on the conference table.

"Ethan didn't touch any of them," Abby told him. "We thought he might have activated the hologram map and made someone aware of its existence. Don't ask me who. I'm just trying to think outside the box. I don't want anyone else breaking into my house."

"I understand," Morgan said. "But we have to know more. Ethan, if you will. This is intriguing." He stepped aside.

Ethan stood at the conference table and touched a white dot on the map. Nothing happened.

"Try this one," Morgan said, spreading out the world map with the green dots.

Ethan studied it and turned to Morgan. "Did you see this?"

Morgan joined him. A smile lit his face. "Cymatics. Each dot has an intricate geometric design."

"Why is that exciting?" Abby asked.

"It's one of the most fascinating things in the universe," Morgan said. "Simply put, sound can create visual patterns. And each dot on these maps has a different geometric design, meaning, they individually have their own acoustical wave." He looked at Ethan. "Did you learn about frequency at school?"

"No," Ethan said. "Music wasn't allowed."

"It's more than music," Morgan told him. "NASA has proven that each planet in our solar system has its own frequency. That includes Earth. In fact, the entire universe vibrates."

"Why can't we hear it?" Ethan asked.

"We're not attuned to some frequencies."

Ethan touched a green dot. "It didn't work." He lifted his finger from the paper. "Why would my dad create nano cymatics smaller than the normal eye can see?"

"Another mystery," Morgan said. He began rolling up the scrolls and placing them back into the suitcase. "Hopefully, we'll find out why he went through all this trouble. But we have a plane to catch, and this will have to wait." He took the suitcase to his office and locked it inside.

In the dark of night, they arrived at the DC safehouse, the last residence on a string of Victorian townhouses.

Abby glanced around at the homes on both sides of the street, watching for lights being turned on. But their arrival hadn't been noticed. The boys walked in front of her in the beam of her flashlight. When Abby entered the house and turned on the lights, she led the boys upstairs.

Will trailed them, carrying suitcases.

The third floor spanned the length and width of the entire home and contained three twin beds and a couch.

"The couch turns into a bed," Will told her. "I'll sleep here with the boys."

"Perfect," Abby said. "It's late. I'll be turning in, too."

Ethan sat cross-legged on his bed. "I'll wait until they fall asleep. By the look of their droopy eyelids, it shouldn't take long."

Abby ruffled his hair and kissed his forehead. "Good

night." She went over to Dillon and Jack, who had crawled into their beds. "I'll see you boys in the morning."

"Pleasant dreams," Will told her as he walked her to the door.

"Thank you for watching over them." She gave him a kiss on his cheek. "Good night." She left him standing at the door, watching her take the stairs to the second floor.

In her bedroom, she reached into her pocket, retrieved her cell phone, and set it on the nightstand. She rummaged through her suitcase, found her pajamas, changed, and climbed into bed.

Abby sat with her back against the headboard and grabbed her phone. Cymatics, she typed into the Internet search. She found a video explaining how sound creates visual images and played it. She watched as someone hooked a speaker to the bottom of a square, thin metal sheet covered with sprinkles of sand. When the low Hertz frequency began, the sand danced and formed a geometric design. Her eyes widened. The higher the frequency, the more complex the image became. "This is so cool," she said. With each tone, the pattern changed, forming distinct geometric shapes. "I'll have to show this to Ethan and Dillon," she muttered. "This is amazing." As she watched the rest of the video and found others of interest, five minutes turned into a half an hour.

Yawning, she placed her phone on the nightstand, turned off the lamp, and slid beneath the sheets.

Chapter 17

In the morning, Morgan returned from his meeting with the surveillance team and asked everyone to gather in the living room.

"Surveillance has trailed our target to DC Labs. We have a window of opportunity to search her home. Make sure you place all items in their original location. We want our visit to go unnoticed."

"I can help if anyone needs me," Ethan said.

"That would be very helpful." Morgan spread out a blueprint of the fifteen-story high-rise. "Okay, there are five of us, and we'll enter the building one at a time. All of us taking the elevator at once may catch security's eye. Each of you will go to your designated floor. Chad, you'll go to the sixth. Will, take the eighth. And I'll be on the tenth. Abby and Ethan will be the last to enter the building. Before riding up, Ethan will hit all the floor buttons. Security will more than likely take it for child's play. As the elevator ascends, each of you will be waiting until it stops at your floor."

Everyone nodded.

Morgan continued, "Ethan will make the cameras flicker as they go up. By the time we all arrive at the tenth floor, the security cameras inside the elevator will be completely off. Once we reach the fourteenth floor, at the end of the hallway, we'll find the staircase leading to the penthouse. And of course, Ethan will disrupt the cameras as we move forward."

"Which elevator goes all the way up?" Ethan asked.

Morgan pointed to the blueprints. "It's here in the lobby, but we won't be using it. We'll take the private stairway to our final destination."

"Why not take the penthouse elevator?" Ethan asked.

"The elevator is closely monitored," Morgan told him, "with multiple surveillance. If too much of their equipment goes down all at once, they'll investigate. Entering through the backdoor, so to speak, won't be expected. The stairs are only used in case of emergency and secured by one camera and a digital keypad lock."

"Easy enough," Will said.

Morgan looked at Holly. "You'll be first up to watch the boys." Then he handed the others latex gloves. "Don't put them on until you reach the stairway. Once inside the home, Ethan will disrupt any interior video cameras his fake mom may use to catch intruders. I think I covered it all."

"Why would she have cameras inside her home?" Chad asked. "Wouldn't that be overkill?"

"Someone who's trying to hide something would be overly protective," Morgan replied. "Any more questions? Remember what you're looking for? Addresses, documents, anything pertaining to her work or any school. I'll search her computer. Let's move out."

Morgan led the way up the penthouse's private stairs to the emergency entrance leading into the home. At the top step, he stood aside, letting Ethan enter.

Ethan hesitated. "There's a camera just inside." He closed his eyes. "It's disabled now. And there's a camera between the elevator and the front door."

"And how would you know that since it's forty feet away, through the living room, and outside the front door?" Morgan asked.

Ethan looked down for a moment, then glanced at Morgan. "I can hear its energy."

"That's new," Morgan replied. "No need to explain. I

believe there's a reason." He looked at Abby, Will, and Chad. "Wait here. Ethan and I will do a bug sweep."

When the door closed, Abby turned to Will. "He can hear electricity? Is that even possible?"

"In the US, electricity hums at 120 hertz," he replied. "The sound would be between a B and B-flat, two octaves below middle C."

"All clear," Ethan said, opening the door and allowing them to come inside.

Abby followed him into the living room.

"Will and Abby, cover the master bedroom," Morgan said, "then move to the second bedroom. Chad, start searching the living room. I'll check her computer."

In the bedroom, before they touched anything, Ethan used his photographic memory. "Got it," he told Abby and Will. "You can touch anything now. When you're done, I'll put everything back where it was."

"Let's start by looking under the mattresses and the bed," Will said.

They found nothing and moved on to search the rest of the room.

Abby began with the books on the nightstand. She flipped through the pages, looking for anything important tucked inside. She hesitated before going through the nightstand drawer. "I'm going to need your memory," she told Ethan. When he came to her, she opened the drawer and let him take a look.

"Okay, Mom," he said, stepping back. "Go ahead."

She rummaged through it, checking every corner and each surface. *Nothing.* Trying to think where a hidden object would be, her attention turned to the closet. She placed her hands on her hips.

Ethan stood next to her.

"Did you restore the contents in the drawer?" she asked

him.

"Yes. She'll never know you went through it."

Abby opened a door a few steps away and stared at a sea of clothing in a huge walk-in closet. "This may take a while," she told him. "I have to search every pocket." She began to go through each garment.

"I'll help Will," he told her and turned away.

Moving quickly, she checked everything hanging before turning to the shoes. She glanced inside each pair. *Nothing again*, she thought.

She peered into the bedroom and saw Will closing a dresser drawer. "Have you found anything?" she asked.

He held up a memory chip. "I'll be right back. I'm going to give this to Morgan to scan on the computer."

She nodded and turned to a stack of purses on a shelf. One at a time, she went through each of them, remembering to put them back where she'd found them. Looking up, she saw a cardboard box just out of her reach.

"I'm finished out here," Will told her as he stood in the doorway with Ethan, watching her stare up at the top shelf. "Need a hand?"

"I want to go through that box."

Will reached up, brought it down, and set it on the floor in front of her.

Abby contemplated the folded flaps, memorizing their position.

"Wait," Will said. "Is that a tell?" He pointed to a piece of lint between the folds.

"Could be." Looking over the box, she hunted for any other subtle clues that would tell the owner if the box had been opened. She grabbed her cell phone and took a photo. "Good eye," she told him. Carefully setting the lint aside, she opened the box and gasped. "Look. It's the missing storybooks." She took them out of the box. "*The Little Boy*, books one, two, and three."

"Can I see them?" Ethan asked.

She passed them to him and watched him read through the stories until he froze, staring at a page.

"There's a map on the little boy's bedroom wall," Ethan said.

"A map of what?" Abby asked.

Ethan touched it, and a hologram appeared above the storybook.

"It's this penthouse," Will said.

"There's a red dot," Ethan said. He glanced around the walk-in closet. "It's somewhere in here."

"Something in the closet is being tracked," Will said, scanning the surroundings.

"While you search, I need to get a better look at this," Ethan said, nodding at the hologram and walking out of the closet.

Abby glanced in the open box on the floor in front of her and felt the blood drain from her face. Reaching inside, she pulled out a photo of her husband and Ethan's fake mom having dinner in an Italian restaurant. "What the hell? When was this taken? Who is she? She's not getting this or the storybooks back."

Will folded the flaps, restored the tell, and placed the box back on the top shelf. "Let's show Morgan what we've found."

"Come look at this," Ethan called from the bedroom.

When Abby rushed out of the closet with Will behind her, she saw Ethan standing by the bedroom window. "What did you find?"

"The dot moved," he told them. "The book's being tracked, or I am."

"Let me see," Will said.

Ethan handed him all of the storybooks with the hologram hovering above them.

"Walk out to the living room," Will said.

Ethan left the bedroom.

Will looked at Abby. "It's Ethan. She's been tracking him."

Abby glanced at the bedroom door. "Where did he go? He must've gotten sidetracked." She heard Ethan shouting in the living room, telling everyone to hide, get down.

Will and Abby reached the open bedroom door together and froze. She raised her finger to her lips, cautioning Will to keep quiet. Peeking out the door and looking down the hall, she saw Morgan ducking behind the computer desk. She strained to listen and heard two people speaking, Ethan and an unknown woman.

"Did you think you could enter my home and I wouldn't know?" the woman asked.

"Don't you recognize me, Mom?" Ethan asked. "It's me, Emory. Are you a hologram?"

"Is it really you, Emory? What happened to your hair?"

"I ran away and colored my hair so I wouldn't get caught," Ethan told her.

"How did you get into my home?" she asked. "How did you find me?"

"Where are you?" Ethan asked. "Are you coming back?"

"I'll be home in about fifteen minutes."

"Okay," Ethan said.

Abby saw Morgan stand. She took the storybooks from Will. When she closed book one, the hologram tracking Ethan vanished. She shoved all three into her waistband under her blouse and put the photo into her pants pocket before slowly walking to the living room.

Chad rose from behind a chair.

"She's gone," Ethan told Abby and Will.

Morgan tossed the memory chip from the bedroom to Will. "I made a copy. Put that one back." He answered his cell phone, then turned to them. "She called the Takers. Estimated arrival is three minutes."

Abby peered out the wall of windows that looked out across the city and saw a hovercraft land on the rooftop landing pad. Her heart jumped into her throat.

"It's the Underground," Will told her, returning to her side.

"Ethan, cut the cameras on the roof," Morgan told him.

Ethan ran out the door then waved to them to follow.

They sprinted outside and jumped into their rescue vessel.

Through their craft's clear dome, Abby saw ten of the Takers' fleet coming from the north. *Seconds,* she thought. *We have only seconds.*

As she held on to her seat, the pilot hovered their craft to the south side of the high-rise and dropped down behind the building.

"We're cutting this uncomfortably short," Chad said.

Below, the streets were clear of traffic. Government agents blocked the roads in a four-block radius.

Abby peered upward. From above, a hovercraft swooped toward them, trailing so close she could see the determination on the Taker's face. She turned to see their craft heading straight into a high-rise. Her eyes widened, and panic filled her. As she held her breath and braced for an impact, their pilot turned sharply, soaring high and diving low, staying out of the Taker's gun sights. Abby glanced over her shoulder. *He's gaining on us,* she thought. "Can you stop him?" she whispered to Ethan.

Ethan stared at the follower's hovercraft. "Stop," he said in a low voice.

Their pursuer's engines failed. Between the buildings, his craft fell fourteen floors to the empty streets below and burst into a ball of fire.

Abby looked back and saw smoke billowing in the sky above the high-rises.

Their pilot soared above the traffic, flying between the buildings to a nearby park. When they landed, a black SUV picked them up.

"We outsmarted them," the driver told them. "They were expecting a getaway car. That's why all the streets were blocked off. No one, including the Takers, knows about our small fleet of hovercrafts except your pursuer, and he won't be talking." He raised his hand to the communicator in his ear and nodded. "It's all clear. I'm taking you back to the safehouse."

Chapter 18

Once inside the townhouse, Abby stood with Morgan in the living room.

He reached into his shirt pocket and pulled out his memory chip containing the downloaded copy. "Well, at least we found something."

Abby retrieved the storybooks from her waistband. "I discovered these in a box in her closet," she told him, "with a photo of her and my husband." She snatched the picture from her pants pocket and handed it to him. "Book one has a map inside it that's tracking Ethan's location."

Morgan opened the storybook and flipped through the pages. When he placed his finger on the map, and a hologram of the safehouse showing Ethan's location appeared, Morgan swore. "This is damn disturbing. She's been watching every move he makes." He gave her back the storybooks. "I'd like to know why these maps exist and why Ethan and the rest of us are being tracked." He held up the downloaded memory chip he brought from the penthouse. "Now, if you'll excuse me. I have to examine the contents of this chip. Hopefully, we'll find some answers."

"Of course." Abby called Dillon and Ethan over to her. "Let's sit on the couch and read your daddy's stories."

On the white sectional, Dillon sat on her left and Ethan on her right. They watched her flip to the first page of book one.

"Wait, Mom," Ethan said, pointing to the cover page. "That's me."

Abby stared at the drawing of a little boy playing with blocks. "It can't be. He has red hair."

"No. I mean, on the wall behind him. See that wave with

a hook on both sides? That's the zodiac sign for Leo, and there's eight of them spread around the wall. It means that it's August. Under each sign are things grouped in four—balls, jacks, hanging pictures—see. August fourth is my birthday. The numbers on the blocks are the year I'll be twelve."

"It could be a fluke. Except, the time on the clock is the time you were born." *The key's the little boy,* Abby remembered Ethan saying. "Your twelfth birthday might mean something. Write that down and put a star by it." She read the story to them while she searched for the answers to the hundreds of questions she had swirling in her mind. She shook her head. "I don't see anything else. Do you?"

"Nothing that makes sense," Ethan said.

Morgan came down the hall and into the living room as Will opened the sliding glass doors and walked inside.

"Find anything?" Will asked.

"Nothing that tells us what's going on," she replied. "The problem is the clues are too vague." She flipped through the pages of the second book. "Like this one. I know this interlinked three-spiral symbol means something. It's on almost every page."

"We need to focus on Doctor Davis," Morgan said, "her connection to the school, and why they chose Ethan to be her son's replacement."

"Do we know anything about her real son?" Abby asked.

"Yes," Morgan replied. "He's the same age as Ethan. Photos on the Web show him at age four having white hair like his mom. But we don't know if he's alive or dead."

"If she believes Ethan's her son, why did she call the Takers?" Abby asked. "She must know he's a replacement."

"She has to be a government puppet," Will said. "She had to be the one who told them about the GPS map showing the location of all the silver-eyes. How else would the Takers School know about the so-called treasure map and send a couple of their students to locate it?"

"She must not have told them much," Abby said, "or they wouldn't have sent children to find it. The technology alone should've brought troops to my door."

"Too much uncertainty," Morgan said. "For now, we treat her like she's the enemy."

"Did you find anything on the memory chip?" Abby asked Morgan.

"Not so far. It contains research for a lecture she gave on animal mutilation around the world in the nineteen-sixties and into the present century. It's a fascinating mystery. Each animal's blood had been drained, leaving no signs of splatter near the carcasses. Wolves and other common predators had been ruled out as the perpetrators."

Abby scrunched her nose. "Seems odd that she would keep something like that on a memory chip under the clothes in a dresser drawer."

"I'm going to go through it again," Morgan said. "Just in case I missed something." He turned and headed into the office.

"Want to relax for a bit on the patio?" Will asked Abby.

"Good idea," she replied. "I'm going to grab a bottled water. Want one?"

He nodded.

They went out to the backyard and sat across from each other at a table under a green canvas umbrella.

"It's difficult to believe how much my life has turned on its head," Abby said. "I hardly recognize myself. Who knew I'd be fighting against the Takers, or able to shoot a gun?" She took a sip from the bottle. "You know you promised to show me some self-defense moves."

He froze with his water bottle halfway to his mouth and grinned. "I'm up for a challenge, but not until we leave DC. We'll need a padded floor."

She bumped her bottle against his. "We have a plan."

They both sprang to their feet, hearing Morgan shouting in the office. They ran inside and found him sitting in front of the computer with Holly, Chad, and Ethan standing behind him.

"I found a locked file within her lecture," Morgan said, visibly shaking. "It's pure evil." He started the video file from the beginning.

The images moved haphazardly. *Someone's taking a video,* Abby thought, *and trying not to get caught.* When the camera focused, Abby nearly vomited. Children were strapped to tables while the Takers withdrew their blood.

"Now we know what the school is doing to the children during the night," Morgan told them. "It gets worse."

The video showed children inside pods, comatose, and floating in fluid.

Morgan stopped the video and pointed at the screen. "Doctor Davis is Ethan's aunt, and that boy floating in the liquid is her son. They threatened to keep him as a breeder if she didn't do their bidding."

Abby gasped.

"What's a breeder?" Ethan asked.

"A breeder produces more children so they can harvest their blood," Will replied.

Morgan nodded and continued. "She saw Ethan's photo among others who would be confined once they turned twelve. By taking her son hostage, they forced her to use her knowledge to enable their shapeshifters to build up their immunity to viruses on Earth. She told them she was very respected in the medical field, and the rumors of her son not being returned at the promised age of twelve years old would make the headlines. She made it appear as if she pointed randomly to the hundreds of photos on their computer's screen to choose a replacement to prevent the scandal. She saved Ethan's life."

Tears streamed down Abby's face.

"What's a shapeshifter?" Ethan asked.

"It's an alien who can take any shape it chooses," Morgan replied. "They're walking among us." When he restarted the video, the footage jumped to a new location.

"Aliens?" Abby asked, her heart in her throat. She continued to watch as Doctor Davis stood in her penthouse.

"They're not human," Abby heard the doctor explain. "They only look like us when they shapeshift into human form. The aliens drained the blood of more than ten thousand animals. Now they feed on our young children's blood. It helps them prolong their lifespan. And now, their taste for blood is the same as our taste for wine. They have to be stopped."

"Damn right they have to be stopped," Will said.

Doctor Davis continued to say, "Ethan will be twelve soon."

Abby's skin prickled. *Why is she talking about my son?*

"He should see changes happening to him already," the doctor said. "Soon, the knowledge that he needs will come to him."

Changes? Knowledge? A fear Abby could never imagine filled her. *What the hell,* Abby thought. "What does Ethan have to do with this?"

"She doesn't say," Morgan replied. He stopped the video. "She wants us to stay away from her because the time isn't right. Her last words on the video are that the future of Earth's children depends on the gathering."

"What's a gathering?" Ethan asked.

"We don't know," Abby told him.

"We should focus on what we do know," Morgan said. "The maps. We know there's at least two hundred of our brothers and sisters. Let's assume for a moment that they'll be the ones who gather together. The second map and the other maps along with it have to do with frequencies."

"What do frequencies have to do with fighting the aliens?" Will asked.

"We intend to find out," Morgan said.

"I understand you're having the cymatics map examined," Will said. "Remember, the runaways at your orphanage have embedded chips. We don't know what the frequencies will do to them."

"We can try the frequencies on the two boys," Chad said, coming into the room, "who were sent to look for the so-called treasure map."

"Perfect," Morgan said. "We'll bring the maps to our orphanage in Utah, where there are no runaways, and none of the children have embedded chips. They can find the frequency that matches each of the cymatics images, and then we'll test the results on the two boys."

He retrieved his cell phone from the desk in front of him and made a video call to his office. "I'd like you to go to the conference room. You'll need the key code to enter. Inside my office, you'll find a black suitcase. I'll wait while you find it."

The woman took her cell phone with her and left her desk. When she entered Morgan's office, she said, "Found it."

"This is a priority one, top secret mission," he told her. "Leave it there. Tell no one. Lock the office and the conference room. I'll send someone to retrieve the suitcase within an hour. Give it to no one other than the person who will tell you that his cat swam two laps in his pool." He waited until she locked the rooms before he ended the call, then made another one. "If you don't mind," he said to everyone, "I'll need you to step out of the room. This is a secured call."

"Want to go back outside?" Will asked Abby.

She nodded. "What's Dillon and Jack doing?" she asked Ethan.

"They're watching a movie."

"I'm glad they aren't involved in the discussions about Doctor Davis's mind-blowing reality," she said. "Let's go out to the patio."

Once outside, Ethan poured three glasses of lemonade from the pitcher in the center of the table, gave one to Abby and one to Will, and sat with them.

"Did you understand what we just saw?" Will asked Ethan. "Does it scare you?"

"A little," he said. "I'm not afraid of changes. What's happened to me so far is kind of cool. And I want to help save my cousin and everyone else. What's scary is the way the aliens fooled everyone. No one knows but us that they're everywhere and can change their shape to look like us. The Cole that left that day didn't even know me. Now I know it wasn't him. I wonder if the real Cole is in a container, too."

"That's a scary thought," Abby said. "I think we should take this step-by-step, or we'll be overwhelmed. The first thing I want to do is learn how to fight. If Ethan's going to be anywhere near an alien, I'm going to be right beside him."

"Easy enough," Will said. "You'll need an expert. I know a guy."

"I can't believe this is happening," Abby said. "I need to practice shooting, too." She turned, hearing Morgan calling them to come inside.

Everyone gathered on the sectional, while Morgan sat on a recliner across from them.

"The Underground is overnighting the frequency maps to Utah," Morgan explained. "The headmaster said he'll have all able bodies focused on cracking the cymatics clues. We should know by late afternoon tomorrow. We're flying back home in the morning." He looked at Ethan. "Looks like you and I will be spending a lot of time together."

"And I have you on speed dial," Ethan said. "I'll call you if anything happens."

"Deal," Morgan told him.

Aliens draining blood? Abby thought. *It's a scene out of a horror movie. Everybody seems too calm.* "Is anybody else as scared as I am?" She watched everyone raise their hand.

Chapter 19

At least I got seven hours of sleep last night, Abby thought. After hearing that aliens are invading Earth, she imagined she'd never be able to sleep again. She finally dozed off around two in the morning and awoke just in time to eat before heading to the airport.

Sitting still while flying from DC to Washington state proved stressful. The adrenaline in her system kept reminding her that the time to fight could present itself at any minute. After they landed, the drive home from the Underground orphanage took another hour.

At home, Abby waited for Will to take her to a self-defense class. Holly had invited Dillon to her house for a play day with Jack. Meanwhile, she went through the storybooks again, looking for clues, and Ethan perused the Internet to find more information about the three-spiral symbol.

She jumped when she received a text from Will. "He's here," she shouted to Ethan.

They hurried out, locked up the house, and climbed into Will's truck.

"I'm not sure," Ethan told them, "but I think we're Druids. At least that's what we were called at one time. The description of who they were back then fits us today—custodians of our planet, keepers of justice, teachers of advanced knowledge, and magicians. Oh, and they had white hair and could foresee the future, just like Daddy could."

"Druids, huh?" Will said, pulling into a parking spot in front of an unmarked building on the outskirts of town. "We're here."

"Will we be able to come again tomorrow and every day

until Ethan's birthday?" Abby asked. "I'll need more than one class."

"He's willing to train you until you're a fighting machine," Will told her. "Ethan, too."

They climbed out of the truck and went inside the building.

Abby glanced around and saw eight instructors teaching classes. "It looks like we're not the only ones who want to defend themselves."

"It's been this way for years," Will said. "Each time the government takes away one of our constitutional freedoms, the self-defense clientele doubles."

A man who looked to be in his twenties approached them. "Good to see you again, Will. Just follow the arrows to the elevator and go to the second floor. When the doors open, have a seat in the waiting room. Our instructors will assist you momentarily."

"Second floor?" Abby said to Will as they walked away.

"It's deceptive," Will said. "Street view, the building's one level. All other floors are below ground."

After riding the elevator down and stepping out into a waiting room, two instructors greeted them. Ethan followed one to a ten-by-ten padded training zone, while Abby's trainer took her to another padded area across the room.

"It's smart of them to put you in an area where you're unable to see Ethan," Will said. "The instructor needs your full attention. Glancing at Ethan for just a second could put you in harm's way."

"I understand." Abby followed her trainer to the middle of a padded zone.

Will sat in a chair against the wall.

"You'll need to remember a list of soft spots," the trainer told her. He pointed to various places on his body. "They're the most vulnerable areas to strike, even on someone who's bigger and stronger than you. When you strike the soft spots, you're giving yourself a chance to fight back and escape."

She pointed to those areas on her body and nodded. "Got it," she said.

"We'll start off with escaping a choke hold," he told her.

By the end of the lesson, Abby needed a shower.

"That was fun," Ethan said.

Will looked at Abby. "It will get easier. I promise."

"I used muscles I didn't know I had," she told him.

"Would you rather skip a day between classes?" Will asked her.

"No," she replied. "There's not enough time."

They climbed into his truck.

Before Will started the engine, his cell phone rang, and he answered the call. "What's up, Morgan?" He listened, then turned to Abby. "They've matched each of the cymatics patterns with their corresponding frequencies, and tomorrow, they plan to test the effects on the boys, Cole and Alex, who were looking for a treasure map. Do you and Ethan want to be present for the results?"

"Yes," Abby said. "I think my husband would want us there."

"Yes, Morgan," Will told him. "We all want to be there." He listened again and nodded. "We'll be ready." He ended the call and slid his cell phone into his shirt pocket. "A car will be by your place in the morning to pick us up at seven."

"Do you want to stay the night?" Abby asked. "There's a sofa bed in the office downstairs if you want to."

"That sounds like a good idea. We can stop by my place on the way home so I can pick up a few things."

As twilight kissed nightfall, sitting in the passenger seat, coming home from the defense class, Abby observed the deserted roads. This time of night, electric vehicles were being hooked up to their energy stations. And gas-run cars and trucks stayed off the roads to keep from being noticed.

Will turned into a long driveway, following it as it trailed away from the road.

At the end of the drive, his forest-green two-story house, with cedar shutters around the windows, came into view. "Your house blends in with the woods," she said.

"It fits me. Plenty of privacy." He parked in front of the porch steps, they climbed out of the truck, and he led them to the front door.

As he unlocked it, Abby admired the cedar-peaked gable roof above the entrance that gave character to the wraparound porch. Once inside, she followed him to a living room at the back of the house and waited with Ethan as Will cleaned up and packed some things.

Tawny-beige walls made the large room seem cozy. She sat on a white couch in front of a stone fireplace that rose to the high ceiling. Above its wood-beam mantle hung a painting of an eagle.

"Look, Mom," Ethan said, standing in front of a ten-foot-wide picture window.

She gazed beyond Will's cedar deck's railings to a sea of grass surrounded by woods and saw four deer. "Cool, huh?" she said. "Why do you think there's no animals around the Takers School?"

"I think it's the hum," he told her.

"It has a hum?"

"Yes. Will thinks it's because it takes a lot of energy to run the holograms."

Abby nodded. "That makes sense. What do you think about the cymatics?"

"Daddy must've had vision like me to be able to engrave those tiny dots," Ethan said.

"I wouldn't doubt it," Abby said.

"Your dad's incredible," Will said, stepping into the living room. "Each cymatics dot he made matched exactly to the frequencies used to create the sand patterns they reproduced in the lab."

"That's cool," Ethan said.

"It is," Will replied. "Morgan wants to use the recording studio at the Utah orphanage to amplify the frequency tones that coincided with the patterns while watching the boys' reaction through the control desk window."

"I hope we learn something useful," Abby said. "We have to find the school."

"But first, if aliens are running it," Will said, "we have to find a way to kill them. Well, let's go." Will picked up his duffel bag and locked the house after they stepped outside. "Are we picking up Dillon?" he asked.

"Holly's bringing him home later," she replied. "With all this moving around and going back and forth to the orphanage, he hasn't spent much time in school. I wonder if life will ever be normal again."

Will threw his bag in the back of the truck, got in, and started the engine.

"I can help him study," Ethan said, sliding into the back seat. "It'll be fun."

"I'm sure he'd like that," Abby said, opening the passenger side door and climbing in.

Pulling out of the long driveway onto the main road, Will turned toward Abby's house.

"Do you have the photo of the cymatics maps?" Ethan asked.

Abby looked at Will, and he nodded. "Yes," she replied. "We both do. Why?"

"Can I see all of them?" Ethan asked. "I think I might've

missed something. I just need to take a look." He took their phones and scrolled through the photos. "Did Morgan tell you what the numbers under the dots mean?"

"They're hertz, the number of waves or vibrations within a period of one second," Will told him. "One hundred hertz means there are one hundred cycles of vibration within that second. The more vibrations within a hertz, the higher the pitch."

"That's interesting," Ethan said. "We didn't learn anything about that in school."

"Did you find what you missed on the maps?" Abby asked.

"No," Ethan said. "But it feels important." He handed both phones back to Abby. "It seems like most of the time I'm starting to feel that there's something I should do or know."

"Hang in there," Will told him. "It won't be long before you'll have all the answers."

"Are there any other changes you've noticed?" Abby asked.

"I can hear the others now," he said. "Just like Morgan. I think there's a lot more of them than the ones on the map."

"How many more?" Will asked.

"Maybe a thousand," Ethan replied.

"All over the world?" Abby asked.

"Yes."

They stopped at a diner before going to Abby's.

"Thank you," she told Will as they climbed back into the truck to leave. "I'm glad I don't have to cook tonight."

He chuckled. "I expect you're pretty sore from attempting to defend yourself in class."

She rubbed her arm. "You might say that."

"If you imagine that you're fighting an alien, it will help you stay on your feet," Ethan said. "It worked for me."

"Good idea." Will glanced at Abby, then started the

engine. "He's right, you know."

"I know," she replied. "I learned a lot today. What time is our class tomorrow? Are we going to be back in time?"

"It takes about an hour and forty minutes to get to Utah," Will said. "Add a couple more hours for the test, plus time for the flight home. We'll make it." He pulled into the driveway of Abby's home, parked, and they got out, heading to the front door.

Abby stood aside, letting Ethan use his ability to unlock the door.

With a duffel bag in hand, Will followed them inside.

They went to the living room, and Ethan retrieved the storybooks. "I'm going to take another look at these." He plopped into the chair by the fireplace.

"Want some iced tea?" Abby asked Will.

"Yes, thank you."

"I'll be right back." When she returned, she handed him his drink, and they strolled out to the patio.

"You know it's all right for him to go over it again a few times," Will said.

"A few times and a few times more," Abby replied. "Feeling like he's missing something all of the time must be driving him crazy." She took a sip of her tea.

"I feel like we're all missing something," he said.

"A plan," Abby told him. "We're missing a plan. What do we do first? Should we search for the school or bring down the Takers?"

"And if the Takers are aliens, how do we kill them?" Will asked.

Ethan opened the sliding glass door and joined them. He sat at the table next to Abby.

"Did you find anything you missed?" Abby asked.

"No. Just stuff I don't understand."

"Like what?" Will asked.

"A globe, a spiderweb, flying fish," Ethan replied. "Morgan was right. Nothing makes sense until it happens. If my eyesight were normal, I wouldn't know what the eyechart means."

"Don't get discouraged," Abby told him. "Maybe that's what your father intended it to be. By drawing and writing what he did, he could've been telling you that he knows what you will be going through. If that's the case, then he succeeded perfectly."

Ethan nodded. "You're right. And that's what I've always wanted." He smiled. "Thanks."

A knock on the door caught their attention, and Ethan ran to answer it. He returned with Dillon and Holly.

Abby gave Dillon a hug.

"I think I might be a Druid," Ethan told Holly.

"I wouldn't hop to any conclusions," she said over her shoulder as he headed inside with Dillon.

"Hi," Abby said.

"Good evening, you guys. You know, I wouldn't let Ethan fixate on the Druids if I were you. I don't believe everything that's been written about them. I suggest we take things one day at a time."

Abby nodded. "It would help me to focus on the here and now. We can't control tomorrow."

"Maybe not yet," Will said. He looked at Holly. "Sorry you and Chad aren't joining us in Utah."

"I suspect that the frequencies will either give Cole and his buddy a headache or make them pass out," she replied. "I doubt we'll miss anything. Have a great trip and see you when you get back."

Abby walked her to the front door. "Thanks for everything, Holly." She hugged her and watched her leave. Before going back to the patio, she went upstairs to check on the boys to get them settled in for the night. "It's time for bed, Dillon," she told him as she entered his bedroom.

Ethan sat on Dillon's bed, drawing with colored pencils.

"If you want to stay up and draw some more, Ethan, you need to take the pencils into your room. Dillon has to go to bed now."

Ethan continued to sketch as he walked out the door, across the hall, and into his room.

Abby tucked Dillon in and kissed him good night. Then, she went back downstairs and joined Will.

"Are the boys in bed?" Will asked.

"Dillon is. Ethan's still up."

Will clinked his glass against hers. "Here's to a quiet evening."

"To tonight," she said.

Ethan rushed outside. "You've got to see this." He placed a colored pencil on the table and put his hand above it.

Abby sipped her drink, and her eyes widened as she watched the pencil levitate. She raised her hand to her mouth, keeping its contents from spraying across the table, and swallowed hard.

"Have you tried lifting anything larger?" Will asked him.

Ethan put his hand over a chair, and it rose from the ground. He giggled and clapped his hands. The chair remained in the air. "Can you believe that?"

"Can you lower it?" Abby asked, stunned.

He put his hands above it again, and the chair returned to solid ground.

Chills went across her skin as frightening scenes from sci-fi movies played in her mind. *This isn't a movie,* she thought. *But how is this possible? Excellent eyesight and mechanical manipulation seen unthreatening. But levitation is different. This is physical.*

Will grinned. "Come on. Let's go inside."

Abby followed them into the house and watched them play like kids, running around and finding all sizes of things to levitate.

"Try to do it without putting your hands above it," Will said.

Ethan stared at the dining room table, and it rose a couple of feet off the ground, where it remained as he and Will stood with their mouths open. Then, Ethan lowered it to the floor.

Abby saw the excitement on their faces while her thoughts whirled with the reality that her son could do the impossible again. "Why don't you help Will make the bed in the office?" She watched them go down the hallway.

Chapter 20

Abby stood with Ethan and Will in a sound studio at the Underground orphanage in Utah. Behind her, in a room meant for an audio recording class, selected officials from Underground Headquarters and a few of Morgan's friends sat in three rows of seats to watch the frequency test and Doctor Davis's video. Seeing those in military uniforms among the group surprised her. "I thought military personnel were the government's puppets."

"The ones here are Morgan's friends," Will told her. "The three-star general's grandson was a runaway from the Takers School. The school gave no recovery assistance or an explanation for what caused the boy to run. The general went on television asking for help from the public to find the ten-year-old. That's when Morgan found the boy and returned him to his family. He and the general have been best friends ever since. The others in uniform have had similar experiences. Their colleagues were told that they're here to be guest speakers at the orphanage's career seminar."

Abby nodded.

On a wall displaying a digital screen, everyone watched Cole and his sidekick, Alex, sitting in chairs behind a table.

"To be clear," Morgan said to Ethan, "you know for a fact that the frequency won't harm humans, right?"

Ethan nodded. "I don't know how I know. I just do. They'll only pass out for about five minutes, then wake up."

"I just wanted to be certain," Morgan said. "It's not that I don't trust you, because I do. I guess we're ready to give it a go then."

Morgan stepped in front of the live stream and addressed the assembly. "Thank you for coming." He pointed to the screen.

"The boys you see here are actually sitting behind me in a soundproof recording room. I'm about to subject them to intervals of frequency to see if it may affect them. The test shouldn't take long before I get to the real reason you're here—to witness our latest video discovery. We'll get started in just a moment."

Abby watched Morgan sit at the sound control desk and test the list of frequencies that matched the cymatics symbols on the map.

Will, standing at Morgan's side, studied the boy's reactions.

"I don't get it," Morgan said. "Why would her husband go through all the trouble of creating this map if frequency does nothing?"

"Maybe it's a combination of sounds," Will replied.

"It's all of them together," Ethan said. "Remember the storybook *Little One Note*? The last line of the story was, *and they all sang together.*"

Morgan emitted the combined frequencies into the recording room.

Alex went limp, his head slumping on the table.

Cole, unconscious and face down on the table, transformed into something that made Abby panic. He no longer looked human. The shapeshifter's stature, twice the size of the child it pretended to be, wore remnants of the clothes that had fit it before it had transformed. It had gray skin and a massive head. Plus, each of its hands on its long, thin arms had only four fingers. Abby thought of Dillon. *He's safe. He's with Morgan's assistant.* She glanced at Ethan, whose brows furrowed as he stared at the Taker. *How am I going to protect them from something like that?* she thought.

Morgan turned off the amplifier.

Gasps came from his guests who left their seats to look beyond the glass window into the recording room. Everyone talked at once.

"I will answer all your questions once our test has been completed," Morgan told them, keeping his eyes on Alex and the alien. "Please return to your seats and remain silent. The data we're collecting is extremely important."

"Are they dead?" Ethan asked.

"I'll check their pulses." Will hurried in and placed his hand on Alex's neck, then turned to the alien. It raised its head, its dark saucer-shaped eyes glaring at him. Will dashed for the exit as the alien leaped across the table toward him.

Standing with Ethan at the glass door, Abby noticed her son make a pushing gesture with his hands and saw the alien fly backwards until it slammed into the far wall. She put her hand across her open mouth. "You saved Will's life," she said.

Will ran back to Alex, pulled him out of his seat, and brought him into the control room. After securing the door, Will looked at Ethan. "Was that you?"

Ethan nodded.

"Thanks." Will led Alex by the arm and placed him in a chair.

Abby's heartbeat quickened as she watched the alien stand. Its dark eyes looked large above a small, thin nose and a lipless mouth. It snatched a chair and hurled it at the window, cracking the glass. Then it charged toward them. Sailing backwards, it hit the wall much harder than before.

Unharmed, it stood and took two steps before Morgan blasted the mixed frequencies nonstop inside the soundproof room. The alien dropped to the ground.

"Do you think he'll get up again?" Will asked Morgan.

"Your guess is as good as mine. I'll leave the sound on."

"Come with me," Will said to Alex. He led him back into the recording room. "Stop crying. I'm not going to hurt you."

The boy sniffled and looked around as if wanting to escape.

Will waited a short time before he brought Alex back into

the control room and closed the door behind him. "No reaction," he told Morgan.

"We should scan his implant and examine his demeanor to see if any influence the Takers have on him has been severed," Morgan said.

Will placed the boy back into the chair. Then he and Morgan entered the soundproof room.

Abby watched as they stopped in front of the alien. She saw Will bend down and search for a pulse, then shake his head. They didn't stay long before they returned.

"It's dead," Will told Abby.

Morgan concluded the testing. "Looks like we have a weapon," he said. "Now, we have to figure out how to use it to our advantage."

"Let me understand what you've learned so far," the general said.

"All of the children who have been to the government's elementary school, which we refer to as the Takers School, have been implanted with a chip," Will told him. "We amplified a combination of frequencies which caused the implanted human to black out for about five minutes before regaining consciousness. When the alien lost consciousness, its real identity was revealed. Those who have no chip have no response."

"We found the human ceased to be affected by the frequencies at that point," Morgan said. "If the sound is turned off too soon, the alien will regain consciousness and attack. That happened twice until I switched on the amp again and subjected it to constant combined frequencies that killed it."

"There's more," Will told him. "Once you've been shown our newest video discovery, you'll see a broader picture of what's really going on."

Ethan walked over to the glass door and stared into the soundproof room. "I was right. It's not Cole."

Will looked at Alex. "Do you remember where the school is?"

He nodded.

"Don't trust him," Ethan said.

"Ethan is supposed to have the knowledge he needs on his birthday," Abby said.

"Do you think he'll learn the location of the school?" Will asked. "We shouldn't wait? Our best scenario is to take the school by surprise before they know we're on to them. That is, if we had someone to help us find it."

"Abby's right," Morgan said. "We can't rush this. We need more pieces to the puzzle." He took a deep breath. "I guess it's time to show them Doctor Davis's video. This will send shockwaves throughout the Underground once our guests return to Headquarters and show them the doctor's video and ours, revealing our test results."

"What about the general?" Abby asked. "Can he get the military involved?"

"No," Morgan said. "Who can he trust? I'm giving him the frequencies. But he's only one man and swimming in infested waters."

Morgan stepped in front of the assembly once again. "The video you're about to see was taken covertly by Doctor Davis. Please pay close attention. Soon, you'll know exactly what is happening to our children." He walked to the control desk and started the video.

Abby looked away. She couldn't watch. The memories of seeing the video for the first time turned her stomach.

The room fell silent. Doctor Davis's whispering words could be heard by all. Once the video ended, the group's reactions varied from tears to retching and rage. Before leaving, they pledged to save the children.

"We have to prepare for the worst," Morgan told Abby

and Will. "The Underground has HERF guns in our arsenals." He chuckled. "I thought they were crazy obtaining those outdated weapons. I guess I was wrong."

"What's a HERF gun?" Ethan asked.

"HERF stands for high-energy radio frequency," Morgan told him. "It's a direct-energy weapon used decades ago to disrupt equipment such as computers. With a little adjustment to the frequencies, the guns will serve our purpose perfectly."

"We should get going," Will said.

"There's a car out front ready to take you to the airport." Morgan returned all of Abby's maps to her. "As far as I know, we won't be needing these any longer."

"If you do, you know where to find them. I guess we're ready to leave." Abby took Ethan's hand. "Let's go find Dillon."

Chapter 21

Target practice and defense classes filled Abby's and Ethan's days until the morning of Ethan's birthday. That's when she opened his bedroom door just after sunrise and found him missing.

"He's in the backyard," Dillon told her. "He wants to be left alone. I went out there just now. His eyes are closed, but I don't think he's sleeping. He didn't hear me, and I tried to wake him up. I think he went away and left his body sitting there."

Abby went into the living room and looked out the sliding glass door leading to the patio. The dew glistened beneath the morning sun. In the middle of the damp lawn, Ethan sat cross-legged on a blanket, his back straight and his hands in his lap. She remembered her husband meditating, sitting in the same position, cross-legged, for hours sometimes. "You're right," she said. "Your dad used to do that, too. He'll be meditating for a while." She turned away from the glass door. "Let's not bother him." Taking his hand, she strolled with Dillon to the kitchen and made breakfast.

When Abby glanced out the kitchen window and saw Will's truck coming up the driveway, she poured a cup of coffee and headed to the front door. After she opened it, she saw the concern on his face and handed him the cup.

"Are your phones dead?" he asked as he came into the house. "The entire town is blacked out." He looked at the cup in his hand. "How did you make coffee?"

"Our coffee maker's working and so is our stove," she told him. "I just made breakfast. Would you like some?"

"That would be nice. Thanks." He followed her to the kitchen and flipped on the light switch. "Your lights are out," he said.

She opened the refrigerator. "Fridge is working."

"Your generator must have kicked on," Will told her. "How's Ethan? Is he up yet? He's going to miss his birthday."

"I think we'll have to go with the flow." She led him to the sliding glass door in the living room and pointed toward Ethan. "He's been out there for over an hour now."

"I remember Doctor Davis's quote," Will said. "He'll receive the knowledge he needs on his birthday." He took a sip of coffee. "I wonder if whatever he's doing has anything to do with our phones and the electricity going out?"

"I think it does," Abby replied. "Our clocks stopped when the sun came up this morning. Dillon told me that's when Ethan went outside, spread the blanket, and sat down."

"Kind of like a power surge," Will said. "Incredible. Everything looks peaceful out there. How are you feeling? Any headaches?"

"It took me a while to wake up. But after two cups of coffee, I'm alive and well. And no headaches." She led him back to the kitchen. As Abby fixed three plates of pancakes, scrambled eggs, and bacon, Will poured glasses of milk and brought them to the dining room table. They sat with Dillon and ate breakfast while keeping a vigil on Ethan in the backyard.

After three hours of meditation, Ethan opened his eyes and stood.

"He's awake, Mommy," Dillon said.

"I see that," Abby replied. "Do you think he's hungry?"

"I'll ask him." Dillon opened the sliding glass door and dashed outside.

Abby went back to the kitchen and heated up the breakfast leftovers, stacked buttered toast on a small plate, and placed sliced strawberries, bananas, and melon into a bowl. When she brought the food to the dining room table, Ethan came inside and ate everything she set in front of him. She gave him more eggs, pancakes, and fruit.

"I know where the schools are now," he said with his mouth full.

"How many are there?" Will asked.

"Five in America."

"The buildings must be huge considering how many children there are in our country," Abby said.

"They're not buildings," Ethan said as he scooped up more scrambled eggs. "I'll show you where they are. I need maps of Washington state, Arizona, Kansas, Ohio, and Mississippi."

Abby went into the office and shuffled through her husband's collection of maps. As she found the ones Ethan asked for, she handed them to Will.

Ethan slid his empty plate aside when Will laid out a map of Washington state. Then he pointed to the school's location. "There."

"So, the other runaways were right," Will said. "It's where they said it is."

"It's cloaked."

"I should have guessed," Will said. "Wait. If it's not a building, what is it?"

"A spaceship," Ethan replied.

"A real spaceship?" Dillon asked.

"Yes," Ethan told him. "The spaceships that belong to the monsters I told you about."

"Invisible," Will said. "It would have to be. We searched every bit of that area except the marsh. Wouldn't we have felt it if we had walked into it?"

Ethan nodded. "The marsh is a hologram," he said. "Has anyone seen balls of light flying around?"

"Yes," Will said. "I saw one when I went in search of the school four months ago."

"You were being watched. The balls of light are spies."

"How are we going to get into the school without them knowing?" Abby asked. She imagined Takers in hovercrafts striking lightning at them as they tried to make it through the hologram and enter the school. *Impossible,* she thought.

"I can cloak us," Ethan said.

"That's new," Will said. "Can they see our heat signatures?"

"No. They won't see us at all."

"How many can you cloak?" Will asked.

Ethan shrugged. "I don't know. I guess we should find out."

"So," Abby said, "we have to take Dillon to school and act like it's just another day, test your cloaking ability, and make a plan. What about the gathering?"

"We have to save the children before then," Ethan said.

"How long do we have?" Will asked. "And what and when exactly is the gathering?"

"In about four weeks," Ethan told them. "Do you know what chakras are?"

"Yes," Abby said. "They're the seven energy centers of the human body. What does that have to do with anything?"

"Earth has chakras, too. They're called vortexes. Some are major. Others are minor. Each vortex is connected to another by straight lines called ley lines that form an energy grid around Earth. My brothers and sisters have to travel to seven major vortexes in America, South America, Australia, England, Egypt, Turkey, and Tibet. That's the gathering. Then they'll send the frequencies across the grid."

"Are those the same frequencies that will kill the aliens?" Will asked.

"No," Ethan said. "It's a call for help. But first, we have to save the children. Soon, the shapeshifters will stop looking like humans, and people will panic. Then, the aliens inside the school spaceships will try to liftoff. We can't let them leave and take the children with them."

"Will there be others like you who will help us find the school?" Abby asked.

"No," Ethan said. "It's okay. I have the information I need now, and I called for the gathering. I'll be leading the others, kind of like a conductor leads a symphony, to spread the frequencies across the ley lines. And I was given the ability to save the children."

"Is Morgan going to the gathering?" Will asked.

"Yes," Ethan said. "I'm going with him. It won't take us long to get to Mount Shasta. Some of the others will have to go to countries far away to get to their gathering places. In four weeks, I'll have to be at Mount Shasta to conduct the frequency."

"We'll have to move fast," Will said. "Morgan needs to form a team to hit the schools, or rather, spaceships. And we'll need the HERF guns. I'll call him when we take Dillon to school and test Ethan's cloaking ability."

"Why Mount Shasta?" Abby asked. "Will you have to go to the very top?"

"It's Earth's major energy vortex," Ethan told her. "Its energy is really strong. I can make it to the base of the mountain to Panther Meadow, and that will be good enough. We're meeting twenty others there."

"That should be easy to get to." Abby looked at the clock on the mantle. "Get dressed, boys. We'll take Dillon to school, and I have office work to catch up on."

"Should I take my lightsaber?" Dillon asked.

"No," Abby told him. "There aren't any aliens at your school."

As soon as they were ready to go, they piled into Will's truck and drove to the Underground's school. A line of transport pods trailed through the parking lot as moms and dads dropped off their children.

Will parked. They climbed out of the truck and headed for the main entrance, passing the sandbox filled with swings, slides, and monkey bars before reaching the school's open double-doors. Dillon ran ahead to walk with one of his friends.

"Once his class gets settled in," Will said, "Ethan will make them disappear."

"How are we going to do this without the entire town knowing Ethan's more than special?" Abby asked, dodging a little boy who almost ran into her. The children's laughter and chatter bounced off the walls, and their footsteps echoed off the gray vinyl floor. Up ahead, she saw Dillon go into his classroom.

"It will be me they'll be watching," Will told her. "We'll declare it magic day. I'll tell them that I'm going to make everyone disappear."

"Good idea," Ethan said. "I can be your assistant. Every magician has one. While they're watching you, I'll cloak them."

"When the children tell their parents that you made the class vanish, no one will take it seriously, I'm sure," Abby said. "But what about the teacher? What are you going to tell her?"

"She works for the Underground," Will said. "She knows how to keep a secret. Anyway, people who know me won't believe her. Pulling a coin out of someone's ear is about the only thing they've seen me do."

Fewer and fewer children filled the hall, the last of them darting into the classroom when the teacher stood at the door, blowing a whistle.

"We need to get synchronized," Will told Ethan. "I'll count to three, raise my hands, and say be gone. Will that work?"

Ethan nodded.

"A little corny," Abby said. "But it will get their attention. How about making the teacher disappear first so the children can get excited?"

"Perfect," Will said. "What do you think, Ethan?"

He grinned. "It's going to be fun."

Abby, Will, and Ethan entered the classroom.

"Do you mind if I disrupt your class for a few minutes?" Will asked the teacher.

"Be my guest," she replied, stepping aside.

He stood in front of the children with Ethan at his side. "Boys and girls," Will said, "today is magic day. And I'm going to make all of you disappear."

The children sat silently, looking bored.

He turned to the teacher. "Would you mind being my first volunteer?"

"Certainly. What do you want me to do?"

"Just stand right here, wave to the class, and I'll say the magic words."

She did as he asked.

He had the class's attention now.

Ethan stood beside Will, and when Will said be gone, Ethan closed his eyes.

She disappeared, and the children went wild.

"Okay." Will counted to three, raised his hands again, and said, "Appear."

The teacher reappeared. "Could you see me?" she asked the class.

"No," everyone said in unison.

She could see everyone and didn't know they couldn't see her, Abby thought.

"Okay," Will told them, "I'm going to make all of you vanish. Stay in your seats."

Ethan studied the class and gave Will a nod. When Will said the magic words, the boys and girls vanished.

He only cloaked the children, Abby thought. *Their chairs look empty.*

"Not possible," the teacher said. "What did you do?"

"A magician never gives away his secrets." Will said the words, and they reappeared. He thanked everyone, didn't give a reason for being there, and left, following Ethan and Abby out the door.

Abby glanced back into the classroom. The teacher appeared dumbfounded.

"Looks like we're good to go," Will told Ethan.

"Twenty members of the Underground, plus me, you, Mom, and Morgan, should be enough," Ethan said. "Chad and Holly, too, if they want to come. We'll save the children before the gathering. Then they will come. No worries."

Will stopped walking. "Who's going to come?"

"You know we're not alone," Ethan said. "We've never been alone."

Where have I heard that before? Something I read in one of my husband's magazines. When she remembered the subject matter in the article, Abby felt blood rush to her head. She imagined scenes out of movies she had watched with Dillon. "Other aliens? A war for our world?"

He nodded. "Soon."

Abby held her breath while flashes of horror shot through her mind, ending with the memories of Doctor Davis's video. "We have to get the children out of there."

Will retrieved his phone. "Morgan, we have a problem."

Chapter 22

The next morning, Dillon stayed with a trusted Underground member while Abby, Will, Ethan, Chad, and Holly drove with Morgan to a warehouse on the edge of town. Twenty others met them inside in an area filled with sacks of grain and livestock feed. The cargo door slid open. The driver of a semi-truck parked at the cargo dock, got out and walked toward them.

Abby recognized him, Keith, the driver of the mobile shooting range.

Morgan ruffled Ethan's white hair. "Thank you for allowing me to reveal your abilities to our friends here."

"It's time," Ethan said.

"Let's save the world, then," Morgan told him. He turned to the others. "You know everyone here except our newest members, Abby and Ethan Muse. Now let's get down to business. Keith will be driving us to our destination. I want to remind everyone that this is a top-secret mission. Our HERF guns have been empowered with frequencies that have the capacity to kill the aliens. But there is a catch. You must keep your finger on the trigger until your target is dead. This will require patience. I know all of you, except a few of us, are military vets trained to shoot and move. If you don't allow the frequencies to kill your target, they'll stand and attack again and again. The upside to your HERF gun is you'll be able to kill all aliens within earshot."

"Will the HERF guns affect us as well?" someone asked.

"Only those who have a chip embedded in their head," Will told them. "That's why you were scanned before joining our team. No one in our party has a chip. But the aliens and the children do. The children will black out for a few minutes. Don't let that startle you."

A man raised his hand. "How will we be able to get into the school? I assume their surveillance is extensive."

"We have an advantage," Abby told them. "We all know that superheroes are people out of comic books. But like most myths and legends, there is some truth within the stories that we don't always recognize. Before I confuse you anymore, let me introduce you to my son, the myth." Ethan stood at her side, and Will joined him as Abby continued. "You will be cloaked, leaving no signs of your presence. Not even your heat signature will be detected. Ethan, if you will demonstrate, please."

Ethan used Will as his aide. As he had done in Dillon's classroom, Ethan closed his eyes and then opened them. Will vanished.

The group stirred. Hands went up.

Morgan took questions.

"How?" a woman in the back row asked.

"Need to know," Morgan replied. "Does someone want to come up and participate in our demonstration?" He chose a man sitting in the front row.

The man bumped into Will and jumped back. "Sorry, Will. I didn't see you."

The group laughed.

"Uncloak me, Ethan."

Ethan did so.

The volunteer inspected Will and poked his arm.

"I didn't disappear," Will said. "Nothing physically happened to me. The cloaking was placed around me. I couldn't see it, but I could see you."

"Those under the cloak will see the people beneath it as well," Abby told them. "We'll follow my son. That means you'll have to stick together until he gives you the okay to spread out."

"Sweet," someone in the back said. "We'll take them by surprise."

"That's the plan," Morgan said. "Ethan has the capability to unlock doors or anything else that's locked. Hiding the bodies is crucial. I don't want a child to see who the Takers really are. Nor do I want any of the aliens' friends to find them dead and raise an alarm."

"What about the children?" a man wearing a gray baseball cap asked. "Will we be removing them from the ship?"

"No," Will said. "There are too many. We need to find their records."

"I know where they're located," Ethan said. "Cole and I found the records room while we were exploring the vents. Lots of people, probably aliens, were in there creating new files and editing others. I watched them from the vent over their heads, and I remember how to get into the computers."

"Good man," Morgan told him. "We're talking about thousands of children, maybe even millions. Finding their families or legal guardians will take time. Once we take control of the ship, the Underground will run it like an orphanage until the children are returned to their homes."

"Plus, we don't want the children to panic," Will said. "They never have to know that they were abducted by aliens."

"Are there any other questions?" Morgan asked.

No one raised their hand.

"Good," Morgan said. "This'll take precision, and you all have tactical experience. Once we get to our drop-off point, we'll communicate with sign language, if need be."

"After Ethan cloaks you," Abby told them, "your cloak will cover you wherever you're told to go until Ethan removes it."

Someone raised their hand and asked Ethan, "Could you determine the layout of the ship while you crawled through the ducts?"

"No. When we find my dorm room on the first floor, I'll be

able to find the records room and a few others."

"Good to know," Will said.

"Show them what else you can do, Ethan," Abby said. "Start by levitating something, then get forceful like you did in the sound room. I don't want any surprises that will distract our team." She faced the group. "If, for some reason, something is lifted into the air or moves, the moment you take to figure out what's going on may cost you your life. Ethan will show you what he's capable of doing, so you won't be distracted. Go ahead, dear."

Ethan and Will teamed up to put on a show just as they had in Abby's living room when he showed them his ability to lift objects. In conclusion to the demonstration, he turned to the semi-truck outside the cargo doors, started its engine, then killed it.

"Ethan will be able to disable their spaceship so they can't lift off," Abby said.

"That'll happen only if we're detected," Morgan told them. "If we cut their source of energy, it will alert them to our presence. We'll go through each floor until we reach the control room. The element of surprise is the only way we'll meet our objective."

"Any more questions?" Will asked.

No one spoke up.

"For those who brought their guns with them," Morgan said, "refrain from using them. You were issued knives when you joined our team. Use them. Silence is mandatory. Gunfire will alert the enemy of our presence."

"I don't think I can stab anyone," Abby whispered to Will.

"You'll be surprised what you'll do to protect yourself and your family," he said.

Each of them went to the staging area where they grabbed a HERF gun off a table, and they were given instructions on how it works. Once equipped and ready to leave, they climbed into the back of the semi.

Abby, Ethan, and Will sat in the cab with the driver. Then Will entered the school's location on the driver's GPS.

The driver backed out and headed for the main road.

Abby kept the images of Doctor Davis's video in her mind to hold on to her anger, pushing out the fear lingering on the edge of her thoughts that threatened to disrupt her focus.

"Which way do we go?" Will asked Ethan.

"South."

After a two-hour drive through the back roads and countryside, Keith stopped the semi-truck. He switched on the video communicator on the truck's dashboard.

Abby saw the entire team on the screen.

"The road on the right," Keith told Morgan, "leads to the meadow. Is this where you want Ethan to cloak the truck?"

"Yes, if you will, Ethan, please," Morgan said.

Ethan gave him a thumbs up, closed his eyes, and opened them again. "The whole semi is cloaked, and so is everyone inside," he told Morgan. "After we get out of the truck, our cloak will stay around us until I remove it. Don't worry. There wasn't anyone nearby when we vanished. We're surrounded by woods about a mile away from the school."

"When we reach the meadow," Keith said, "I'll find a secure place to park."

Once they arrived at their destination, on the video communicator, Abby saw Morgan turn to the team. "Remember," he said to the twenty-plus team members sitting inside the trailer, "we're here to kill the aliens. There'll be humans among them who probably don't know the Takers are shapeshifters. Escort them to safety. I don't want them hurt. From here on, we stay quiet. Now, let's move out."

Abby followed Keith, Will, and Ethan to the back of the trailer, where Keith slid open the cargo door. She stood aside as the team members streamed out and gathered a few feet from the semi. They stayed together while they forged their way across a field so large it dwarfed the size of the pines along its southern edges.

Abby scanned the area. *Are those trees beyond the marsh real?* she wondered. *Is the entire marsh a hologram?* The marsh covered over a third of the clearing. *About the size of three football fields,* she thought.

The team continued hiking through a sea of wildflowers when Ethan raised his hand, giving them the sign to halt.

Abby looked up at the late morning sky and saw nothing but white clouds drifting by. In an instant, coming from the south, a hovercraft appeared over the field, descended, and landed about one hundred and fifty feet from them. She readied her HERF gun. Even though she knew they couldn't see her and the others, she held her breath and watched the Takers exit the craft along with two small children. Her attention turned to her son, who motioned to Morgan that he wanted to follow them. *I'm not letting him out of my sight,* she thought. When he turned to go, she joined him with Will at her side.

Chapter 23

They hurried ahead until they were steps behind the Takers. When they walked through the hologram, Abby saw the size of the spaceship and slowly inhaled to calm her racing heart. *If this is smaller than the mothership, our world is in big trouble.* Not seeing windows or an entrance baffled her until the Takers approached the ship, and the smooth metallic surface shimmered, revealing a doorway.

As the Takers went inside, Ethan caught the door before it slid closed.

Will turned, cupped his hands around his mouth, and whistled like a bird.

In a moment, the others joined them.

As Abby walked with Ethan ahead of the team to kill the surveillance, she studied their surroundings. *Stark white, even the floor. Are they afraid of germs?* When she and Ethan returned, he led the others inside and held up his hand, gesturing to hold their position.

Moments later, the Takers from the hovercraft exited a room and walked toward the team.

Abby raised her HERF gun, and the others did the same.

The Takers collapsed. Their alien bodies, larger than the human forms they had replicated into, tore through their uniforms, leaving remnants of clothing draped across their lifeless remains.

Will tapped Abby on the shoulder and motioned to a door beside them. She opened it, fired her gun, looked around, and gave Will the all-clear sign. Grabbing the alien's thin gray arm, she helped Will drag one of the bodies inside, and then the second.

Up ahead, some of the others opened doors across the hall. Once their frequencies filled the rooms, they went in to secure the area and closed the door on the way out, leaving the dead aliens inside.

Morgan gave a signal to move forward.

As Abby rounded a corner, she came to three more bodies. She looked straight ahead. More alien carcasses littered the hallway. *Within hearing range,* she thought.

They stashed the terminated aliens behind closed doors. Then half of the team moved forward down the hallways, opening doors while their frequency guns blared. Ten others followed behind them, checking the corpses and looking for humans.

Chad dashed out of a room and ran to Ethan. "I need your help," he whispered. "There's a human woman passed out in there. She should be waking up any minute. Uncloak me."

Morgan joined them.

Holly leaned in. "No. Uncloak me instead. I can get her to trust me. Hopefully, she'll tell us where the children are."

"Our first human," Morgan said. "We shouldn't be too far ahead of you. Bring her with you after you speak with her and catch up with us."

Abby, Ethan, and Holly entered the room where they found a dead alien and a young human female who awoke on the slick, hard floor.

"Don't hide the body," Holly told Ethan. "I need proof that I'm telling her the truth." Uncloaked, she went to the woman, who sat up glancing around, and led her to a chair where she sat while Holly told her the facts.

"Not possible," the woman said, standing. "This is staged. Where's the admittance controller? What have you done with him?"

A man in a black suit entered through a door at the back of the office, and the woman ran to him.

Abby raised her gun, filled the room with frequency, and watched the man's transformation as he slumped to the floor at the woman's feet.

Screaming, the woman dashed to a side door and hurried into a room filled with rows and rows of shelves fully stocked with metallic boxes.

Ethan uncloaked and stood in the threshold. "We're not going to hurt you," he told her.

Trembling, she peeked out from under a desk a few feet away.

Ethan sat on the floor next to her. "I'm Ethan," he told her. "We don't have much time. You'll be safe if you come with us."

"Uncloak me," Abby said. "She should know that there are more of us."

The woman's teary eyes widened when Abby appeared.

"Come with us," Abby said. "We need to save the children."

Holly wandered farther into the room and took a metallic object off a shelf. "What's inside this?" she asked the woman.

Rising from a squatting position, Ethan stepped back.

With Abby's help, the woman stood and glanced into the other room, where the bodies of aliens remained lifeless.

"What's your name?" Abby asked her.

"Sylvia," she replied.

"Well," Holly said. "What's in this?"

"Personal files," Sylvia told her.

"Whose files?" Holly asked.

"The children, I think."

"The students' files are in the records room," Ethan said.

Holly turned the box-shaped object upside down and sideways. "How do you open it?"

"I don't know," Sylvia said. "I'm not allowed to touch the boxes."

Ethan joined Holly, and she handed him the metal cube-shaped container.

"There's writing on the outside," he said.

"It doesn't look like writing to me," Holly told him.

"I can read this," he said. "Senator Thomas Chain." He closed his eyes, and the container opened.

Abby moved closer and saw a photo of a man she had seen on the six o'clock news last night. "A shapeshifter has replaced him in the Senate. Where's his real body?" she asked Sylvia.

"I don't know what you're talking about. What's a shapeshifter?"

"Aliens who can change what they look like," Ethan told her. He pointed toward the other room. "Just like your boss over there." A sample of blood, a photo of a woman, and a lock of hair accompanied a disk that Ethan extracted from the box. "I remember seeing someone put a disk like this into the computer in the records room." He closed the container, set it back on the shelf, and walked the length of the room, looking at other metallic boxes.

"Do you know where the children are?" Abby asked her.

Sylvia nodded. "On levels one and two."

"What does your job entail?" Abby asked.

"I enroll new students, give them uniforms, and assign each of them to a dorm room."

"That means you know your way around the ship," Abby said.

"It's a school," Sylvia said. "We have classrooms on two floors. Our teachers and school officials reside on the third floor. I have a map of the interior if you'd like to see it."

"It's a spaceship, Sylvia," Abby told her. "And if they find out we're here, there's a good chance they'll try to lift off."

Sylvia glanced again at her dead boss, who no longer looked human.

"How could you come here every day and not know it isn't a building?" Holly asked.

"It looks like any other school," she replied. "I know it's a bit more modernized than most with the dorms and medical combined. But it's the same as any other school."

Except it's round and metallic, Abby thought, remembering the overwhelming size of the ship.

"The building exterior is a hologram," Ethan said to Sylvia.

Sylvia shook her head.

She needs time to absorb this, Abby thought. *Time that we don't have.* "We'll need the map," she said to her.

"Yes, of course."

Abby followed her out to a desk, where Sylvia retrieved a map from a drawer and gave it to her. Turning, Abby handed it to Holly. "We'll be right back. Ethan and I have to get the team. Make sure you tell her about them. She's had enough surprises."

Holly nodded.

Cloaked again, Abby and Ethan left the office, ran down the hall, and saw the others up ahead.

"Wait here," Ethan told her. "I'll go get them." He sprinted off.

Everyone hurried toward her, followed her back to the office, and went inside.

"This is Sylvia," Abby told all of the team after they uncloaked. "She worked for the admittance controller. She gave us a map of the ship."

"Post a guard outside our door," Morgan told Will. He cleared off the controller's desk.

Abby spread out the map. "Where's our location?" She stepped aside and let Sylvia draw an X.

Will, Ethan, and Morgan studied the ship's layout.

"There are four levels and a single elevator up to the bridge," Morgan said, as his fingers moved across the interior diagram.

"I know nothing about any levels above the second," Sylvia said.

"There are locked doors on both sides of the hallway as we enter from outside," Will said. "Where do they lead?"

"They lead to a corridor encircling the entire school, giving access to all the dorms on the first floor."

"Encircles?" Holly asked. "Are you sure?"

Sylvia nodded.

"Are you listening to what you're telling us?" Holly asked. "There's not one circular brick school building in the entire United States." She turned to Abby. "She still doesn't believe it's a spaceship. Shouldn't we continue our mission without her?"

"No," Abby said. "We may need her help."

"What's behind these locked doors?" Morgan pointed to a door leading to the core of the ship.

"Labs, as far as I know. I'm not authorized to enter."

"Where's the records room?" Ethan asked.

She pointed.

"My dorm must be here," he said, placing his finger on the map. "E-7."

"Yes," Sylvia told him. "E-7 and ten other dorms are located in this area."

Morgan looked at a text. "There's a man wearing a suit coming down the hall. Do you know who it is?"

"It's the dean," Sylvia told him. "He has an appointment with the controller."

"Stash the controller's body and the other one somewhere, Will," Morgan said.

Will took hold of the controller's legs while Chad grabbed the arms. They lifted the limp body, its black suit shredded by the transformation, to a supply closet and crammed the body inside. Then, they went back for the other, throwing that corpse on top of the controller and closed the door.

"Ethan, will you cloak us again?" Morgan asked as he procured the map from the controller's desk. "All except Sylvia. I'm going to text the guard in the hallway to let him come in. I agree with Holly. Our friend here still needs a little more convincing that things aren't what they appear to be. I want to make sure she understands. We need to stand back."

Cloaked, everyone spread out.

The dean walked into the office and looked at the controller's desk. "Hi, Sylvia. Where is he? We have an appointment."

"He knows," Silvia replied. "I'm sure he didn't go far."

Abby raised her gun and filled the room with frequency.

The dean dropped to the floor, his human persona changing into an alien corpse.

Sylvia jumped back, her eyes fixing on the body as if she finally saw the truth.

"Now do you believe us?" Morgan asked, uncloaking along with the others.

"How many humans work here?" Abby asked her.

"Forty. We're bused in."

"We're not here to hurt them," Abby said. "Is there somewhere they'll be safe?"

"The auditorium."

"Show us where the aliens are on this level." Abby followed her back to the map that Morgan spread out on the controller's desk again and watched her give a head count in each department.

Morgan pulled Abby to the side. "Have her send all those who commute by bus to the auditorium," he said. "Holly's good at impromptu distraction. Knowing her, if I send her in there, she'll turn all of them into allies."

"Good idea," Abby said.

"And Doctor Davis will be here soon," he said. "Her son's

somewhere on the ship."

"Cole is, too," Ethan said.

"So, what's the plan for now?" Abby asked.

"You stay with Sylvia as she leads the way," Morgan said. "She trusts you. Ethan, Will, and I will join the others. We'll clear out the aliens on the first level as we move forward."

Abby nodded, then she went back to the map and told Sylvia about the auditorium. "While they'll be gathering in a safe place, will you take us to those who weren't bused in? I'll be right beside you. You won't see me, and the team will be following behind us."

"Yes," she replied. "But make sure you don't shoot anyone until I give you a sign. I'll scratch my head if we run into a non-human. Otherwise, I'll just act normal. I don't want any of my friends getting hurt."

"I can't make any guarantees," Abby replied. "If the aliens find out we're here, no one will be safe. You get the humans out of the offices, and the team will eliminate the blood suckers. Is this the only auditorium on the ship?"

Sylvia nodded. "Why did you call them blood suckers?"

"Before the children go to bed at night, they're given sleeping pills. In the middle of the night, while they're sleeping soundly, the aliens drain their blood."

Sylvia stared at her.

"It's true," Abby told her. "Morgan, do you have Doctor Davis's video? If she's going to help us, she should know the truth."

Morgan reached into his pants pocket, retrieved the memory chip, placed it into the computer, and played the footage.

"I know her," Sylvia said, watching Doctor Davis on the screen.

"Then you know this video is real," Morgan said.

She nodded and put her hand over her mouth. "I feel sick."

"There's no time for that," Morgan told her.

"My best friend is inside one of those containers," Ethan said. "I have to save him."

"I'm sorry," Sylvia said. "I didn't know."

Morgan took the memory chip out of the computer and placed it back into his pocket. "Ready to save the children?" he asked her.

Sylvia straightened her stance and raised her chin. "I am now."

Abby and Sylvia walked to the office door with the others.

"You'll have to open it, Sylvia," Abby said. "Remember, the cameras are on. After the team leaves, follow them out and close the door." *It'll look like just another day at the office,* Abby thought.

As they walked down the hallway, passing offices they had already cleared, a man came out of a door on their right.

"Clark," Sylvia said, "I'm telling all of the bused employees that we'll be meeting in the auditorium shortly. The controller would appreciate it if you pass the word."

"Will do," he replied. "I'll let everyone in the breakroom know."

"Where to next?" Abby whispered to her after he walked away.

Sylvia turned down a short hallway to their right that ended at a secured door about four hundred feet away. She went room-by-room, extracted each human, and sent them to the impromptu meeting, then whispered, "Okay."

Ethan disrupted the surveillance while the team filled the ten offices with frequency, killing a total of nineteen aliens. Then he returned the cameras to their previous state once the bodies were removed from each office and piled into a vacant room.

Sylvia opened another door, went inside with Abby, who remained cloaked, and talked to two more humans. "There's not much time before the meeting starts. You'll have to hurry."

"What's this about?" their supervisor asked. "I tried to contact the controller, and he's not in his office. Then my communications failed to reach the dean." He walked out into the hallway and stood with Sylvia as his staff strolled toward the meeting. "I've been contacted by security. Our surveillance cameras are blinking off and on. They're coming to assess the problem."

Sylvia watched her fellow employees turn down a hallway.

"What's going on?" the supervisor said. "I demand an answer."

She scratched her head. "Sorry, but I can't tell you."

The team raised their guns. The supervisor's transformed body dropped to the floor.

Will rushed to Abby and Morgan and told them, "Five humans are down in the hallway."

"They were within hearing range of the frequency," Morgan said. "If we try moving them, there's a good chance they'll wake before we can get them to the auditorium."

"I'll take care of this," Sylvia said. "Leave them where they are. Once they're awake and start asking questions, I'll make something up. Maybe I can say a chemical leak is causing people to pass out."

"Good idea," Abby said. "We have to move fast. Security is on their way."

Chapter 24

Abby stood at the intersection of two hallways. She watched five employees, who had passed out from the weaponized frequency, stand with Sylvia's assistance.

Morgan checked a message on his phone. "Doctor Davis is at the door outside. I told her to wait there."

"Does she know where the controller's office is?" Abby asked.

Morgan sent a text, then received an answer. "Yes."

"The outer door and the office are locked," Ethan said.

Abby heard a door close down the hall to her left. "Security. I'll go with Ethan. You and the team get to the controller's office. We'll meet you there."

Deciding which direction to go, Abby had to calculate her next move. They had cleared out all of the offices and needed to look at the map again before moving on. If the team went to their right, within seconds, they would reach the outer door near the controller's office where they began the siege, but they would run into the surveillance crew if they did. "Ethan and I will sneak by the crew while they inspect the cameras," she said.

"Are you sure you want to do that?" Will asked. "It's dangerous."

"We'll be quiet," Ethan said. "They won't hear us. If they do, I'll levitate them and pin them to the ceiling."

"Not a good idea," Morgan told him. "They have to make it back to the security department, or an armed patrol will be sent to find out why they didn't return."

"Okay," Abby said. "We'll go the long way. We need to get out of here now."

Morgan signaled to the others.

As Abby ran with Ethan, she couldn't hear the team. *Are they following?* she wondered. She glanced over her shoulder. They were running behind her. *High ops retired military. Of course, they'd move quietly,* she thought, feeling a burn in her tired legs. *I haven't run this far since I was in track at college.* She slowed and walked for a minute before she started to run again.

"Come on, Mom," Ethan said. "We're almost there."

Will caught up with Abby and ran alongside her. She stopped suddenly, and so did he. Up ahead, the surveillance crew stood in front of the outer door, looking up at the camera in the hallway. She watched Ethan tiptoe closer to the surveillance crew. Knowing that he remained cloaked and invisible to anyone other than the team, Abby still felt he could somehow be detected. She stepped toward him.

Will grabbed her arm and shook his head.

"How about now?" she heard one of the crew ask while standing on a ladder, looking into the camera.

Another voice came over an intercom on the crewmember's wrist. "Not yet."

Ethan closed his eyes and opened them again.

"I don't know what you did," the voice on the intercom said. "Everything has stabilized."

"Must be internal," the crewmember replied. "It's not the cameras. We're done here." He stepped down from a ladder, another worker folded it up, and the four-man crew walked toward Abby, Will, and the team.

Ethan backed against the wall as the workers walked past.

Abby and Will hugged the wall along with the others.

Ethan unlocked the controller's office door, motioned to Abby and Will, then slipped inside. After the surveillance crew passed by them, Abby and Will also ducked inside.

Abby peeked out of the cracked door and watched them stop to give a thumbs up to another camera nearby, then they waited for a response over the intercom. She held her breath until the crew finally passed the cloaked team lining the wall.

One of the surveillance crew stopped and turned. "What was that?" He looked at the controller's office door and walked toward it with the rest of the crew.

Abby backed away. She tried to slow her racing heart as she saw a hand about to open the door.

"Can I help you?" Abby heard Sylvia ask.

The crewman stepped back.

Abby swallowed hard and looked out into the hallway again.

"The admittance controller is in a meeting with the dean," Sylvia told them, "and doesn't want to be disturbed."

"We're securing the area," one of the crew replied.

"Why?" Sylvia asked. "What's going on?"

"The surveillance cameras are malfunctioning," one of them said.

"So, you're going into the controller's office to tell him you can't find the problem?"

"No," one of the crew replied. "No message. We're finished here."

They walked away a little faster than before.

Sylvia pushed the door open and came inside. "Where are you?" she asked.

"Step away from the door and let the team come in," Will told her.

Sylvia walked to the controller's desk as the door opened wide.

When the office door closed, Ethan removed the cloak.

Morgan glanced around. "We're all here. Doctor Davis is waiting outside. The outer door is locked."

"I'll open it." Ethan closed his eyes and opened them again. "Okay. She can come in."

Soon, the office door opened, and Doctor Davis entered. Stepping around the desk, she stood at Morgan's side.

Morgan made the introductions. "We're about to update our progress." He studied the map of the ship spread out on the controller's desk.

Abby moved closer to get a better look.

"It's a round ship about the size of a superdome," Morgan told the doctor. "The interior is laid out in circular bands. We know that the outer yellow band on this level is where the dorms are. The green band next to it incorporates the classrooms, the kitchens, common areas, and the auditorium. This thinner blue band is where we are. It encompasses the administration offices on the west side and more classrooms to the east. Classes were over, and the rooms were empty by the time we reached that side of the ship. We've annihilated every alien within this band and sent the human employees to the auditorium. Where are the containers?"

"The labs and medical departments encircle the containment area that surrounds the core of the ship." She pointed to an area encompassing more space than the rest of the bands combined. "And it goes up three floors."

"Amazing," Morgan said. "What would happen if we fired our HERF guns inside the containment area?"

"Each child has an embedded chip, as you're aware," she said. "If your HERF guns discharge the lethal frequency to kill the aliens in that area, the children inside the containers may fall into a coma. Or, it could kill them. The good news is there are only four aliens on duty until the rest of the staff starts their shift at midnight."

"What's the surveillance like?" Ethan asked Doctor Davis. "Are there lots of cameras in the containment area?"

"Yes," she said and pointed to the map's inner band. "But it's monitored internally in the red zone. This part of the ship is considered classified. Even the administrators, like the dean and the controller, aren't authorized to enter the containment area."

Morgan opened the door leading into the room filled with shelves and shelves of metallic boxes. "Have you ever seen these before?" he asked Doctor Davis.

She entered the room and picked up one of the metal cubes. "Yes. I was there when my son's personal file was assembled." She set the container back on the shelf. "These are the original life-forms' files containing personal information on the humans who have been contained and replaced by shapeshifters."

"Like Cole," Ethan said.

"Yes, like Cole," Doctor Davis replied.

"You read some of the names on the metal boxes when we were here last," Abby said to Ethan. "Were there any other senators?"

He nodded. "And congressmen mixed in with others that weren't. Every box has photos and a chip in it that will probably tell you more."

"Another thing I can help you with," Doctor Davis said.

"What is the reason why some of the children are given photos of women who aren't their mothers?" Morgan asked.

"There are several different reasons. For one, the children whose parents fought to keep them out of the hands of the Takers are placed into pods to become breeders once they turn twelve." The doctor looked at Abby. "Ethan was on that list."

Abby swore under her breath. *It's a good thing he ran. I never would've seen him again.* She pushed her anger to the side to focus on the here and now.

"Why are they taking the children's blood?" Will asked.

"The mimics only live so long before our viruses and diseases kill them. They believed drinking children's blood allowed them to live longer. But it didn't solve their longevity problem. It only became the drink of choice. Now, the children's blood has become a commodity within their empire. The plasma they compile is transported to a mothership and flown back to their planet. In order for the aliens to stay and harvest blood, their mimics have to live longer. It's essential they find the answer so they can stay on Earth long enough to enslave the human race. That's why they took my son to force me to use DNA sequencing to manipulate their lifespan.

"The aliens codify human blood the same way we categorize wine," Doctor Davis continued. "When they find someone with the right blend, so to speak, they're also sent to the containment area when they turn twelve—another reason for sending a replacement to an unknowing mother."

"So, Earth has become their winery," Will said.

"They took my son hostage to force me to find a solution for their dilemma. For six years, I've been helping them find a way to create hybrids. But so far, all attempts have failed, thank goodness."

"Do you know about this, Sylvia?" Abby asked.

She shook her head.

"She wouldn't know," Doctor Davis said. "Everything is done at night. Once a month, after all human employees have left, a cargo ship arrives to retrieve the amassed plasma harvest."

"Is there a set pick-up date?" Morgan asked.

"They were here three days ago," Doctor Davis told them. "They'll be back in four weeks."

Abby looked at Ethan. "Will we have time to raid all five schools and get you to the gathering?"

"The gathering?" Doctor Davis asked. "When?"

"In three and a half weeks," Ethan told her.

"That's cutting it close," she said.

"It's possible, but we have to hurry," Ethan said.

"Then, let's get back to business," Morgan told them. "We'll hit the containment area before we take out security."

"Would we be endangering the lives of all those in pods if we eliminate the aliens monitoring their vitals?" Will asked. "Is it possible to release them from captivity without alien help?"

"Over the six years of my frequent visits to monitor my son's wellbeing," the doctor replied, "I've gained the staff's trust. They've shown me the steps to control my son's environment and his vital signs. And over time, I've witnessed the process to contain and release individuals."

"They didn't see you as a threat," Abby said.

Doctor Davis shook her head. "The staff was arrogant and thought the information would be useless to me. Fortunately, they've simplified the applications, eliminating the chance of error that would damage the humans inside the pods." She looked toward the room filled with metallic cubes, then looked at Will. "So, in answer to your question…you won't need them. I'm capable of maintaining the welfare of those contained and willing to train others to help release them."

"How many of the contained have been duplicated?" Abby asked.

"A large majority," the doctor replied. "Others will be used for breeding."

"Are you saying there are hundreds of them?" Abby asked.

Doctor Davis shook her head. "You'd have to see the containment area to realize the magnitude," she replied. "But the doors lock once they're closed and must be opened by authorized personnel going in and out. I don't have clearance."

"That isn't a problem," Ethan told her.

Morgan, Will, Ethan, and Abby studied the map.

"There's a hallway outside the locked doors," Morgan said. "We'll need to get the four workers outside of the containment area."

"I can handle that," the doctor replied.

"Lead the way," Morgan told her.

Doctor Davis started for the door.

"You'll have to open the doors for us again, Sylvia," Abby said. "Our tampering with the cameras has put security on alert. A door opening by itself would tell them the trouble isn't internal."

"I'll act like I forgot something and leave the door open while I go back for whatever it is," Sylvia said. "Make sure you let me know when the last of you has left the office."

"Good plan," Morgan said. "Let's move out. Cloak everyone but Sylvia and Doctor Davis, please, Ethan."

They made their way into the main hallway. Sylvia, with Doctor Davis beside her on her right and Abby, cloaked, to her left, casually walked. When they came to a single door, Sylvia stopped and opened the door to another side hallway. While she held it open, she retrieved her cell phone from her pocket, pretending to answer a call, letting everyone enter before she closed the door and stayed behind. At the end of that short hallway, Doctor Davis stood in front of the containment's security cameras and waved. The locked door opened, and she went inside.

Abby and the team waited, standing as far away from the locked doors as possible. When it opened, the four staff members walked out, talking and laughing.

Frequency filled the hallway once the doors closed and locked. The four staff members, three female and one male, dropped to the ground, their human forms changing into gray alien beings.

Abby texted Sylvia to rejoin them, then heard the doctor's knock on the locked doors.

Ethan closed his eyes, then the doors unlocked and slid open.

"Where are you?" Doctor Davis asked.

Ethan lifted the cloak.

"Come," the doctor told them.

Four of the team dragged the bodies inside.

Ethan closed the doors. "The doors don't lock anymore," he told the doctor.

"Perfect. Thank you." She led everyone out of the control room and into the containment area.

Abby stood next to Will, looking up at thousands of individual pear-shaped pods. The vastness of the storage area overwhelmed her. Identical pods in vertical stacks lined the spaceship's interior walls to the ship's domed ceiling. All pods were a shade of blue. On the front of each, a long oval window revealed nothing. An opaque liquid swirled within, concealing the person inside.

"How were you able to see your son?" Abby asked the doctor.

Doctor Davis pointed to the center of the room. "That metal trunk has expandable arms that reach out and pluck a pod from its coded dock. Then, it brings it to the landing over there and places it into a temporary port. In a few minutes, the liquid stops swirling and clears. He's okay and has grown over the years."

Ethan searched the ocean of pods. "I found the meaning of the three swirls in Daddy's books." He pointed. "They're the markings above Cole's pod."

"How did your dad know about this?" Abby asked. *Who was he?*

"I have to help take over the ship," Ethan told the doctor. "When we're done, can I come back and save my friend?"

"I'll make sure of it," Doctor Davis told him.

Chapter 25

While in the containment area, Morgan turned to the team. "Our next move is to the medical station. After that, we'll clear the records room. We'll need a way to eliminate as many guards as we can before we take level four. Plus, we'll need eyes focused on the elevator leading to the bridge."

"Who else has access to surveillance, Sylvia?" Abby asked.

"The dean," she replied. "He makes sure the students don't go where they're not allowed."

Morgan looked at Ethan. "Is it possible to disable the security office surveillance without affecting the dean's office accessibility?"

Ethan nodded.

"Chad, you'll be our eyes," Morgan said.

"I won't be able to see you on the footage," Chad said. "The camera doesn't pick up our cloaked images or our heat signatures."

"I can make the camera closest to us flicker twice to let you know our position," Ethan told him.

"That should work," Morgan said. "Chad, would you mind taking charge of the dean's office?"

"It'll be my pleasure." He left the containment area and went out through the unlocked doors.

Abby watched the security monitor and saw Chad open the door leading into the main hallway. He peeked out and quickly closed the door.

A minute later, he returned. "There's a crowd of people in the main hallway."

"Holly must've instructed the employees to return to their jobs," Morgan said.

Chad retrieved his cell phone and checked a text message. "Holly wants to know our location."

"Sylvia, would you please help her find her way to us?" Morgan asked.

She nodded.

Within minutes, Sylvia and Holly came in through the doors.

"I formed a small militia group out of the employees," Holly told them. "They're all in after I showed them Doctor Davis's video. Once we left the auditorium, they hid me from the cameras in the hallway before they went back to their jobs. The employees in the dean's office are sending out memos to all students and teachers, cancelling classes for the rest of the day."

"Perfect," Morgan said. "We'll initiate our plan on level two, eliminating the chance of the humans getting hurt on this floor. After that, we'll head for security and the bridge. The third floor is the Takers' den." He looked at Doctor Davis. "Do you know how many aliens are on board the ship?"

"That's hard to determine," she replied. "At night, there are twelve assigned to the containment area. About one hundred are in the infirmary at night and only four during the day."

"There are forty-one," Ethan said, "who work at night in the records room."

"And twenty who work the day shift," Sylvia added. "Plus, three hundred teachers. Those in the kitchen and the others throughout the dorms are humans."

"I estimate six hundred," Morgan said. "The third level will be tricky. I'm assuming it resembles a small city—residences, eateries, and entertainment. If we seize that floor before taking security and the bridge, we could be detected and have to fight the six hundred plus the armed guards, who might number another two hundred."

"Divide and conquer," Will said. "Take out the guns first

and leave level three unprotected."

"Will and Abby, stay with Doctor Davis and protect the pods," Morgan said. "Holly, come with us, or stay here. Your choice. Okay, let's go."

"I'm staying," Holly replied.

Fighting the urge to go with her son, Abby looked at Ethan. *Morgan will protect him,* she thought. "Be careful," she told him.

"Ethan, cloak us," Morgan said.

Abby watched all of them vanish, and the entrance doors opened and closed. Then, Doctor Davis walked past her and sat at the control panel.

"I can't leave my son here," the doctor said. "Not this time."

The massive machine in the center of the room began to turn, a mechanical extending arm extracting the pod from its storage location. She followed the doctor to the landing where the arm set the pod on a port.

Doctor Davis placed commands into a panel on the side of the pod. The liquid inside stopped swirling. When its opaque substance cleared, she entered another command.

Inside the pod, Abby saw the doctor's son dressed in a white shift and resting in suspended animation. As the liquid receded, the contents of the boy's lungs and stomach spewed from his mouth. His eyes remained closed, and he breathed normally.

"It will take about two hours before he awakens," Doctor Davis said.

Abby jumped when she heard the entrance doors open and spun around to see three armed security guards storming toward them.

Doctor Davis took a stance in front of the pod that held her son.

Abby bolted toward the security guard to the left, rammed

it, and bounced off its hard body, landing on the ground.

The guard seized her arm, pulling her to a standing position.

Remembering her self-defense classes, she hooked her leg around the guard's, jerked its leg out from under it, and shoved it backward. It fell, taking her with it. The impact freed her from the guard's grasp, and she rolled to the side, then stood. Before she could pull out her smart gun holstered in her waistband behind her back, the guard aimed its weapon. Leaping aside, she watched its shot miss her and disintegrate what appeared to be some kind of gurney. She quickly moved away from Doctor Davis and her son. Raising her gun, she shot the guard in the chest.

Hardly fazed, it lunged at her.

She sprang out of the way, avoiding its grasp, aimed, and fired again, striking her assailant in the head.

The security guard collapsed, dead, revealing its real identity.

Abby searched for Will and saw him with a knife in his hand, standing over another alien body. He looked her way and rubbed his left shoulder.

She nodded.

He rushed to assist Holly, who fought to keep her attacker near the unlocked doors. When the guard moved close enough to the entrance, she slid past him and reached up, hitting the control panel, opening the door.

Will shoved the guard into the hall and followed him out. The door closed behind him.

Holly rose from the floor and joined Abby. They waited, ready to take on whatever came through the door.

When Will reentered, dragging the alien's carcass back into the containment area, Abby lowered her smart gun, placing it back into her waistband. He received a text. "It's Chad. By the time he got to the dean's office, the three guards we encountered had gotten past his surveillance. Our level is secure now. On level two, they're ready to shut down security's monitoring system." He looked at Abby. "Want to join them?"

"Go if you want to," Holly said. "I've got this. There's no one left on this floor who can hurt us. The first floor is ours."

"Thank you," Abby told her. "I keep thinking about Ethan."

"I meant what I said," Holly told her. "I've got this."

Abby adjusted her frequency gun slung across her chest. "Let's go," she told Will.

They made their way to the second floor and, following the curving hallway, they ran to join the others up ahead.

"Remember," she told him, "we're not cloaked. We won't be able to see them."

"Listen," Will replied. "Voices."

Abby came to a halt. "I hear Ethan." Suddenly, she saw the others about fifteen feet in front of her and realized she and Will were cloaked again. They joined the gathering.

"To trick the aliens into coming to us, Ethan has blacked out security's surveillance equipment monitoring this level," Morgan told them. "Chad said it's working. Guards are on their way. They'll be here any minute. Ethan, disrupt their communications."

Ethan closed his eyes. "The guards, the security office, and the bridge's communications are down, and they can't lift off."

"Perfect," Morgan said. "Spread out. Cover all of the elevators."

The team ran off in both directions, leaving Abby, Will, Morgan, and Ethan to cover the elevator they stood in front of. They waited. Then, the doors opened. Inside, five security guards drew their weapons.

Abby held her breath, trying to quiet her pounding heart.

"All clear," one of the guards said. He raised his hand to a device on his ear. "Still not working. First, the surveillance on level one failed. Now, this level's out, and our command systems have gone down. It doesn't make sense."

"No sign of perpetrators," one of them said as they stepped into the hallway.

"If we're being invaded, we would've seen them by now," another guard said. "The problem must be internal."

"Where are our first wave responders?" one of them asked. "Have you noticed how empty the halls are?"

"They're probably in the security office getting face-to-face orders," another said. "And, I understand that the dean has canceled all classes today. That would explain the empty halls."

"Let's search each room on this level and then head to the dean's office to find out why classes were canceled."

We can't let them do that, Abby thought. She waited until Morgan nodded, then pulled the trigger, filling the hallway with frequency.

While stepping over the alien bodies and dragging them into an empty classroom, Morgan received a call. He lowered his hand from his earbud as the rest of the team rejoined them. "Chad said the second floor's ours. We'll take this elevator up. When we reach the fourth floor, we'll move in unison so Ethan can cloak the bodies as we advance. Front line, fire on the aliens. The flank, clear the hallways. Let's go."

"Can they retake the first and second levels?" Will asked.

"No," Ethan said. "The elevators don't work anymore. Only this one does." He smiled. "Must be an internal problem." He laughed along with the others.

Abby, Will, Ethan, and Morgan stepped inside the elevator, leaving half of the team there to wait for its return. As they ascended, they raised their HERF guns. When the door opened, they fired, killing ten guards waiting to take the elevator down.

Ethan signaled Chad.

Morgan put his hand to his earbud and nodded as he sent the elevator back for the others. "We're good to go," Morgan said. "There are at least one hundred guards in small groups in the hallway, trying to take the disabled elevators to level two."

Once the rest of the team arrived, they walked the hallway, killing every security guard within range of their lethal frequency. Heaps of bodies had fallen in front of each elevator.

Ethan cloaked the dead, allowing the team to see them but blocking any fellow alien guards entering the area from viewing the bodies. Meanwhile, the team swarmed to hide the slain and opened doors as they moved forward, killing all aliens within each room.

When they entered the security headquarters, blasting frequency as they came through the doors, they found only three guards inside, trying to restore the communications before their bodies slumped to the floor.

"Seriously," Morgan said. "I thought it would be harder than this. Okay. There's only one elevator leading to the bridge." He hesitated, then looked at Ethan. "Are you sure they can't lift off?"

Ethan nodded.

"Good to know," Morgan replied. "As long as we're cloaked, we'll catch them off guard." He stepped aside, letting half of the team members and Ethan take the elevator. "Make sure you return it to our floor so we can follow you."

Ethan glanced at Abby and rubbed his left shoulder.

"I understand," she replied. *The cause is great*. She watched the elevator doors close. Her heart pounded as her anxiety heightened.

"Don't worry about him," Will told her. "He's got this."

On the next ascent, Abby had her hand on her frequency gun when the doors opened. She stepped out onto the bridge.

Dead aliens littered the room.

Ethan went to the control panel. "Incoming," he said, turning to Morgan. "A hovercraft landed in the field. There are two Takers and two children."

Abby texted Sylvia and asked her to stall them.

"Something's wrong," Ethan said. "They're not coming in. One of the Takers is going back to the hovercraft."

Abby texted again. "Sylvia's going outside."

"We need to get down there," Morgan said. "We can't let them take off."

Leaving the bodies of the dead aliens where they lie, they rushed to the first floor and exited the ship through the door Sylvia had left open.

Abby, standing only a few feet from Sylvia, texted her. *<Tell both of them to come inside because it will take a while to reboot the systems.>*

Sylvia showed the text to the Taker. "We're resorting to text messages."

The Taker motioned to his buddy, who shut down the engine and stepped out of the hovercraft. As soon as his feet touched the ground, both Takers were hit with frequency.

Sylvia slipped a memory chip out of the dead Taker's armored uniform, took the hands of a little boy and girl, and walked away from the craft. She looked up, and so did Abby as she stood with Will by the alien bodies.

Above them, a hovercraft fired on Sylvia. She started to run with the children, staying ahead of the craft's weapons blasting craters in the ground behind her.

Ethan closed his eyes. The bombardment stopped.

"Good job," Morgan said. "In case there are children on board, bring it down slowly."

The craft leveled out. With every movement of his hands, using his levitation ability, Ethan brought it down. "No children," he told Morgan. "Just two Takers." He delivered the craft to the other members of the team, who opened the hatch and exterminated the aliens.

"The children must be terrified," Abby said to Ethan. "Uncloak me." She walked with Sylvia and took the little boy's hand. Glancing at him, she saw the fear on his face as he looked over his shoulder. "He's the same age as my youngest, Dillon," Abby told her. "This can't happen to another child."

"Only one more level to exterminate," Sylvia replied, approaching her office. "And things here will never be the same again."

"One so-called school at a time," Abby said. "We still have four more to go." She turned when she heard Morgan's voice. "Sorry, I have to go."

Again, Ethan cloaked her.

"Let's get to it," Morgan said, walking toward her with the rest of the team.

Abby fell in line between Ethan and Will.

"Almost home," Will said.

"We've got this, Mom," Ethan told her.

Chapter 26

The next day after confiscating the Takers' spaceship, Abby sat with Will on the patio at her home. The afternoon heat cooled as the day faded into night.

"It feels good to be home," Abby said, pouring Will and herself a glass of lemonade. "Dillon's in bed, and we finally have some alone time."

"Yes," Will said. "I didn't get much sleep last night. How about you?"

"Not a wink. I kept replaying the attack in the containment area over and over in my mind."

"I was proud of the way you handled yourself," Will said. "You took down that alien like a pro."

"You weren't too shabby yourself," she told him. "And the third level…."

He chuckled. "They didn't see us coming."

"It's amazing what abilities and knowledge Ethan has acquired," she said.

"I asked him about that, and he said it's being downloaded into his mind."

"By who?" she asked.

"They didn't tell him," he replied, leaning back in his chair. "He was told there are seventy-five different types of aliens visiting our planet, some walking among us. All are multi-dimensional. We can't see most of them. But we're related to one of the races through DNA. They call it blending. They're the protectors of our planet—our forefathers—the missing link, so to speak."

"So now we know what came first—the chicken or the egg—the egg." Abby sipped her drink.

"Like humans, there are good and bad aliens. It's the debauched aliens who are replacing the world leaders with shapeshifters. The people we have trusted to keep us safe are not who we think they are. They've cheated and lied, turned humans against humans, and have made our next generation mindless."

"It all makes sense now," she said. "If they can't read or do simple math, they won't be able to run the country, allowing the aliens to rule the world."

"One World Order, they're calling it," Will said.

She sighed. "And our lives have been placed into the hands of a twelve-year-old, my son. Much like David and Goliath."

"I wouldn't say that," Will said, and took a sip of his drink. "According to Ethan, there has been a standing agreement among the alien nations to do no harm to the human race. The line has been crossed, and all in the pact stand against the invaders."

"And they've chosen my son to expose the truth."

"Are you worried about him?" Will asked, pouring himself more lemonade.

"He's safe with Morgan. Ethan texted me that they've located the other four schools, and they seem to be smaller than the one we raided yesterday."

"Morgan texted me," Will told her. "And they're taking the next school tomorrow. He wants us to help Doctor Davis free the captives in the containment room. According to Sylvia, the metal boxes in the controller's office are those of high-ranking officials throughout the United States."

"Will we be freeing them first?" Abby asked.

"Not all of them," Will said. "There's more to it than just releasing people from their pods. Once we discover where they live and find their families, the aliens who have taken their identities must be tracked down and killed. Then we can return the captives safely to their loved ones. It's a delicate situation. Morgan wants you to assist me while I give each of them a physical to make sure they're ready to go home."

"What about the students?" she asked. "Are we giving them physicals, too?"

"I don't believe it's necessary. They were the aliens' blood providers, and they were well taken care of. Sylvia and the human staff, who are still being bused in, are helping retrieve each child's records while the Underground members are checking DNA to make sure they're sent back to their true families. It's a huge undertaking. They really need our help."

"How will we get there?" Abby asked.

"Chad's taking us in one of the hovercrafts the Underground confiscated."

"What time?" she asked.

"He's letting us sleep in," he told her. "He'll meet us at your dock at noon. It gives us a chance to have one or two meals before we go."

"I'll probably wake up just in time to eat and run," she said.

"I should go," Will said. "Call me when you're up in the morning."

Abby walked him to his truck parked in front of her house and waved as he drove away.

Turning, she headed back inside the house. Not quite sleepy enough for bed, she sat by the fireplace, picked up one of her husband's storybooks, and flipped through the pages. On the third page from the end, she noticed a newspaper article pinned to the wall behind the child playing with blocks. A photo of a journalist by the name of Terry Brookes topped the headline. *This wasn't here the last time I searched this book for clues,* Abby thought. She studied the page, looking around the room where the child played, trying to find something more about the journalist. Squinting at the editorial below the photo, Abby tried to read the fine print. Frustrated, she went to her office down the hall, found a magnifying glass, and went back to the living room.

Abby picked up the storybook once more and returned to the news article, taking a closer look. The words were illegible. *Why?* she thought. *Why show me her photo and not give me a clue to its meaning? Why can't you just spell it out for me?* She tossed the storybook on the footstool by her chair, its pages folding aside, revealing the mysterious new clue. As she glanced again at the open book, the letters on the child's blocks caught her attention like a light in the dark. *F, I, N, D, H, E, R.* Abby sounded it out in her mind. *Find her.*

"Who is she?" She glanced at the clock on the mantle, then picked up her phone resting on the end table next to her chair, and dialed Will's number.

He answered quickly. "What's wrong?"

"I have a mystery," she told him. "I was looking through one of the storybooks and found something new. It's a photo of a journalist named Terry Brookes. It was pinned to the wall behind the child whose building blocks spelled out find her. I've never heard of her. Have you?"

"Yes," he replied. "She was a late-night radio talk show host who went missing for about a week. She was found in a hospital looking as if she had been hit by a truck. Her memory was gone, and she had no identification."

"Is she a member of the Underground?" Abby asked.

"No. Her show was focused on conspiracy theories. Nut jobs stalked her everywhere she went. Maybe one of them caught up with her."

"Did she ever get her memory back?"

"No," he replied. "And her show went off the air."

"This doesn't make sense," she said. "Why would my husband want me to find her if she can't tell us squat?"

"I'll look into it and see if her condition has changed," he told her.

"Okay," she told him. "Thanks. I'll see you tomorrow."

Abby returned her phone to the end table and decided to check the web on the computer in her office. She glanced at the clock on the mantle again. *Eight-thirty,* she thought. *I'll search the Internet for an hour, then I'm going to bed.*

When she opened the door down the hall and went into the office, she eased herself into the swivel chair in front of her desk. On the keyboard, she typed, Terry Brookes conspiracy theories. The number of websites that popped up surprised her. She began to read theory after theory. The majority came from people who believed the government had a hand in Terry's disappearance and injuries. *They wanted to shut her up*, she thought.

Abby glanced at the time. "That's it for now. I've got to get to bed."

Chapter 27

Abby rinsed and drained the blueberries that she planned to add to the breakfast pancakes, chuckling to herself when she saw Dillon wearing a cape, pretending to be a superhero. A car door closing in front of her house caught her attention. She looked out the kitchen window and saw a woman about her age exiting a black car, and Will lifting a suitcase out of the bed of his truck.

"Good morning," Will said when Abby opened the front door. "This is Jill. The Underground sent her to watch Dillon while you're away."

Abby put out her hand, and Jill shook it. "Come in. Would you care to join us for breakfast? We're having blueberry pancakes."

"I would love to. Thank you."

Dillon darted into the living room.

"I want you to meet Jill," Abby told him. "She's going to stay with you while we're gone." She turned to her. "I'll leave you two alone to get to know each other." Abby motioned to Will to follow her into the kitchen.

"What can I do for you?" Will asked.

"Nothing," she said, pulling out the batter from the refrigerator. "Haven't I seen her someplace before?"

"She works at Headquarters," Will replied. "And, yes. She was in the audience at Morgan's alien reveal. She's here because Dillon's your son and Ethan's brother. You can bet our surveillance team is watching your home. He couldn't be in better hands."

"That's good," she said. "Have you found out anything about Terry Brookes?"

"Oh." He took out his phone.

She raised her hand. "No, that's okay if you haven't spoken to anyone. I have a better idea. I was wondering if Jill can get access to Terry's records or personal information since we'll be occupied helping Doctor Davis. I really have to get on this, and we'll be too busy."

"I agree," Will said. "I'll go have a word with her."

Abby flipped the last pancake onto a plate and garnished everyone's serving with blueberries and whipped cream.

In a few minutes, Will returned. "She said she'd be happy to assist us. She already made a call to Headquarters."

"That's fantastic," Abby replied. "All we need is an address."

At noon, when Chad flew in on a hovercraft, they were waiting for him on the dock. Once they arrived at the spaceship, Abby and Will stopped in to see Sylvia, who sat at her desk in her office with a frequency gun by her side.

"We've contacted forty families," Sylvia told them, "and our team is returning their children to them as we speak."

"How about those who are in the pods?" Abby asked.

"That's taking longer," she replied. "It's an extensive process."

"The cause is great," Will said.

Sylvia smiled. "It's good to see you guys again."

"It's good to see you, too," Abby told her. "We'll be here until Friday."

Sylvia nodded. "Yes. We're rotating volunteers so they won't be away from their families long. Doctor Davis is expecting you. She's in the containment room. The door is still unlocked, thanks to Ethan."

Abby checked a message on her phone at the same time as Sylvia and Will received a message alert. "That can't be possible," she said. "They've raided the second ship already?"

"They entered it at six-thirty this morning before the staff arrived," Sylvia told them. "It was a split-second decision."

"That's certainly good news," Abby said.

Will nodded. "It is. We'd better let Doctor Davis know we're here."

As Abby walked with Will down the hallway, the memories of the takeover filled her mind. She glanced up at a camera. *It was only the day before yesterday,* she thought.

"A day we'll never forget," Will said as if he had read her mind.

They met Doctor Davis in the containment room.

Will trailed away, joining other members of the Underground on the landing. The giant mechanical arm went in search of a chosen pod, retrieved it, and set it gently on the recovery port in front of him.

"How's your son?" Abby asked the doctor.

"He's back to normal. The last memory he recalls is crawling into bed when he was five years old, the night they had kidnapped him almost seven years ago." She handed Abby a document. "It's a list of those scheduled to be freed from containment."

Glancing at it, Abby noticed the names were all female. Her attention focused on the name Terry Brookes. *So, they made it look like an accident and replaced her with a shapeshifter,* Abby thought. "Will, come here." When he stood at her side with his medical bag in hand, she pointed to Terry's name.

"Who is she?" Doctor Davis asked.

"Someone we're looking for," Abby replied. "When can we speak with her?"

"It takes two hours before the pod can be opened. Then twenty-four hours of sleep is required in order for her mind to readjust to the here and now."

"Why two hours?" Abby asked.

"The aliens use frequency to heal the human body," Doctor Davis replied. "All levels of healing are activated the moment the liquid is drained from the pod, and the individual has spewed the contents from their stomach and lungs."

"Frequency," Abby said. "Who knew?"

"There are 210 different types of cells in the human body, and each type vibrates at a different frequency," Will told her. "Plus, each organ has its own vibration. The key is to find those certain vibrations that will work to restore each part of the body to its healthiest state."

"It sounds complicated," Abby said.

"Maybe someday we'll find the answer," Will told her.

"Not if our alien invaders have their way," Doctor Davis said. "Frequency healing is something they don't want us to know about. Never forget their objective is to use our world as their winery. They are cold-hearted and view disease and viruses as another way to eliminate the old and those who have faulty genes and unhealthy blood. Plus, keeping the discovery of healing frequency from humans has stopped mankind from advancing mentally, since the technology also enhances the mind. The more ignorant we are, the easier it is to control us."

"Well," Will said, "the truth will be revealed soon."

"Some are hard-headed," Abby said. "What are they going to do when they find out they've been brainwashed by aliens?"

"I'm certain we'll know soon enough," Will said.

"What about Miss Brookes?" Abby asked.

The doctor checked an inventory of names on the computer. "You're in luck. She was one of the first we freed today. You'll be able to speak with her tomorrow morning. She's sleeping right now."

I wonder if she'll remember why they imprisoned her, Abby thought. *One of her conspiracy theories must have been right.*

"How can we help?" Will asked.

"You're needed in the recovery room to make sure those who are awake will be physically ready to go home," the doctor replied. "After you give them a once-over and take DNA samples, they'll go to Sylvia and the other staff to tell them their stories so their replacements can be tracked down."

"Lead the way," Will said.

Abby and Will followed Doctor Davis down the main hallway until she came to the door leading to the dorms. They stepped into a corridor that encircled the entire ship. Doors on the right and left were labeled with a letter and a number. They entered the first door they came to. The interior looked identical to the drawing Ethan had sketched. The white room had forty beds, twenty on each side of the room. In its center, tables and chairs were now used for dining, and a place for those recently freed who wanted to read to catch up on recent events.

"We put together a private area in the washroom near the shower stalls," Doctor Davis told them. A woman approached and joined the doctor. "She'll show you to the makeshift exam room and bring in your first patient."

"Thank you," Will told her.

Once they settled in, Will retrieved the equipment from his medical bag to check the vital signs of each individual. After five hours of examining twenty-five men from ages forty to seventy years old, he and Abby packed up and left the dorm.

"It's scary to think that everyone you've examined today is a senator, congressman, or someone within the White House," Abby said, walking down the corridor with Will. "How are we going to remove the impostors from the government? We'll never get close enough."

"We'll have to catch them at home," he replied. "It looks like it will take more time than we have before the war for our world begins. If we can't stop the government from getting the military involved, who's to say what will be left of humanity?"

"All we can do is our best," Abby said.

"We can't let hope die," Will added.

"Are we staying on board the ship tonight?" she asked.

"No," he replied. "Sylvia found us rooms at a hotel in town. We'll be taking the bus with the rest of the staff, who will be leaving soon." He looked at the time on his watch. "In about twenty minutes. She said she'd track us down to make sure we don't miss our ride."

"We'd better get back to her office and get our suitcases we left there," Abby said. "I'm eager to hear what Terry Brookes will have to say tomorrow."

Chapter 28

The next morning, after breakfast at a family diner next door to the hotel and a bus trip, Abby and Will walked into the recovery room inside the spaceship they helped seize a couple of days ago. They found the journalist, Terry Brookes, sitting cross-legged on her bed and watching TV.

"I'm looking for a news channel," she told them when they walked up. "I've been asleep, so to speak, for two years. What in the hell is going on?"

"Hi. I'm Abby Muse, and he's Doctor Will Henderson. We'll answer your questions."

"Doctor Davis told me about you," Terry said. "You belong to an underground organization that's fighting against the Takers."

"Yes," Will said. "The same organization that annexed this ship and set you and all the others free."

"Thank you," Terry said. "I can't remember anything after they captured me. Can you fill me in on what I've missed?"

"The aliens killed livestock, drained their blood, and left them mutilated in the fields," Abby told her, not knowing how far back to go to bring her up to date.

"That's been going on for decades," Terry said.

"Those same aliens have the ability to change their shape and become replicas of people like yourself," Will told her.

Terry glanced around at those who had recovered and others still sleeping. "Many here were on my list of government officials who had seemed to change their minds and their entire demeanors overnight. I became obsessed with finding out why."

"Two years," Will said. "A lot has happened while you slept. The aliens replaced at least half of the politicians in the

Capitol and officials throughout the country. Plus, those who control the governments in nations all over the world."

"I have about a thousand names of the people I spent days, weeks, months, and years investigating," Terry said. "I found it strange that as soon as their personalities changed, each of them sold their homes and moved to a new location."

"To get rid of friends and neighbors who would question their complete change of character, I would guess," Abby said.

"On my talk show, I presented my listeners with my theories, and from their input, I added names and addresses to my list."

"Do you think they confiscated your research?" Will asked.

"I hope not. I went to a lot of trouble to hide it."

"Where is it now?" Abby asked.

"During the early nineteen hundreds, in the town where I was born, the streets were raised about fourteen feet in order to prevent the sewage from mixing in with flood waters every time it rained. For over a hundred years, there's been an underground city that few people know about. I hid my research in a century-old room under a historical home downtown where my sister works."

"You won't be able to retrieve it until we get your life back for you," Will said. "If they notice there are two of you now, they'll know this ship has been seized, and they'll reclaim it."

"I'm sure you're right," Terry said. "But I'm curious to know if my work has been found."

"If you want," Abby said, "we can join forces. With your list, we can hunt down a great number of the government's alien impostors. It would help us immensely."

"We have to take back our government," Will said. "We don't have much time. There's an alien war for our world coming within weeks, and we need to stop our government from getting the military involved."

"Why?" Terry asked. "I'd expect them to defend our country and the world."

"It's not our military right now," Will told her. "It's controlled by the aliens."

"Where are you getting your information?" Terry asked.

"You're not going to believe it," Will said.

"Doctor Davis gave me a tour of this ship. After seeing where I was contained for two years, it won't take much for me to believe anything you say."

"Fact," Abby said. "An eleven-year-old is leading a team of men to capture three more spaceships disguised as government schools like this one. He's taken two already. It's a fact that aliens are downloading information to him to help him save mankind."

Terry raised a brow. "Sounds like something out of a comic book."

"And aliens capturing you and placing you into suspended animation inside a pod sounds like a scene out of a movie," Abby said. "What's your point?"

"No point," Terry replied. "Fiction often mimics reality. I've spent my entire career uncovering the truth within the pages of outlandish stories. Can I meet this eleven-year-old?"

"He's kind of busy right now," Will said. "If you'll get together with Doctor Davis and the staff to locate the impostors that took over the lives of those on your list, we can start taking back our country immediately."

"Count me in," Terry said. "When can I get out of here to resume my life?"

Will answered a call on his cell phone. "Yes," he told the caller. "Now's a good time. Send me an address, don't forget to leave a key for the door, and any vehicle she's driving." He listened. "Great. We'll be ready." Will ended the call, peered at a text message, and turned to Terry. "As of right now, you're the only you in the world."

"That's the best news ever."

He checked another text message. "I received your address. A car is picking us up and taking us to our hotel to gather our belongings, then taking us to the airport just out of town. We'll take you home so you can change your clothes before we look for your research. Are you okay with that?"

She glanced at her white shift. "Yeah. That's fantastic."

"You have time to eat something before we leave," Abby told her.

"Good idea," Terry said.

"We have an impossible amount to do in a very short time," Abby whispered to Will as they left the dorm room. "There has to be a faster way to eliminate the impersonators."

"If you come up with something, let me know," Will said.

They reached the main hallway and stopped by Sylvia's office. After explaining the details of their plan to her, they went to speak with Doctor Davis.

"She'll help speed things up," the doctor told them. "We're sending students home every hour. By the end of today, we'll have four more dorms to use as recovery rooms." She looked over at the mechanical arm in the center of the room that pulled another pod from its storage area and set it on the landing port with two others that had been retrieved. "We have people working day and night."

"Impressive," Will said. "There's so much to do. That reminds me, we have to go. We'll keep you in the loop."

Abby said her goodbyes. Then she and Will went back to get Terry and left the spaceship, finding a black SUV waiting for them outside.

Will sat up front in the passenger seat. "Well, Chad, it looks like they've made you our chauffeur again."

"I added four more hovercrafts to our inventory today. I was in the area."

"Keep it up," Will told him. "To get the children home, we need as many hovercrafts as we can commandeer."

"This is Terry," Abby said, sliding into the backseat with her. "She's going to be a big help with tracking down the impostors."

"Nice to meet you," Chad said. "That will be one hell of a job."

"They took two years of my life from me," Terry said. "I believe in karma."

Once back at the spaceship after locating Terry's research, Abby and Terry walked down the hallway with Chad and Will, heading for the containment room. As they entered, Doctor Davis and Sylvia turned away from the computer's 3-D screen.

Terry handed the doctor three thick files. "I hope this helps."

"Thank you for coming back," Doctor Davis told her. "You know you didn't have to."

"I know, but you're fighting the same fight I fought before I was taken, and I have to see this through to the end. It's personal."

As the doctor flipped through the pages, Abby glanced at the documents covered with names and information.

"To be realistic," the doctor said, "I think we need to find a way to gather the replicas of our government officials all in one spot. If we try to eliminate all of the impostors one at a time, we won't be done before the gathering. And it's imperative that they retake our government before then."

"What's the gathering?" Terry asked.

"Have you heard of ley lines?" Abby asked.

"Yes. Earth's electromagnetic energy fields throughout the world form an energy grid that surrounds the entire planet."

"The major energy fields located in different places on

Earth are where the gathering will take place," Abby said. "At a precise moment, a select number of people forming a multitude of groups around the world will send a frequency message into the grid that will ask our alien allies for help. That will trigger a war for our world."

"Are you serious?" Terry asked. "Do we know who will win?"

Will shook his head. "But we're taking away the reason the Takers have invaded Earth—the children."

"I don't understand," Terry said. "Why the children?"

"At each Takers' School," Abby explained, "while the children sleep, the aliens take them to the infirmary and draw their blood. Horrifyingly, the aliens found that our young children's blood extends their lives. Once a month, they transport the plasma to their planet. In the process, their people have developed an addiction. Secretly, the Takers are invading our world to control the human race and satisfy their craving for immortality."

"To gain access to our children, they created the so-called schools," Will told her. "As of right now, we have one Takers School left to seize. We're reclaiming our children and taking away their reason for being here. And the war will convince them not to return."

"And if they don't leave?" Terry asked.

"We have ways to terminate them," Will said, touching his frequency gun.

Abby answered a call on her cell phone and put it on speaker.

"Mom, it's me," Ethan said.

"It's good to hear your voice. Are you coming home soon?"

"Yes. We finished raiding the last school a couple of hours ago. We added five more hovercrafts to our fleet. But we're not done yet. The amount of students we saved from all the Takers' Schools doesn't add up to the number of children they've taken from all over the world. I know now that there's a mothership above our planet with hundreds of thousands of children on board."

Abby felt sick. "How are we going to save them?"

"How big is this mothership?" Will asked.

"It's too big to measure."

Abby gasped. "We can't fight against something that size."

"We won't have to," Ethan told them. "That's what the gathering is for. Morgan, Holly, and I are landing at OFS in less than a minute."

"OFS?" she asked.

"Our First Spaceship." Ethan laughed. "We have a bunch now."

"How do you feel?" Abby asked.

"Hungry."

Chapter 29

Abby stood with Doctor Davis and Terry in the containment room, looking at the captives' names remaining on the list who still needed to be freed.

"We're back," Morgan said as he came through the double doors.

Holly strolled over to Chad and put her arms around his waist.

Ethan ran to Abby and gave her a hug.

"I've missed you," Abby said. "Love you."

He smiled. "Love you, too, Mom."

"This is Terry," Abby told him. "I found her name on a page in one of your father's books. Now she's helping us track down the impostors."

"Hi. I'm Ethan."

"Thank you for rescuing me," Terry said. "How was it possible for only a handful of you to take a ship this big?"

"Should I show her, Mom?"

"Go ahead," Abby replied. "She's one of us now."

Ethan vanished and then reappeared.

Terry's jaw dropped. "What just happened?"

"We operate on a need-to-know basis," Will said. "All you need to know is we can be cloaked. Don't bother to ask how it's done."

"Top secret," Terry said. "I understand perfectly."

"Well," Ethan said, "we have more to do. And not much time." He glanced at Will. "Morgan wants to talk to everyone."

"Gather around," Abby told everyone. "Grab a chair or anything you can sit on and bring it over here in front of the monitor." She sat beside Ethan and Will.

Morgan stood in front of the group. "We've captured all five Takers' Schools."

Everyone cheered.

"And now they're in the hands of the Underground," he added.

Doctor Davis stood. "We have two hundred House and Senate members ready to reclaim their lives," she said. "We should have over a hundred more released before the gathering."

"It's taking too long to return the captives to their former lives," Morgan said.

"The perfect scenario would be to exterminate their impostors all at once," Doctor Davis said. "We won't have enough time otherwise."

"I know of an excellent place for an ambush," Terry said. "The Capitol Building. I heard on the news when I went home to change my clothes that there's going to be a Joint Session in the House at the end of next week concerning military funding. They want to be over and done with it so they can go on summer break, which starts the next day. Both the House of Representatives and the Senate will be there."

"Ambushing the aliens at the Capitol the day before the gathering is cutting it close." Morgan hesitated for a moment before he said, "I like Terry's idea. If we do this, I want only our TV footage to be seen on all channels across America, and if possible, the world. We'll need to hack into every network and override the control the Takers have over the media. The news about the war for our world can't be released until the morning of the attack. The Takers must be caught off guard, or they may stop the gathering."

"I know just the people who can help us," Terry said. "I'll have to call around. I'm willing to bet the fake me hasn't talked to anyone who would know I wasn't myself. So, no one has seen me or talked to me in two years. It will be great to see them. I'm sure

I can get a TV crew together. Can I tell them what's going on?"

"If they're willing to help us, you'll have to," Morgan said. "They'll be watching it unfold live while they film. I don't want anyone to drop their camera and run. Make sure they believe what you say." He handed her a copy of Doctor Davis's video and the footage of the alien reveal. "After they watch this, they'll be convinced. I'll call Headquarters, and they'll collaborate with your techs and hack into the One World communications satellite."

"Perfect," Terry said.

"All of the released congressmen and senators will need business attire," Sylvia said. "I'll get my staff to inform Headquarters to spread the word that we need to form a nationwide clothes drive." She looked at Morgan. "How much time do I have to pull this all together?"

"Schedule it for this Saturday."

"I'll get on it." She left quickly.

"What else do we need?" Morgan asked.

"A way in," Will said.

"We have Speaker of the House Witfield," Doctor Davis said. "He's been brought up to date, and I'll make sure he's dressed appropriately." She touched the 3-D computer monitor and stated the speaker's name. His image appeared on the screen. "He's in dorm room B14."

"Will, Abby, and Ethan, you'll need to get the speaker back to his family and into the Capitol under the Takers' noses," Morgan looked at Chad and Holly. "You'll be in charge of locating and terminating his replica."

"Understood," Chad replied.

"I'll let him know you're coming," Doctor Davis said.

"When he comes to the door," Morgan said, "bring him into the hallway to discuss the procedure. I want all conversations to be confidential."

Abby turned to leave with Will and Ethan.

When they reached the corridor, they passed Terry's old dorm and kept walking until they came to B14.

Will knocked on the door, and a man opened it. "I need to talk with Speaker Witfield."

They waited, and the speaker, wearing a gray suit, joined them in the hallway.

Abby made the introductions.

"Are we ready to go?" he asked.

"We have a few things we have to go over before we take you home," Will said.

"Sure."

"Is there a procedure you have to follow to inform the House that you're ill or taking time off?" Will asked.

"Yes. It's a common practice."

"We're in the process of locating your double," Abby told him, "and finding a way to make a seamless switch."

Will received a message on his cell phone. "That was fast. They've located the shapeshifter already. He's on a flight home to Northern California. We'll follow him after he lands. He won't be going to the same address you remember as being your home. He and all the impostors relocated and started fresh with new friends and neighbors."

"After you reclaim your life," Abby added, "you'll need to call in sick to delay your return to work."

"I'm a doctor," Will told him. "If you have to fake a broken leg or catch an imaginary flu, I can take care of it and make it look official."

"Understood," the speaker said.

"Don't take any phone calls unless it's from us," Abby said. "You can't trust anyone. If the Takers realize what we're doing, innocent lives will be lost." She handed him her cell phone. "If you watch this video, you'll understand why the aliens are taking over our world. They need to control our government in order to harness our children."

As the speaker watched, his eyes widened. "This is a horror. Who knew it would come to this? I was against mandated federal schools. Now I know why I was replaced."

"Let's go," Will said.

They walked back to the main hallway and met Sylvia in her office.

"Have a seat." Sylvia handed him a sheet of paper and a pen. "We'll need a list of your closest colleagues. If they're in containment, we'll free them. Then we'll open a line of communication so you'll have people around you who you can trust."

"Thank you and everyone for this," Speaker Witfield told them.

"We're glad we could help," Sylvia said. "Are you married?"

"Yes," he replied. "I have two children. Both are living at home."

"What are the odds that all of them, or maybe just your wife, have been replaced?" Sylvia asked. She called Doctor Davis and gave her the names of his family members. "Yes. I understand. Thank you." The call ended, and she turned to the speaker. "Your wife is in containment. The doctor is releasing her tomorrow."

"Actually," Abby said, "that will work out great. You'll need time to explain things to your children after we terminate their mom's lookalike."

"They're not going to believe it," he said.

"You may be surprised," Abby said. "Speaking of surprises…. I'd like to tell you about my son, Ethan."

Will drove an Underground's black SUV up a long drive

that curved through an acre of green grass. He parked in front of a colonial white mansion with black shutters and a red front door. Woods surrounded the vast yard, allowing complete privacy.

Will handed the speaker a ziplock bag. "They took everything out of the shapeshifter's suit pockets. One of the keys on the ring should open your front door."

He took the items out of the bag and shoved everything into his pockets. "Ready," he said.

As Abby stepped out of the vehicle, she looked up at the second-story window and saw a curtain move. She followed Will, Ethan, and the speaker while scanning the area for prying eyes.

At the front door, the Speaker fumbled through the keys on the ring. His hands shook.

"I've got this," Ethan said. "Go ahead. It's open now."

He opened the door as if coming home from work and smiled at a blonde woman who came down the stairs.

Before the woman could say a word, Abby raised her gun and filled the foyer with frequency. The wife's lookalike collapsed, her lifeless body slumping on the stairs.

"Search the house," Will said. "We'll see if your children are home. Stay here."

Abby rolled the alien's body aside and climbed the stairs, the strap of her gun slung across her chest, and her finger on the trigger. She and Ethan searched four bedrooms and connecting bathrooms before they returned downstairs. "All clear," Abby told them.

"Maybe the children aren't home," Will said.

"What now?" the speaker asked, following Will to the living room.

"We hide the body," Will told him. "And wait."

Abby sat in a leather chair where she could see anyone coming into the house.

A blonde teenage girl wearing a sweaty jogging outfit

came through the door. "Mom, I'm home."

Witfield rose from his seat. "So am I," he called out. He reached the foyer and stopped her before she went upstairs. "I'd like you to meet a few friends of mine."

Abby fired her HERF gun, but the frequency didn't affect the girl. "Clear," she said.

"What did she just do? Was she trying to shoot me?"

"No. Things aren't always what they appear to be." He introduced everyone. "Come into the living room where we can talk. Where's your brother?"

"He should be home any minute," she replied, entering the room and plopping onto the couch.

"Good," he said. "We'll wait for him. We have good news to share with both of you."

"What is that thing?" she asked, pointing to Abby's gun. "Weren't those used in the late twentieth century?"

"Do you have an interest in firearms?" Abby asked.

"We're learning about past failures in the military. And that was one of them. In the future, guns will be replaced with new technology."

"Protecting our country is part of my surprise, honey," Witfield said.

Her brows furrowed. "You're not sending us to military school. I won't go."

"I wouldn't dream of it," he replied.

She crossed her arms. "That's not what you said yesterday."

He looked toward the front door as someone entered. "Go get your brother."

She left the room. "Hey. Don't go upstairs. Dad has something he wants to tell us," Abby heard her call out.

After explaining the situation to the children, Speaker Witfield walked Abby, Will, and Ethan to the front door. "Thank you for everything," he told them. "I'm eager to see my wife again. When do you think she'll be home tomorrow?"

"Later in the day," Will said. "She needs time to be briefed and to absorb the reality of it. We'll see you soon."

He closed the door as they stepped away.

"That went well," Abby said as they proceeded to their vehicle. "I thought what the children said about the complete difference they saw in their dad and mom was frightening. They knew something was wrong. It had to be a living horror."

"Seeing the alien's body made them feel better, I think," Ethan said. "It gave them proof that they weren't crazy."

"Let's head back to Headquarters, grab a hovercraft from the fleet, and fly home," Will said.

Abby nodded. "Sounds good. I'm looking forward to a quiet evening."

At Headquarters, Will picked out a hovercraft from the fleet. He threw back the camouflage tarp and opened the hatch. Once everyone climbed in, he started the engine, lifted off, and cleared the top of the trees, heading toward home.

Abby looked at a message on her phone. "Sylvia was given permission to have our town's clothing drive at Saint Martin's Church near Suzie's Restaurant. I hope we get a good crowd. We need a boatload of clothing for all those freed from containment."

"I wonder what the government will think when they find out the drive will be nationwide?" Will asked. "I'm sure they'll investigate."

"It is for the homeless," Abby said. "That's not a lie."

"It's not that," Will said. "You know what the government thinks about the homeless. They've allowed drugs to cross our borders and given the homeless free syringes."

"Why?" Ethan asked.

"In the eyes of the government," Will said, "the only useful humans are the ones who pay taxes. They know they can't kill off the homeless themselves, or the country will turn against them. So, they're hoping the drugs will do it for them."

"Do you think they'll try to stop the clothes drive?" Ethan asked.

"They may try," Will said. "But it will look bad if they do. There's no other way we can find clothes for the thousands of people contained in the pods. They can't reclaim their lives wearing the white shifts they've worn throughout their captivity."

"How are we going to advertise?" Abby asked.

"We can stop by Suzie's to have a bite and tell her about it," Will said. "She'll spread the word. Beats putting it in the newspapers."

After flying for about three hours from Northern California to Washington state, Abby looked out over a sea of trees and the vast lake that fed into the river flowing by her house. In the distance, she saw another hovercraft and hoped they'd make it home before being noticed. "Where are you going to stash our hovercraft?" she asked Will.

"In my backyard," he told her. "It's surrounded by trees. No one will spot it."

In a couple of minutes, nestled within the pines, Abby saw his forest-green two-story house dressed with cedar shutters.

Will hovered the craft over his backyard and slowly descended, landing in the shadow of the trees. He raised the hatch, and they exited the craft.

As they walked across the lawn, Abby glanced up at the back of Will's home. Steps led up to a cedar deck. She slid her hand across the smooth wooden railing made from finely-sanded tree limbs. The rest of the railing enclosed a twenty-by-ten feet deck. At the top of the stairs, she glanced through the large window and thought about her last visit when she sat on the couch with Ethan, looking out at the deer.

"Remember?" she asked him. "They were playing over

there."

"I see them now," Ethan said. "They're watching us."

Abby peered into the shadows.

"They're in the trees," he said.

"Sometimes I forget how well you can see," she told him.

Will led them to his truck. When the garage door rose, he backed out and drove down the long driveway to the main street.

Abby recalled the bridge ahead of them and the lake on both sides of the road, surrounded by tall white pines. But this time, instead of seeing a bald eagle soaring in the sky, black smoke billowed toward the clouds.

Will pulled up in front of a police car parked sideways to block traffic. He lowered his window and asked, "What's going on?"

"Lightning struck Suzie's restaurant," he said. "Burned the whole place down."

"Did anyone get hurt?" Abby asked.

"No, thank goodness," he replied. "The health department closed down her restaurant yesterday. The place was empty when the strike hit about an hour ago."

"Have you seen Suzie?" Will asked.

"Yes," he said. "She's talking to the reporters on live TV in front of the charred remains of her restaurant. We can't get her to leave."

"Can we speak with her?" Abby asked.

"If you can take her home," the officer said, "she'll be better off. She's not making much sense. She's claiming the government is to blame. I hate to see her like this. She's such a nice lady. Drive around my car. I'll give them a heads-up that you're here to take her home."

"Thank you, officer." Will drove past the blockade and parked by a firetruck. A few feet away, Suzie stood with news reporters. "Stay here," Will told Abby and Ethan. He climbed out of the truck and joined Suzie in front of the TV cameras.

Abby lowered her window to hear the interview.

Will put his arm around Suzie's waist and whispered into her ear.

She nodded, then continued to speak. "Disaster can strike anyone. That's why I want to tell you about the clothing drive at Saint Martin's Church on Saturday. Business attire is needed for the homeless to help them enter the workforce. Shoes and undergarments are also needed. And don't forget the children. I'm going home now. Thank you to everyone who has visited my restaurant and has become my family and friends."

Will walked with her to his truck. "Thanks for the plug. It was very important. You remember Abby. And this is her son, Ethan."

"Yes," Suzie said. She looked at Ethan. "Pleased to meet you. I'm not as upset as I appear to be. I've been expecting this since I took a photo of those three government agents who came into my restaurant."

"Are you in the mood for payback?" Abby asked. "First, you need to go someplace where the Takers can't watch you."

"If that were only possible," Suzie said.

"It is," Abby told her.

"We know where they can use your cooking talents," Will said. "But it's a need-to-see-it-to-believe-it place that no one knows about. Up for a challenge?"

"Yes. I'd like to see what you have up your sleeve." She glanced at the TV crew. "Does the clothing drive have anything to do with the challenge you're proposing?"

"Everything," Abby said. "Get in. They believe we're taking you home."

Will looked at his watch. "The sun doesn't set for a couple of hours. Let's go back to my place."

"Good idea," Suzie said. "I'm sure my house is bugged."

"There are things we have to discuss before we take you home," Abby said.

With ash still on her face, Suzie climbed into the backseat with Ethan.

Will started the engine and turned around, heading home. When the garage door opened, he pulled inside, then led them into the house, where they gathered in the living room.

Suzie scanned her surroundings. Her mouth gaped as she looked out into the backyard. Slowly, she walked to the large window overlooking the deck and an acre of grass surrounded by trees in the backyard.

"It's one of an entire fleet the Underground has in its possession." He told her about the Takers School. "You know we've been trying to find it for years. It's been cloaked." Will placed a laptop on the coffee table and plugged in a memory chip. "Our government is being taken over by aliens. Have a seat. We have something to show you. Watch this footage, and you'll understand what's going on."

As the video played, tears streamed down Suzie's cheeks.

"This is more than just a fascist government trying to shred our constitution," Abby told her. "There's going to be a galactic war for our world in a week." She removed the memory chip from the computer and handed it back to Will.

"A war?"

Abby nodded. "The Underground now controls the so-called schools, which are actually cloaked spaceships. The ship we'll be taking you to is the one that houses thousands of pods containing humans. They were used as templates, allowing the aliens to shapeshift into clones of government officials as well as children who were being kept for breeding. Each child had been replaced, and their replicas were sent home as replacements."

"This is horrifying. How can you tell the difference between the copies and originals?"

"You can't," Abby said.

"Then how do you know what you're telling me is true?"

"I think that is something you'll have to see for yourself," Abby told her.

Suzie glanced at her ash-sullied hands. "I need to wash up."

Will directed her to the bathroom. "How much should we tell her about Ethan?" he asked Abby.

"Nothing. I'm sure she'll figure it out as we go along."

Suzie returned to the living room.

"Are you still up for a challenge?" Will asked her.

"More than ever."

"Let's take you home," Abby said. "You'll need to pack."

"We'll take the hovercraft," Will said. "They'll think we're Takers. We won't be followed."

"Are you crazy?" Suzie asked. "If they find us in a stolen hovercraft, they'll kill us."

"Right now," Will said, "you'll be safer in the sky than on the roads. They're probably hiding somewhere waiting for us to drive by. I'd rather not take the chance."

"He's right," Abby told her. "You'll have to trust us sometime. Might as well be now."

Suzie followed them outside and through the yard to the hovercraft. "This has got to be the stupidest thing I've ever done," she said, climbing into the backseat with Ethan.

Once Abby slid into the passenger seat, Will lowered the hatch and lifted off.

The setting sun painted the sky with shades of pink and gray. But night hadn't fallen yet, and Abby could still see the roads below trailing through the tall trees.

"There's a black SUV hiding behind that highway sign down there," Ethan said. "You were right. They're waiting for us."

"Do you know where I live?" Suzie asked Will.

"I know where everyone in town lives." He circled around and came toward her house from the opposite direction. He flew close to the tree tops as he approached.

"Do you see it?" Ethan asked.

"I see it," Will replied.

Below, Abby saw what they were looking at. A hovercraft hid behind a wall of pines on the north side of Suzie's house.

"Is there anyone inside it?" Will asked Ethan.

"No."

"How can you be sure?" Suzie asked.

"My son has very good eyesight," Abby told her.

Will landed next to the Takers' craft.

Abby grabbed her frequency gun, and Will did the same. When the hatch rose, they climbed out.

Ethan took the lead.

"Shouldn't we sneak up on them?" Suzie asked. "We're in plain sight."

"Trust us," Will replied.

"My keys," she said.

"You won't need them," Will told her. "We'll go in through the back door."

Keeping quiet, they walked along the side of a two-story brick bungalow and followed a stone walkway to the backyard.

Ethan opened the kitchen door, touched the corner of his eye, and pointed up.

Will nodded and gave Ethan the sign to disable the surveillance.

When Ethan gave the okay, Abby raised her gun and filled the house with frequency. She heard something fall in the living room and a thud above them on the second floor. "Two," she said.

They went into the living room, where a dead alien had

collapsed by the front door.

Standing over the body, Suzie gasped. "It's true."

"There are different types of aliens visiting our planet," Abby said. "This alien and his race are the only ones invading Earth. They broke the pledge they made with the others who swore not to interfere with the human race."

"I'll check the second floor." Ethan walked up the staircase, looking all around as he went. When he came back down, he said, "All clear. I found three bugs down here and three up there. I killed the visual surveillance in the kitchen, the living room, at the top of the stairs, and in her bedroom."

"Well, I hope they got a good look," Suzie said, crossing her arms.

"I'll call Chad," Will said. "He and Holly should be home by now. She can drive him over. We need someone to fly the other hovercraft. Grab whatever's necessary, Suzie. You shouldn't come back here for at least two weeks. They'll be all over this place."

"You'd better empty the refrigerator so the place doesn't stink when she returns," Abby told Will and Ethan. "I'll go upstairs and help her."

Suzie pulled two suitcases out of the closet and threw them on her bed. "How long have they walked among us?" she asked Abby as she went to her dresser and started to empty the drawers.

"We think at least a thousand years," Abby said, helping her pack her suitcase. "Who knows, maybe more. They shapeshifted into human form and shared knowledge with mankind, enabling us to advance. Seventy-five different alien races are peacefully visiting our planet. But this race of aliens," she pointed to the body in Suzie's bathroom, "formed a secret society with enough power to take over our planet. Then they began replacing our elected officials and leaders of countries around the world by transforming themselves into their exact lookalikes and stealing their lives. But they didn't count on us."

"How many aliens have infiltrated our government?" Suzie asked, turning to the closet and taking garments off their hangers.

"We don't know for sure," Abby replied. "There are several hundred congressmen, senators, and support staff in the Capitol Building. And there's even more in the Pentagon, FBI, CIA, and every other government agency in America. But they haven't invaded just the US. They're taking over our world."

Suzie pulled a duffel bag out from beneath her bed and froze as footsteps came up the stairs.

Chad entered the bedroom. "Hello, ladies. Just thought I'd clean house." He hauled the dead alien out of the bathroom and dragged it down the stairs.

Suzie stuffed the duffel with more clothes and documents, then zipped her final bag just as Will and Chad came up the stairs to carry the luggage to the alien's hovercraft.

"Ready?" Abby asked. "Let's go." She left the bedroom with Suzie beside her, and they stopped at the top of the stairs, seeing Will returning and waiting by the newel post.

Will looked up at them. "Chad's flying Suzie's things to the ship. I told him we'd meet him there."

"I'd like to stop by my house and pick up Dillon," Abby said, descending the stairs.

"I think he'll be excited," Will replied. "He's never been in a hovercraft."

Abby, Suzie, Ethan, and Will flew south. When they reached Abby's house, Will landed the craft a few yards away from her patio.

Inside the house, through the sliding glass doors, Abby saw Dillon jumping and dancing with excitement. Behind him, the sitter waved.

After Will raised the hatch, Dillon opened the door and ran outside to join them.

"Can I go?" Dillon asked, followed by the sitter coming outside right behind him.

"That's why we're here," Abby told him. "We're taking Suzie to the spaceship, and we came to get you." She walked the sitter to the front door. "We'll need you again tomorrow. We'll still be in town, but we'll be involved in a clothes drive. I'd take Dillon if I could, but it's not safe for him to be seen in public. Hopefully, things will be back to normal soon."

"I understand," she said. "I'll see you in the morning."

Abby locked up the house and helped Dillon climb into the hovercraft's backseat with Ethan and Suzie.

Will lifted off.

"Tell me more about the students on the ship," Suzie said.

"All five of the so-called schools are sending as many of them home as possible," Will told her. "It can't be rushed, or we'll be noticed. They're working day and night, but the children are taken home only from sunup to sundown. And each time a dorm is vacant, it's filled with the people who were freed from the pods."

"It will take time," Abby said.

"After the war is over and if we prevail, we won't have to hide our actions any longer." Will flew above the treetops.

"Help me look for other hovercrafts," Ethan told Dillon. "They could be the Takers."

Abby looked over her shoulder and saw her two sons searching the sky. "Things will get back to normal someday," she said to Will.

"Only one more week," he replied. "If…."

She looked out over a lake that went on for miles. Across the sky, the sunset's pink hues intermingled with soft yellows and bright oranges. The sun hung well above the horizon, leaving time enough to take Suzie to the ship. *And then go home and spend an evening with the boys,* Abby thought. She relaxed and enjoyed the bedazzling western sky.

Chapter 30

The next few days, Abby and Ethan joined others in the Underground at the clothing drive, followed by a couple of days of sorting the items by size and gender, then delivering everything to the ship. In the evening on the last day of the task, Abby finally relaxed. The boys had gone to bed an hour earlier, and the silence throughout the house gave her time to think about all the possibilities of things that could go wrong in the coming week. She sat in front of the fireplace, the fire licking the logs, and the heat warming her toes. While sipping a cup of tea, she thought about Morgan's plan. *Speaker Witfield will reclaim his seat just before the reveal. And who knows what will happen after that. This had better go smoothly. Ethan needs to get a good night's sleep before the gathering.* Will's phone call interrupted her thoughts.

"I just talked to Morgan," he told her. "He spoke with the general you met at the orphanage in Utah to get an idea of how our government would react to a war for our world. We're secretly eradicating the alien impostors who replaced the top officials throughout the Pentagon and returning the newly released to their rightful lives."

"How about the president and first lady?" Abby asked. "Were they replaced?"

"We're sure they were," Will replied. "But the real president and first lady aren't in the containment area with the others."

"They're on board the mothership," Ethan said as he came into the room, "along with the other world leaders."

"Could it get any more complicated?" Abby asked.

"Baby steps," Will said. "One thing at a time, or it'll be too overwhelming. The good news is we have the next couple of days to ourselves. Thursday, we'll be at the Capitol Building. Terry and her news crew will accompany us, along with our team, who helped us confiscate the Takers' Schools."

"The gathering is on Friday," Abby said. "Will Ethan and Morgan make it home in time to rest?"

"If everything goes as planned," Will said, "we should be home by sundown."

If everything goes as planned, Abby thought.

Wednesday night, the Underground team, plus the speaker and Terry's media crew, flew to DC. They stayed in a hotel near the Hill and met in Morgan's room to go over the plan.

Morgan spread out a map of the Capitol Building's first and second floors. Separately, he laid out the Visitor Center's floorplan.

"If we go through the Visitor Center," Abby said, "Ethan can disrupt the security screening. That way, while we're cloaked, we can all slip past the scanner."

"It might only take a minute," Will said, "but shutting down the security system for even a short time could cause an evacuation. Plus, the place is huge, and there's too much ground to cover to get to the Capitol Building."

"Yes," Morgan said. "Good point. We know how touchy security is when there's even a hint of a threat to the Capitol Building. That eliminates deactivating the alarm on any locked door. The nature of the bill being voted on will bring everyone to Congress. This is the only opportunity we'll have to reveal the reason there will be a war for our world. We can't make any mistakes."

The speaker cleared his throat. "I would suggest following other members of Congress inside. Before reaching the scanner, we'll have the opportunity to trail off to the left. Security is a little lax since the public isn't allowed to enter through those doors."

"Good." Morgan looked at Speaker Witfield. "When we go inside, you'll proceed to the House floor while the team goes up to the gallery. Terry, do you and your media crew want to remain cloaked once you're inside?"

"Yes," she said. "I want to play it safe until all the Takers on Earth are annihilated. And to help in that effort, if you have an extra frequency gun, I would love to exterminate those scumbags for locking me inside a pod for two years."

Abby remembered when she hungered for justice and found it when she joined the Underground. She handed her HERF gun to Terry, hoping she would find a small piece of satisfaction herself. "Look up at the gallery and watch for our signal to shoot."

"Thanks for this," Terry said as Abby showed her how the weapon worked.

"Ethan," Morgan said, "will you be able to disrupt everyone's lines of communication?"

Ethan nodded. "In the whole building?"

Morgan shook his head. "Just in the House. If we do this right, security will be kept in the dark." He looked at Will. "Tell them what's next."

Will stood. "Once everyone is in position, the doors will be locked."

"As soon as dead aliens start to litter the place," the speaker said, "everyone will bolt for the exit. When they start banging on the doors to get out, security in the hallway will respond."

"Isn't it the speaker's job to control the floor?" Will asked him. "Say and do anything you can to get them back in their seats. Think about your plan tonight before you go to sleep. Make them realize that they're the leaders of our country, and they can't run. They need to be strong. And they'll need to keep this quiet once they leave the House. They can't trust anyone—not even their families."

"But, to be prudent," Morgan said, "the team will covertly cover the exits."

"While you're controlling the room, Mr. Speaker," Abby said, "we'll be gathering the alien bodies. All identification and personal items on each body will be bagged and given to their rightful owners who are being released from containment."

As for the cleanup crew," Will said, "we'll remain cloaked. Our faces will never be seen. That doesn't mean we won't speak to anyone. We'll have to ask them to move or find another seat so we can drag the bodies from the aisles."

"That will scare them to death," the speaker said. "Not only will they be surrounded by alien bodies, but the invisible man will be giving them instructions."

"This entire mission will be traumatizing," Morgan said. "There's no way around it. But if we don't show the world that our planet is being taken over before the war begins, there'll be panic in the streets, plus suicides. Our goal is to give people hope and a chance to stay calm."

"We're not saying that someone won't shoot their neighbors, using the excuse that they thought they were aliens," Will said. "There will be chaos no matter what we do. But the human race needs to know what's going on."

"We need to tell everyone not to fight back," Morgan said, "Defending our world will lead to humanity's annihilation. They must be told that we are not alone. Our alien allies are protecting us. You'll be streaming worldwide, Speaker. It's important that they get this message."

"So, do you agree to the task in front of you?" Abby asked.

Everyone nodded.

Abby turned to Morgan. "Should we call it a night?"

Chapter 31

In the morning, after hiking from the parking lot, the cloaked team led by Abby, Ethan, Will, and Morgan stood on the east side of the US Capitol Building.

Abby looked at her watch. *About an hour before the Visitor Center opens*, she thought. Glancing around, she noticed several Congress members climbing the south wing stairs. No media crews had arrived to get a response to the vote.

"Too early yet," Will whispered as if hearing her thoughts.

In front of the south wing, Abby's gaze followed the massive stairs leading to the Corinthian marble columns and the Greek portico. At the top of the stairs, double doors led inside. "What entrance are we going in?" she asked.

"Congress members used to take the underground subway to the Capitol Building," Witfield said, looking up at the portico. "But, after the terrorist bombing that trapped fifteen Congress members underground and killed twenty more, they commonly use those doors now." He led them up the grand stairs to the entrance, where four members of Congress waited to go through the scanner.

Abby skirted by them unnoticed. At the entrance, she hugged the door frame, slipping inside, following Morgan and Ethan. To her left, the guard on duty stood with his hands behind him, facing the Congress members exiting the scanner and holding his stance as Ethan and Morgan snuck by him. She took a step forward when the guard shifted his position, blocking her. Stifling the swearwords that filled her thoughts, she looked past him at Ethan, who put his hand up signaling her to wait.

Ethan pointed to a thin, old congresswoman with pale skin and arched, pencil-thin eyebrows drawn high above her eyes, giving her a constant look of surprise. She raised her hand to her neck, but not in time to stop her necklace from falling to the ground, white beads spraying across the stately tiled floor.

Everyone stood still, except the guard standing in Abby's way. He sprang to the congresswoman's aid and searched the floor, gathering the beads while the people in line waited under the portico.

Abby held back a laugh and motioned to Will and the others outside to hurry in. Scanning her surroundings, she thought, *Good. We're early. The halls are empty. No obstructions to get by. Perfect.*

Moving as a unit, they reached the House doors, and Speaker Witfield, uncloaked, walked inside. Behind him, enough of the invisible team to cover all the exits entered with Terry and her media crew trailing them.

Morgan signaled the others to follow him and ran for the stairway. When they entered the gallery, they spread out.

Abby and Ethan walked across the balcony as far to the left as possible, avoiding visitors waiting for the session to begin. Looking down upon the entire chamber, she saw the speaker take his chair with American flags behind him. Against the back wall, Terry and her crew stood out of the way as the Congress members mingled before taking their seats.

As the chamber filled, the speaker banged his gavel, getting everyone's attention and signaling Terry's crew to start filming. "Please be seated," he said to the stragglers. When the room hushed, he began to speak. "Today is an important day. It's a day that will go down in history as a turning point for our country. We must all remember that we are the leaders of a free nation. We must work together with dignity and strength to protect our citizens throughout America and those around the world." He glanced up at the gallery, then back at the crowd. "Take a look at the person next to you. Do you see a coward who will scream and run when facing a challenge? Or will it be you who pounds at the doors to escape your duty to lead our nation? You're about to be tested. Remain in your seats no matter what happens." He banged his gavel. "I can't stress this enough. Please remain in your seats and try not to scream." He looked up at the balcony again and nodded.

Abby saw Terry looking up at her, waiting for the sign to fire her weapon. When Morgan gave the word, Abby signaled to her.

Frequency filled the air. The impostors lost their human façade, their alien bodies drooping in their seats.

Everyone sprang to their feet. Those flanked on both sides by lifeless aliens climbed over their chairs. Screams echoed through the chamber.

The speaker pounded his gavel. "The doors are locked. Find a seat and remain calm." The commotion lingered, and he banged his gavel again and again. "Remain calm."

Abby gasped as she saw over one hundred aliens awaken. Her pounding heart threatened to leap from her chest.

"The room's too large," Will said. "The frequency wasn't strong enough."

Those within arm's reach were taken hostage, the aliens' four-fingered hands clenching the combating members of Congress as they struggled to escape. Chaos filled the room. Aliens leaped from row to row, looking for prey.

As people ran in all directions, Terry marched through the chamber blasting her gun, and Aliens dropped as the frequency bombarded them.

Unarmed, Abby and Ethan remained in the gallery while the team rushed downstairs.

Ethan unlocked the doors, and with guns blaring, the team burst onto the floor of the House of Representatives.

"Don't let anyone leave," Abby told him. "We have to

contain the chaos."

He locked the doors again.

Time dragged as Abby waited for the chamber to quiet.

The Speaker of the House called for everyone's attention as Terry's media crew, still invisible to House and Senate members, continued to shoot footage of the revealing. Slowly, the members crossed the room, sitting in areas uncluttered by alien bodies.

Speaker Witfield cleared his throat. "I was taken and contained inside a pod for a year while one of these creatures stole my life. A colleague of mine, also freed from containment, went home to find his wife was an impostor, also. I'm telling you this because you can't trust anyone. Not even your family. When you leave here, say nothing about the invaders because you may be speaking to an alien."

The chamber rumbled as whispers became swearwords. Hands raised.

"Each of you will have a voice. I will call on you to come to the lectern to ask questions until no questions remain. But not yet. I have more to say and a video to show you."

As the speaker adjusted the microphone, Abby glanced around the chamber and watched the team go through the clothing remaining on the alien bodies. All personal items were bagged. Then the bodies were moved to the east wall and dumped in a pile. She looked at the House floor. "Wait until they find out that the president is an alien."

"And the real one's in the mothership," Ethan added.

Soon, everyone signaled they had watched Doctor Davis's video on the overhead screen.

"As you have seen," the speaker said, "the bill we passed promising education for all our children at no cost to the public is a front enabling the aliens to harvest our children's blood. As of this moment, the five Takers' Schools that have been hidden from every parent in the United States of America have been raided and are controlled by a highly classified special unit dedicated to protecting our citizens and upholding our Constitution. As we speak, our children are being returned to their families."

A hand went up.

"Please step up to the lectern."

The congressman approached and adjusted the microphone. He stared at the bodies across the room. "How are they being levitated?" he asked, his voice cracking.

A rumble erupted on the House floor. Many stood and watched the bodies being carried by an invisible source.

"This is a delicate operation," the speaker told everyone. "Our attack squad and cleanup crew are cloaked. Because of their top-secret status, they are undetectable and will remain unseen as they search the bodies and move them out of the way. After everyone leaves, this room will be locked, and everything that has happened today must remain a secret until tomorrow. Once the sun rises, a war for our world will be fought by our alien allies against our invaders. Go home and watch TV tomorrow morning. Everything that has happened in this chamber today will be broadcast around the world to let everyone know that this is a war for the future of mankind." He stared into the TV camera. "I address the human race around the world. Be calm and do nothing. This war is between our alien allies and the evil invaders. Our defensive actions will only provoke the evil to turn their attention on us. It could mean the end of humanity. I repeat, be calm and do nothing."

A congressman stood.

"Approach the lectern," the speaker said.

After adjusting the microphone, the congressman asked, "Should we inform the president?"

"Right this minute," the speaker said, "the president and first lady are on board an alien mothership." He glanced around the room. "We are the only ones who know the truth. The vice president has been released from a pod and will be coherent tomorrow. Meanwhile, the fraudulent president will not be recognized within these walls."

A senator came to the lectern. "Can we stop the impostor from ordering our military to act?"

"At this moment, we are unable to enter the Pentagon and take down the invaders without alerting the other impostors that we're aware of their existence. If they find out that we know what they are up to, their mothership may leave, taking our children and world leaders with them. We're in the process of eliminating the problem by other means."

When the congressman sat, other members formed a line leading to the lectern.

Looks like he's got it under control, Abby thought.

After the speaker answered all the questions and repeated his plea to the world, Will entered the gallery. "We're finished here," he told her and Ethan.

The Speaker of the House banged his gavel. "Step away from party lines and unite as representatives of humanity. Soon, we will have a clearer understanding about the future of the human race."

"It's up to Terry and her TV crew now," Will said. "They have just enough time to get the footage edited and pass it on to the hackers."

"Let's go." Abby looked down at Terry and gave her the sign to withdraw.

Terry nodded. She made her way to the speaker and whispered in his ear.

Ethan unlocked the doors.

"The House is adjourned for today," the speaker told everyone. "Let's leave in an orderly fashion. You'll be notified by text when to return to Congress." He banged the gavel one last time.

"As soon as everyone's out, I'll lock the doors again," Ethan said.

After flying home from Washington, D.C., to Washington state, Abby, standing in her kitchen peeling potatoes for dinner, thought about what had happened at the US Capitol. *It was so unreal*, she thought. *Like a scene out of a movie. People turning into aliens and dropping dead, everyone screaming and running. I almost had a heart attack when the aliens woke up. I'm ready for all of this to be over.*

Dillon ran into the kitchen. "When are Will and Morgan coming?"

"In a while," she replied, placing a potato with others in a pan on the stove. "They wanted to clean up before coming over."

"Can I play in the backyard?"

"Yes. But come inside before Will lands his hovercraft on the grass." He ran ahead of her as she walked out of the kitchen into the hall. Out of the corner of her eye, she saw a sleeping bag floating down the staircase, a backpack gliding behind it. They landed in the corner by the front door.

"Will's bringing me a tent," Ethan told her as he came downstairs. "And a lantern."

"I'm not surprised," Abby said. "He's ready for anything. What's Morgan bringing?"

"Lots and lots of food," he replied. "Will thinks we'll need to eat and drink after the gathering, because it'll take all of our energy to send a message to space."

"He's pretty smart," she replied, walking into the living room.

"He's probably right, but our message won't be going into outer space. They're here on Earth."

She stopped and pivoted toward him. "What do you mean they're here on Earth?"

"They're in the oceans," he told her, "and inside volcanoes and mountains, and some are below ground."

"They've been here the whole time?" she asked.

He nodded.

"Why did they wait so long to stop the Takers? They had a thousand years."

"All I know is the Takers decided they have enough children and breeders and don't need our planet anymore. They're planning to set off nuclear bombs when they leave, killing everyone on Earth."

"How soon?" she asked.

"They don't know about the war," he told her. "The timing could change. By the end of the year, is their plan now."

"Within the next four months?"

He nodded. "But it won't matter after tomorrow."

"What if they win?" she asked. "Where are the bombs they're planning to set off?"

"Remember Daddy's map of Earth with all the white dots on it?"

Her jaw dropped. "There's over a hundred of them all over the world." Abby crossed the living room and grabbed the suitcase containing the maps. As she carried it to the dining table, she looked over her shoulder and saw a hovercraft land in her backyard. "Morgan and Will are here." As Ethan ran outside, she placed the suitcase on a dining room chair and sorted through the maps, pulling out the one tied with a black string. She spread it out on the table and began counting the dots.

"What's up?" Will asked when he came through the sliding glass door.

"Ethan just informed me that the Takers are going to set off nuclear bombs around the world as they leave. I found the map that gives the location of the warheads."

Morgan and Will swore under their breaths as they

scanned the map.

"Has all this been for nothing?" Abby asked.

"In 1967," Morgan said, "UFOs, as they called them then, activated and deactivated ten nuclear warheads at Malmstrom Air Force Base in Montana. Probably practicing. They must have been working on this plan since then."

"How do we know if they were the good guys or the bad guys who did it?" Abby asked.

"We don't," Will replied.

"This is horrifying news." Morgan turned to Ethan. "What do you think?"

Ethan closed his eyes for a long moment, then opened them. "Some of the good aliens are trying to break through the shields surrounding the Takers' mothership. So far, they can't. They said I need to lead the gathering to call in our other allies. They need more ships to stop the bombs."

"So, Plan B is to locate each silo and disable all warheads while there's a war going on?" Will asked.

"They know where they're located," Ethan said, "or Dad couldn't have made this map."

"This isn't something we can worry about now," Morgan said. "We have to keep a clear mind if we're going to accomplish our objective tonight."

"Dinner is ready," Abby said. "You'll need to eat before you go." She cleared away the map, and Will helped her set the table.

After dinner, Ethan gathered his things and placed them into the hovercraft.

It's useless to worry about something you can't control, Abby kept telling herself. She climbed into the hovercraft with Dillon and Will to fly Ethan and Morgan to the gathering.

Will lifted off.

As they flew toward Mount Shasta, the streets below were

filled with unsuspecting people who had no idea their world might end tomorrow. And the blue sky, easing into a peaceful evening, would soon be a war zone.

Abby shook her head, trying to brush aside the what-ifs and live in the moment surrounded by the ones she loved. But her heart broke as she said her goodbyes to Ethan, knowing she couldn't be with him if he needed her. When he gave her a thumbs-up as he walked away with Morgan, she returned his gesture and blew him a kiss.

Tears filled her eyes as she got into the hovercraft to return home. *I have to stop thinking this way,* she thought. She sat in the backseat with Dillon, his head on her lap while he slept. *All we need is a miracle.*

Once Will landed the hovercraft in her backyard, he carried Dillon inside, placed him on the couch, and covered him with a blanket.

"Good night," Abby told Will.

"Sleep well," he replied, turning and heading into the office to stay the night.

Abby kissed Dillon before she went upstairs to her bedroom. With the feeling of dread weighing on her, she undressed and crawled into bed.

Hours later, after tossing and turning, Abby sat up in bed, feeling drained and alone. She threw back the covers, climbed out of bed, grabbed her pillow, and then headed downstairs. The full moon's soft glow streaming through the sliding glass doors lit the path to the office. Trying not to wake Will, she snuck into the room and crawled into bed, curling up next to him.

He put his arm around her, and she fell asleep.

Chapter 32

Before the sun rose, Abby and Will went out to the living room and turned on the TV, lowering the volume while Dillon slept. Terry, her media crew, and the hackers did their jobs. Their footage of the unveiling in Congress played over and over in a loop on all channels. An update streamed on the bottom of the TV screen. All planes around the world had been grounded. People had been told to stay inside.

"I received a message from Terry," Will said. "They put the video on the air early this morning. By now, most of the world has seen it."

"The Takers must be panicking," Abby said.

Will grabbed his phone on the coffee table. "It's Sylvia. She texted me that there are Taker spaceships hovering over all five so-called schools. They're sending communications and waiting for a reply."

"Will they attack because they're not getting a response?" Abby asked.

"No," Will replied. "They don't know yet that their ships have been confiscated, and the children and the people in pods are invaluable to them."

"Is there a team inside with Sylvia and the others who will protect them if the Takers decide to investigate?" Abby asked.

"Yes," Will said. "Once the aliens enter any of the schools, they're dead."

They stared at the TV screen as videos showed spaceships breaking through the surface of the Pacific Ocean. Footage after footage taken of oceans and seas around the world showed spaceships rising from the depths.

Terry's video played in a loop once again. More recordings

from America and abroad showed shape after shape of different sized spaceships flying out of the sides of mountains, rising out of the ground, and soaring from the mouths of inactive volcanoes.

Dillon sat up. "Are you watching a movie?"

"No," Abby said. "This is real."

Dillon crawled out from beneath the covers and ran to the sliding glass doors. Looking up at the sky, he said, "I don't see anything."

"Come watch TV," Abby told him, not wanting him to be seen by the Takers.

A list of the names of world leaders who had been replaced scrolled across the bottom of the TV screen.

Abby watched clips of stranded drivers standing beside their vehicles, staring up at the battle in the sky. The bodies of aliens were shown slumped inside their cars. "What are those people doing outside?" She gasped as a spaceship crashed into the San Fransico Bay, just missing the Golden Gate Bridge.

Another loop of Terry's video played, reminding everyone to stay calm, followed by images of dead aliens littering the streets and sidewalks, inside offices, restaurants, and every interior around the world.

"Ethan said they'd have nowhere to hide," Abby said.

"Except inside their ships," Will said.

They ate cereal while they watched the news, then took showers and dressed.

Just before noon, Will received another text message and said, "The mothership

has been forced down in Oceanside, California. Ethan wants us to go get him and Morgan, then fly there."

"How are we going to make it there with all of this going on?" Abby asked, pointing at a sky filled with chaos.

"They're sending an escort," he told her.

"Look, Mommy," Dillon called out. "There's a spaceship

above our house."

"And it's here now," Will said.

"Are you serious?" she asked him. "Is that our escort?"

He nodded. "The cause is great. We need to get to Oceanside fast. This is the only way."

She took a deep breath. "Okay. How does this work? Are we going to be beamed up?"

"Your guess is as good as mine," Will replied. "Ethan texted me that we need to get into the hovercraft and not to worry about anything." He slid open the glass door and led the way.

Abby took Dillon's hand as he kept his eyes on the disk-shaped spaceship that hovered over an entire city block, its core centered above them. *Why do I have a bad feeling about this?* she thought.

Once Will lowered the hovercraft hatch, they climbed in and buckled up.

A force gripped their hovercraft, pulling it upward and bringing them through the spaceship's open cargo door.

When they touched down on the inner deck, the cargo doors remained open.

"Mommy, look," Dillon said, pointing up.

A soccer ball-sized glowing sphere floated above them, startling her. It zipped around their craft as if inspecting the visitors.

"There must be some kind of consensus within the pact to limit contact with our civilization," Will said.

"Prime directive number one in most sci-fi movies," Abby said, "prevents contact with less advanced civilizations in order to preserve their normal development." In the obscure surroundings, she scanned the vastness. The walls and ceiling loomed in the gray shadows. Although the area on the right and left resembled docks, no other crafts but theirs remained in the hangar.

The bright orb hovered in front of their windshield before it sped away.

"I feel like we're being watched," Abby said.

"We are," Will said. "The ball of light is a surveillance device like the one I saw in the meadow by the school." He checked a message on his phone. "It's Ethan. He and Mogan are joining us shortly."

A Takers' hovercraft, identical to theirs, glided into the cargo bay and touched down.

"Do you think it's Ethan and Morgan?" Abby asked.

"That doesn't make sense," Will said. "We dropped them off. How did they get a hovercraft?"

"Ethan could've commandeered one," Abby replied.

"Morgan would've contacted me before making a dangerous move like that. There's a war going on. He knows the Takers are flying in packs. Bringing down one hovercraft would've made them a target."

Abby squinted, trying to peer into the shadows. The bad feeling she had before they left home started to mushroom, sending a chill up her spine as the craft parked about thirty feet from them.

After a brief moment, two humanoids exited the craft.

"Do you see them?" Dillon asked.

"Yes, we see them," Will replied. He grabbed his frequency gun from the backseat.

Abby retrieved hers, too. The closer the two came, the better she saw their features. "It's Ethan and Morgan," she said, putting her gun down on the floorboard. She reached for the hatch control when Will caught her wrist.

"Morgan and I have a secret code to make sure we're who we say we are," Will told her. "I'll say this day couldn't get any better. Then, he should reply, my big toe tells me it's going to rain. If he doesn't say that, it's not him." He raised the hatch, leaving it open as he stepped away.

Abby saw him casually hold his HERF gun at his side and noticed his finger near the trigger. Focusing, she watched him extend his right hand while walking forward as if greeting a friend. Then, she heard him say the code words.

Morgan didn't reply.

She watched her son's image and Morgan's morph into dead aliens and collapse on the deck. Before she could grab her frequency gun, a jolt to the back of her seat made her whip around to see a gray four-fingered hand wrapped around Dillon's mouth and a Taker lifting him out of the craft. She vaulted over the front seat, but the kidnapper slipped out of her grasp and turned to run. Pulling her smart gun from the waistband of her jeans, she aimed at the alien's head. *Come on, come on,* she thought, waiting for the accuracy voice to say ten. At the precise moment, she pulled the trigger. *Dillon,* she shouted in her mind. As if in slow motion, he dropped out of the Taker's grasp. "Dillon," she called out, seeing him in a heap on the ground next to the dead alien. When she leaped out of the hovercraft, Will sprinted past her and knelt at her son's side.

Dillon stretched out his arms and hugged Will's neck.

With one swift move, Will hoisted him onto his back. "Follow me," he told Abby as he waited for her to grab her frequency gun from the front seat. "The force is still holding our hovercraft. We'll have to take the other one."

As she turned to follow him, she fired her frequency gun and heard alien bodies dropping all around them. For a moment, silence surrounded her. Then she heard a swarm of footsteps running toward them. Blasting her weapon, Abby advanced toward the movement coming in her direction and kept her finger on the trigger until nothing moved. She caught up with Will and Dillon.

When Abby reached the vehicle, she glanced into the

backseat and saw Ethan and Morgan bound and dazed. "Are you hurt?" Leaning in, she hurried to release Ethan. "Stay down," she told him while untying his hands. "They're trying to kill us."

Dillon ducked down in the front seat as Will cut the binding around Mogan's wrists.

Shots whizzed by so close that Abby felt a streak of heat across her back, and she smelled the deck's smoldering metal. She scrambled into the front seat as Dillon jumped into the back with Ethan and Morgan.

With everyone inside and the hatch pulled down, Will started the engine.

"They're after me," Ethan said.

"They're after all of us," Will said. "Can you disable their weapons?"

The firing stopped.

Will pulled up on the controls, and the craft hovered. Yanking the lever back, he spun the hovercraft around and hit the accelerator, slamming Abby against her seat, and the next second, throwing her toward the windshield when he slammed on the brakes.

She looked at Will and followed his gaze. The closing cargo door lowered, vanquishing the last sliver of daylight. Panicking, she looked around. A dim gray light filled the vastness, allowing her to calculate the danger. "They're coming," she said, seeing aliens streaming into the cargo bay behind them. "Like an army of ants."

Aliens with pointed teeth and long, four-fingered hands grasped the craft and swarmed over the hatch, trying to pry it open.

"Pin them to the ceiling, Ethan," Abby said.

Using his telekinesis abilities, he levitated the Takers, their weapons raining down as they ascended toward the rafters.

"Can you open the cargo door?" Will asked him. Slowly,

sunlight flooded the bay, and he flew out into the daylight, dove down to street level, and found a safe place to land.

"Are you okay?" she asked, looking into the backseat.

"A little unsettled but fine," Morgan replied.

"We got a message from you, telling us our alien allies were sending an escort," she told Ethan.

"It wasn't me."

"They must know by now that we confiscated their so-called schools, and we're about to take their mothership," Will said. "Were they telling the truth? Is the mothership down in Oceanside?"

"Yes," Ethan replied. "I sent that message before they took my phone."

"They ambushed us," Morgan said. "His dad was right. Ethan is the key. He's the only one who could start the war, and he's the only one who can stop it."

"How?" Abby asked. "By holding another gathering?"

"His father was apparently a very important man," Morgan replied. "Ethan translated what they were saying while they stunned our friends and left them by our campfire. They called his dad Wave Master. He tunes and guides universal frequencies."

"The controller of chaos, the Takers said," Ethan added. "They've been looking for him for hundreds of years."

"They found him and killed him," Abby said. "And they didn't even know it."

"He's not dead," Ethan said. "He's an energy being. He's been sharing his powers with me." He closed his eyes, then reopened them. "He told me that he can't return to human form."

Memories of the years they had spent together flooded her mind. Tears streaked her cheeks.

"It's all right, Mom," Ethan told her. "He's watching over us. All he wants is for us to be happy."

"If the Takers can capture Ethan, it would guarantee their passage out of here," Morgan said.

"The hell with that," Will said. "Let's kill the bastards."

Abby held on tight as Will flew above the treetops. The war for the world intensified the closer they came to Oceanside. The alien ship's wreckage littered the sky as Will snaked their hovercraft through the raining debris.

Packs of Taker crafts high above them swarmed like bees among the chaos. "Look," Dillon said.

"They're looking for holes in our allies' defenses to save their mothership," Will said.

"They're coming," Dillon cried out.

"Where?" Abby searched the sky.

"From the west," Ethan told her.

"Good to know," Will said. "How close are they?"

"Three minutes away," Ethan replied.

"I know they can't see us," Morgan said, "but it would be safer if we just stay out of their way."

Will landed their craft on Highway 101.

"It's a ghost town," Abby said. "Cars crushed by the debris and abandoned vehicles are everywhere. Looks like panic to me."

"This is the frontline," Morgan said. "Who in their right mind would be outside with all this going on?"

She glanced around, and before she could take another breath, a gasp filled her lungs. Spaceship carnage the size of a car door fell from an explosion in the sky and struck the highway. The debris's sharp edge pierced the asphalt, only three mangled cars away from them.

"They're here," Ethan said, looking toward the ocean, "and I think we're in trouble."

Chapter 33

In the distance, Abby saw seven hovercrafts change their direction as if zeroing in on them.

Morgan, sitting in the backseat with Ethan and Dillon, passed her a HERF gun, then handed one to Will. "They're acting like they see us."

"When we escaped from the Takers' spaceship, I cloaked us," Ethan told them.

"So, now they know we can cloak," Morgan said.

Ethan nodded. "And they found a way to detect us."

"You said detect," Abby told him. "Can't they see us?"

"No. The cloak looks like a smudge on their tracking screen."

"We can't move, or they'll know it's us," Will said.

"Let me try something," Ethan told him. "I'm going to cloak that blue truck by the chunk of spaceship that fell from the sky."

"Why not a car farther away?" Abby asked.

"I added a second layer to our cloak when we landed. I thought maybe it would help protect us from the space junk, but it only made us show up on their tracking screen."

"If you remove our extra layer," Abby said, "and double the cloak on the truck, they might think the truck is us. Is that what you're thinking?"

"Good idea," Will told him.

"Okay," Ethan said. "The truck's cloaked. And now we'll see."

Abby watched the hovercrafts swoop down and land on the highway far enough away to make her squint to see the features of a dozen Takers climbing out of their crafts.

"We have to get out of here." Will edged away slowly. "Ethan, watch to see if any of them look our way."

"One of them raised his hand to his ear," Ethan told him. "Now, all of them are looking at us."

Will gained altitude as he increased speed. "What are they doing now?" he asked Ethan.

"They're getting back into their hovercrafts. They're coming after us."

"We have to make it past the frontline," Will said. "It's our only chance."

"Go faster," Dillon called out.

"I'm going as fast as I can."

"Turn to the left now," Ethan told him.

Just as Will veered off, shots from the Takers' hovercrafts whizzed past them, missing their craft by a foot.

"Dive," Ethan said.

Will dove while maneuvering around debris coming from a disabled spaceship high above them. All seven of the Takers' crafts fired on them. Their shots missed as Will followed Ethan's directions.

"There's a disabled hovercraft above us," Morgan said. "Use it as a decoy, Ethan. It might buy us some time to get away."

Abby held on as they ascended at a speed that shook their craft. Bracing herself, she couldn't stop from ramming into the hatch in front of her as he came to a complete stop directly behind the craft's mangled leftovers, with its hatch torn off and half of its body gone.

"Why is that thing still in the sky?" Abby asked, rubbing her head.

"Beats me," Morgan said. "Cloak it, Ethan."

He nodded. "Got it."

Will backed away, dodging debris, then flew south. "How's it looking?" he asked Ethan. "Did they take the bait?"

"They fired on it and knocked it out of the sky. All of them are following it down. The cloak is holding. Cool."

"Let's find the highway again and keep low," Morgan said. "We can't stay in the middle of all this. It's too dangerous."

Descending, Will flew toward the Pacific Ocean and followed the coastline, then veered inland until he came to Interstate 5.

When they reached Oceanside, Abby looked out the hatch while they flew toward the shoreline. The mothership had taken out the pier as it slid to a stop on the sandy beach, leaving splintered wood scattered on the shore.

"Have you noticed that we haven't been fired on since we crossed the frontline?" Will said. "Here we are flying straight toward the mothership in a Takers' hovercraft, and no one seems to care."

"They know it's us," Ethan said. "They download information to me all the time." He tapped the side of his head. "They always know where I am."

"The chip in your head," Will said. "You mean they've been watching you since you were three years old?"

"I know," Ethan said. "When I found out, it kinda freaked me out too. But then, I found out that Dad uses it to share his powers with me. That makes it cool."

Will flew beneath a fleet of allies' spaceships hovering above the mothership that stretched a mile out into the Pacific.

"Ethan was right," Abby said. "It's the size of England." It stood about as tall as the Empire State Building, but it floated above the water as if it weighed less than a cloud. Its massive hull seemed to go on forever.

Will turned back toward the shore.

Below them, a caravan of military trucks poured onto the beach.

Morgan pointed to someone waving to them near the

remnants of the pier.

"Is that the four-star general we met in Utah?" Abby asked.

"Yes," Morgan said."And he brought all of Camp Pendleton with him."

Abby glanced back at the mothership that stood stone still, hovering about ten feet above the water. "We're going to need more troops."

Will flew above a few palm trees and landed on a strip of grass. When they got out, they trudged through the sand toward their team while scanning the ship that hovered above the waves.

"Do you have any idea how we'll get inside?" Morgan asked.

Ethan closed his eyes for a moment. When he opened them, he said, "There's a door on the belly of the ship."

"General Rand's with our team over there," Morgan said. "We should let him know."

"Hi, guys," Chad said, approaching them. "It's about time you got here."

"We had a little problem on the way," Will told him.

"What happened?" Chad asked.

"We were momentarily delayed," Will told him. "I'll tell you about it later. Ethan said there's an entrance on the ship's belly. We need to talk to the team."

"I'll watch the boys," Holly told Abby.

"Thanks so much." Abby bent down and asked Dillon, "Will you be okay with that?"

"I have to tell Jack all about that spaceship and being chased by monsters," Dillon told her.

"Okay." Abby stood. "He's all yours, Holly."

"We'll be in that transport truck over there. Come on, boys." She led them away.

"General Rand wants to speak with you," Chad told Morgan.

"Just the man I want to see," Morgan said.

"Does he know I can cloak?" Ethan asked.

"Yes," Morgan replied. "I told him everything. Now he understands why a twelve-year-old boy is on our team." He chuckled. "It's a good thing we've been friends for decades. It took me a while to convince him I was serious."

Ethan nodded. "Good."

They joined the general under a sheltered picnic table near some palm trees. Abby and the team stood around him.

"I want to thank you again for giving me a heads up about the HERF guns," General Rand told Morgan. "I've supplied the entire base with them."

"Someone has to have some common sense," Morgan told him. "You wouldn't have heard it from anyone in the Pentagon."

"You're right about that," the general said. He pulled out a handwritten plan from a manila folder. "Morgan, your team will be going in first."

"Do you have anything I can draw on?" Ethan asked General Rand.

"As a matter of fact, I do." He opened the file, pulled out a blank piece of paper, and set it in front of him.

Ethan drew a detailed map of the mothership's interior, flipping the sheet of paper over to sketch more levels. "The children's sleeping quarters and the containment area are on the first floor, where we'll enter. This won't be like any of the schools we raided. This time the Takers know we're coming, and they'll be waiting for us."

"I was briefed about your gifts," the general told him. "It's hard to believe."

"See this pen?" Ethan asked him. "Keep looking." He cloaked it, and the pen vanished, then reappeared.

The general looked at Morgan.

"Told you so," he said.

"Well then, let's get down to business." General Rand studied the map with Abby, Ethan, Will, and Morgan. "This helps immensely," the general said. "Your team will be heading directly to the helm to stop them from launching the nuclear missiles." He highlighted a pathway to the bridge.

"Give us a fifteen-minute head start," Morgan said. "Once we're cloaked, they won't see anyone entering their ship. They'll still see you here on the beach going over the plans. It will buy us some time if they don't think the raid has begun yet."

"Good idea," General Rand said.

"After we take control of the helm," Morgan told him, "we'll come back to the first level to help. The door leading to the containment area will be locked. Ethan will have to open it for us."

"Looks like we're all set," the general said.

"Team," Morgan said, "let's make our way to the truck where Holly and the boys are and slip between the vehicles so we won't be seen vanishing into thin air."

Abby and Ethan went first, strolling along the sand, making their way through a parking lot of military vehicles emplaced on the sandy beach. In an area out of sight of General Rand's troops, she and Ethan vanished.

"Over here," Ethan said to two more members of the team who walked among the trucks. As they casually followed his voice, he brought them under the cloak.

In a short time, all twenty-five of the Underground team joined together and made their way to the underbelly of the mothership.

Ethan stood on the dry sand near the foaming backwash and closed his eyes.

"Do you see it anywhere?" Abby asked him, scanning the underbelly. The smooth metallic skin gave no clue to the door's location.

"Got it," Ethan said, opening his eyes.

A ramp lowered and rested on the sand about three feet out in the water.

"We can't get our shoes wet," Morgan said. "The slightest squeak or wet footprint will give away our presence."

Ethan turned to Morgan and the team. "You're going to have to jump." The team formed a line and, one at a time, took a running start. Before they reached the wet sand, Ethan levitated them over the frothing waters and set them down on the ramp. Once everyone made it across, Ethan joined them, and they entered the ship.

Inside the stark white ship interior, guards in human form, wearing armor resembling reptilian skin, hurried through the hallway toward the lowered ramp. Abby held her frequency gun, her finger on the trigger, and noticed everyone else did the same. *If we kill them,* Abby thought, *they'll know we're here.*

Forming a single line with Abby and Will trailing, the team hugged the wall and snaked their way through the armed Takers running past them.

When the line stopped in front of her, Abby heard a noise behind a door beside her. Leaning closer, she tried to eavesdrop. The door opened, sending her heart into her throat, and a Taker plowed into her. When he reached out, feeling the space in front of him, she grabbed the alien's arm, twisted it, and pushed him back inside the room. Will, following behind her, closed the door, and she fired her frequency gun. Ten aliens within the room fell dead.

"There was no other choice," Abby told Will.

"I agree," Will replied. "Let's go."

They snuck out into the hallway again and caught up with the others.

Through the line, a message from Ethan made it back to Abby and Will, telling them that he couldn't break through the

Takers' ship's shield. They would have to go all the way to the helm to prevent the launch.

The number of Takers around them dwindled, allowing the team to move faster.

In front of Abby, she saw the others hold up two fingers. She glanced behind her. Will covered her back with no others trailing him. She gave him the sign over her shoulder, and he nodded. Again, she saw the signal, but with only one finger raised. *A countdown*, she thought. Abby slowed, ready to stop at any moment. When hands went up to signal a halt, Chad and three of the team dashed across the hallway to a closed door, opened it, and went inside.

She glanced at the front of the line and saw Ethan coming toward her. As he crossed an intersection of hallways, a Taker sprinted around the corner, collided into him, and sent him sailing until he slammed into the wall. The alien stopped, turned in a circle, then continued running toward the breached underbelly and General Rand's men, making their way inside the ship.

Abby darted to Ethan's side. As he looked up at her, his silver eyes closed. She stifled a scream, and tears filled her eyes.

"I've got him," Will whispered, scooping him up into his arms.

She held open the door that Chad and the other three had entered, letting Will carry Ethan inside. With the rest of the team behind her, she entered a large circular area with hallways leading away from it like rays of sunlight. An empty glass elevator went upward, and she knew that whoever called for it might be coming down any minute. She searched for a way out. As Will carried Ethan up the spiral ramp, she hurried alongside him, and the reality of the situation struck her. "I have to stay with him," she told Will. "I can't leave him like this."

"We have to find a place to hide," Will said. "We're out in the open."

When Abby reached the second-floor landing, she pointed to a door, opened it, and fired her frequency gun. The empty white room looked familiar. *Like the dorm rooms in the Takers School,* she thought.

Will came in behind her and set Ethan on a bed while Morgan, with the rest of the team, streamed inside and closed the door.

"How is he?" Morgan asked.

"He hit his head hard," Will said. "It knocked him out."

The team can make it without me, Abby thought. She looked over her shoulder and grabbed her HERF gun as the door opened. The Taker, entering, glared at them, then reached for his weapon.

The team fired their frequency guns, and the alien dropped to the floor.

"Now it's confirmed that our cloak is gone," Morgan said.

Chad closed the door and locked it.

"The fighting is on the first floor," Abby said, "but it'll be making its way to the second soon. There's no time. We have to move to the next level."

"She's right," Will said. "Grab the ends of the bedcover. We'll use it as a litter."

Chad opened the door a crack. "All clear." He moved aside, letting two of the team carry Ethan into the hallway. "Get back," he told them as footsteps echoed up the ramp a few yards away. He closed the door, listened, then opened it a sliver. "Okay. Let's go."

The team filed out of the room and followed a ramp upward to the next floor.

"Spread out," Morgan said. "We need an unlocked room. Be discreet and stay vigilant. If an alien notices someone trying to enter their room, be ready for a confrontation."

"I'll assess the rooms closest to the ramp first," Abby said, "before searching farther down the hallway." She tried the door closest to her and stepped away when she found it locked. To double-check, she took a couple of steps back, tried to open it again, then turned away. Too late, she heard the door open, and a gray four-fingered hand went over her mouth.

The Taker ripped her HERF gun from her shoulder and dragged her into the room. Before the alien closed the door, Abby grabbed its hands, leaned to the right, and pivoted, twisting the hand as she turned. As hard as she could, she kicked its legs out from under it.

The alien leapt up, grabbed her arm, then flung her across the room.

Abby hit the wall, rolled to the side, and crawled behind the bed. *No HERF gun,* she thought. *No problem.* She reached behind her back and pulled out the smart gun from her waistband. Swallowing hard, she held the gun steady, waiting for the Taker to attack her. Out of the corner of her eye, she saw it coming around the corner of the bed and fired, wiping the snarl off its face.

Will bolted through the door, shouting, "Abby."

"Over here." She stood and leaned over, placing her hands on her knees, trying to assess the pain in her arms and legs while waiting for her dizziness to subside. Bruised but all right, she stepped over the body.

"Are you okay?" He put his arms around her.

"I got us a room," she told him.

Chuckling, he brushed the hair out of her eyes and wiped the blood off the corner of her mouth. Then, he looked at the Taker. "Good shot."

Morgan, with the rest of the team behind him, entered the room. After the men carrying Ethan entered, he closed the door and locked it. "Is anyone hurt?" he asked.

"We're okay," Abby replied.

They placed Ethan on the bed, where Will checked his

pulse while Abby knelt next to him.

"We have to keep moving." Morgan waved over a team member, then he looked at Abby. "Warren's a retired medic. He'll watch Ethan if you decide to go with us. It's up to you."

"He'll be in good hands," Will said.

"You know how hard this is," Abby replied.

"There'll be four of us here with your son," Warren told her.

"I know you don't want to leave him," Will said. "He'd want you to go."

Visions of the thousands of children and the people they kidnapped for breeding filled her mind, followed by the world exploding. She stroked Ethan's forehead, brushing his white hair out of his face. Abby stood. *He'd want me to go,* she thought. She nodded.

"They'll be expecting us to take the elevator to get to the helm," Morgan said. "They'll be waiting for us."

Abby looked up at a vent cover. "How about the duct?"

"Chad," Morgan said, "crawl in and find out if we can follow it from floor to floor, then report back."

"Will do." Chad grabbed a chair, climbed on it, and began pulling off the vent cover leading to a duct twice his width.

Abby heard voices in the hallway outside the door. "It's not safe here," she told Will.

Chad disappeared into the duct.

Abby looked over her shoulder, hearing a knock on the door. She grabbed her frequency gun and stood with the rest of the team, her finger on the trigger.

"Let them in," Morgan said.

A woman from their team stepped toward the door. The knocking stopped.

Morgan put his hand on her shoulder and shook his head.

For a minute, Abby heard mumbling in the hallway, then

the sound trailed away. She looked at Ethan.

"He used all of his energy at the gathering," Will whispered to her. "Let him build up his strength again. He'll be okay."

She nodded, recalling that Ethan had mentally connected with all the Silver-eyes who had gone to a number of Earth's chakras around the world. Each of the Silver-eyes hummed with an inaudible frequency. *Their own soul song, Morgan called it, that Ethan redirected upward into Earth's ley lines,* Abby remembered, *sending a signal asking for help from our alien allies.* She tried to imagine how drained he must have felt after that. *He didn't even have time to rest before the Takers kidnapped him and Morgan, like they did to us.* "You're right," she told Will. "We have to get him to a safe place."

Chad climbed down from the vent. "We'll have no trouble going level to level. The ducts are as squeaky clean as the rest of the ship. On each duct leading up to the next floor, there's a ladder, probably used by their maintenance crew to maintain and sterilize the unit. It'll take us all the way."

Morgan nodded and looked around at the team. "We're not here to fight. Our mission is to get to the helm before they nuke the world, and there's a lot more levels we have to go up before we get there. First, we have to find a safe place for Ethan."

"We can place him in the ducts with Warren and a couple of the others to guard him," Chad said.

Three men lifted Ethan and handed him off to Chad inside the vent, where he slid the litter holding Ethan into a duct branching off in another direction. After the team crawled inside, Abby and Will replaced the vent cover, then trailed the others.

"Notice anything?" Will whispered to Abby. "The ducts are soundproofed."

"Good to know," she told him. With Will at her side, she followed the team around a corner and hesitated when she saw movement out of a vent to her right. "The containment area," she said to him, in a low voice. He looked over her shoulder as she peered through the metal grate. She compared the containment area to four football stadiums stacked on one another. But instead of seats, pods lined the perimeter. The site encircled the center of the ship, and at the heart, the robotic arm looked to be twenty times bigger than those inside the Takers' Schools. It made her stomach turn.

"We have to move on," Will whispered. "According to Ethan's map, we have two more levels to go."

When the team reached the floor below the helm, Morgan talked to them in coded sign language and a whisper.

Will, Abby, and Chad with me, Abby read as Morgan signed. He pointed at the rest of the team, then directed them to take the duct to the helm and patted his gun. "They'll see us by the elevator," he whispered. "We'll be the decoy. Don't wait for us. Go surprise the hell out of them."

Abby peered through the vent cover, counted eight guards, put her frequency gun against the vent cover slats, and fired. The guards collapsed.

One by one, she, Will, Morgan, and Chad jumped down into the hallway.

Will looked up. "Surveillance cameras. If we take the elevator now, they'll be waiting for us when we reach the helm."

"Let's take a minute to think of a plan," Morgan told him.

Code for let's give the others time enough to catch the aliens by surprise, Abby remembered. She tried to estimate if the team made it to the helm yet. *Morgan's right,* she thought. *They need more time.*

Morgan used sign language, which Abby believed would annoy the aliens watching the surveillance footage. Eventually, he glanced at his watch. "Let's go," he said, giving the others a five-minute head start.

They boarded the elevator and ascended to the helm.

When the doors slid open, they stepped over the alien bodies.

Abby hesitated a moment to make sense of the domed room. She faced a panoramic screen on the walls and ceiling displaying the Marine-covered beach and the blue sky filled with fighting beyond the palm trees. *Live footage,* she thought. When she turned in a circle, she saw nothing but ocean. Above her, the domed ceiling revealed the allied spaceships hovering above, keeping the mothership captive.

They hurried to the master control panel while the rest of the team climbed down from the vent.

From the inside pocket of his vest, Morgan pulled out Ethan's drawing showing the location of the launch button. It flashed red. Putting his hand to his ear, he received communications from the general's audio command post and looked at Abby.

His stunned expression told her everything. "We're too late," she said.

Morgan nodded and retrieved one of the maps her husband had drawn. The dots showing the location of all nuclear warheads around the world had turned from white to gray.

"I have to get back to Ethan and Dillon," Abby said. A sense of urgency to hold them in her arms before the world exploded consumed her. She turned toward the elevator and saw the doors open.

Ethan, along with four of the team, stepped out.

"It's too late," Morgan told them.

"No," Ethan shouted. "No, no, no." He rushed to the control panel. "Stop," he commanded, staring at the flashing light. Nothing changed. He stepped back, and all those around him moved aside. Closing his eyes, he stood with his arms stretched out and his palms up. The lights flickered. The room warmed.

"Look at this," Morgan said, motioning to the map.

One of the gray dots turned black, then another, and

another.

"What does it mean?" Will asked. "Have they exploded?"

The panoramic footage disappeared, and the helm's lights went out as a blue glow expanded around Ethan.

"Look," Morgan said, holding the light from his phone over the map.

A single dot began changing color from black to gray and then to white. Another varied its color, its gray fading. They stared at the map until all the dots showed the countdown had stopped.

Morgan touched his earbud. "It's official. The countdown has ceased, and the nukes have been disarmed."

The helm's lights turned back on.

A roar of cheers came from the Underground team. Then Ethan collapsed, and the room fell silent.

Abby and Will dashed to his side.

Bending down, Will checked his pulse. "He's okay."

Slowly, Ethan opened his eyes and tried to stand.

"There's no hurry," Will told him. "Take your time."

"You did it, honey," Abby said, helping him stand.

Will raised his hand to his earbud and said, "The ship's ours."

The team celebrated.

"It's not over yet," Morgan said. "We have to secure the containment area." He followed Ethan, Will, and Abby into the elevator as he continued speaking. "Doctor Davis and Sylvia are flying in to take control of the containment area. And Suzie is coming with them to take charge of the kitchen. We have a long road ahead of us to get our children home. After the containment area is seized, I'll be staying to help reunite the children with their parents."

The elevator doors opened when they reached the lowest level. They met General Rand in front of the locked doors leading to the containment area, the alien's last stronghold.

"You can't fire your frequency guns inside or shoot any weapons that use bullets," Morgan told the general. "Both the bullets that strike the pods and the frequency blast will kill the captives. Ethan disabled the aliens' weapons as soon as we entered the ship. You'll have to meet the aliens head-on, hand to hand."

"Understood." The general ordered his men to enter. "We'll take it from here," General Rand told Morgan.

"Looks like we're finally finished," Abby said to Ethan and Will.

"When will the world leaders be sent home?" Will asked Morgan.

"Now. They don't want to spend another minute on this ship. I don't blame them. They'll be taken to hotels where they'll connect with their governments, who will fly them back to their countries. Buses are here to transport them."

"Cool," Will said. "We'll walk out with them. How many leaders are there?"

"There might be more than three hundred," Morgan said. "I don't have the exact count. They know there are reporters outside. And they're looking forward to the photo shoot to let the world know they're still alive."

Abby, Ethan, and Will walked out of the mothership and down the ramp beside the first lady and the president of the United States, with the other world leaders right behind them. The thousands of Marines, who captured the mothership, stood on the sand, on the back of trucks, and on the roofs of vehicles, wildly cheering. The vast number of media crews and cameras were pushed back as the leaders made their way to the tour buses.

"I'm kind of hungry," Ethan said as they stepped onto the sand.

"I bet you are," Abby replied. "Let's get Dillon and go

home."

Chapter 34

The next morning, no signs of spaceships were seen in the blue skies. And, the media had enough coverage of the war without repeating the footage. Abby, watching TV, cringed at the sight of destruction throughout the world. *A small price to pay for our existence,* she thought. Hearing a knock on the front door, she let Will in. "I was just about ready to join the boys in the backyard," she told him. "The BBQ is all fired up."

"You go ahead," Will told her. "I forgot something in the truck. I'll be right there." He hurried away.

When she stepped out into the backyard, her sons' laughter couldn't have sounded sweeter. *No more running,* she thought. *And no more hiding.*

Will came out through the sliding glass door carrying a cardboard box.

"What's that?" Dillon asked.

"It's for both of you," he told them, setting the box on the grass. "Go ahead, open it."

Ethan dropped his soccer ball and joined Dillon, lifting back the flaps.

Dillon screeched and danced around as Ethan pulled a blond puppy from the box.

"He's a golden retriever," Will said. "You'll have to give him a name."

Abby put her arms around Will.

"I know a guy," Will told her.

"I know a guy, too." She gave him a kiss on his lips that put a smile on his face.

He leaned in, giving her a kiss that she hoped would last a lifetime.

THE END

Shirley lives in Northeast Ohio. She turned to writing after taking an early retirement to care for her mother, who had been stricken with Alzheimer's. While writing first started as a pleasant form of stress relief for Shirley, it soon became her creative passion. She thanks God for her family and her close friends, who have given her support and inspiration.

www.ingramcontent.com/pod-product-compliance
Lightning Source LLC
LaVergne TN
LVHW090555110826
845146LV00001B/139

9798891265189